THE HOLDER'S DOMINION

To Katieanns!
Women unite!
Thrilled to meet
you and keep in
touch!
— Genese

THE HOLDER'S DOMINION

GENESE DAVIS

BEAVER'S POND
PRESS
EDINA, MINNESOTA

ISBN: 978-1-59298-580-7
Library of Congress Control Number: 2012922278
Cover art by Fabio Barretta Zungrone
Book design by Mayfly Design
Typeset in Bembo
Printed in the United States of America
Second Printing: 2015
19   18   17   16   15   5   4   3   2

Beaver's Pond Press
7108 Ohms Lane
Edina, MN 55439-2129
(952) 829-8818
www.BeaversPondPress.com

To order, visit www.itascabooks.com
or call (800) 901-3480. Reseller discounts available.

To all the friends and family who have supported and believed in me, I give my heartfelt thanks. Your spirits live in these pages.

To my creative producer, Eric Kieron Davis: You are a master director. Your encouragement and ability to propose solutions are pure magic. You inspired artistry even when the well seemed dry.

To Fabio Barretta Zungrone, Kellie Hultgren, Sarah Cypher, and Christie Golden: Your insights and talents are abundant and unparalleled. Thank you for your devoted work and passion for this story.

CHAPTER ONE

THE BOY WAS ON HIS KNEES in the middle of the grocery store aisle. Something was wrong. His face was pale and moist with sweat. He was my age—college age—but looked frightened as a child. *Did he trip? Fall? Faint?* My mind raced. *How should I help?* Other shoppers stopped and stared.

An employee approached. "I'm going to have to ask you to leave, sir," he said, pointing toward the exit.

Leave? The guy looked too disoriented to *move*, let alone leave. "Please, go away," he stammered, "...have to finish the morphis, please, go away." The pleading in his eyes and exhaustion in his voice—I had to help.

That voice. It sounded familiar. I approached, studying his pale face and ash-brown hair. *Could it be?* He slumped over on the tile and waved away the employee.

"Excuse me?" His gaze flew to mine when I spoke. I could tell he recognized me, too. "Elliott? From Mason Middle School, back in Tacoma?"

He put his palm to his forehead and whimpered

1

something inaudible. Helping him to his feet and wedging my shoulder under his arm, I walked him outside.

After resting a while, Elliott seemed more aware than before. He stared at me, guarded and skeptical. Almost as if he was expecting me to say something hurtful.

"Do you remember me?" I asked.

His face relaxed a little. "Kaylie Ames." He said my name with warmth. "Valentine's Day—your first day at our school."

"It's been a long time." I smiled.

"I was sorry to hear you lost your dad."

Sharp pricking stung my chest, as if I'd been stabbed with a needle of grief. I swallowed hard. "Thank you." I grappled for any other subject. "So, what happened in there?"

"It was nothing. It's just an old childhood thing. Don't really want to talk about it, okay?"

"Are you all right?"

"Yeah. I won't be trying that assignment again."

"Assignment? From who?"

THE NEXT MORNING, I stared at the ceiling, wide awake at 5:45 a.m. It was pointless to even try to sleep at this hour. It was getting harder to ignore the fact that I wasn't one of the campus girls giggling at parties or blushing on cell phones. For one thing, they all had fathers. I kept up appearances, blended in, but the cost of grieving too little was insomnia and daydreaming—or day-*scrutinizing*. And the whole ordeal with Elliott yesterday suited the latter.

I had only known him for a brief time in middle school, but I remembered him well. He had helped me with my science homework, and I had helped him make friends. After he moved away, we lost touch. Running into him yesterday—bizarre as that was—I was most bothered by the conversations we'd had afterward. I checked my phone on the nightstand, proposing more questions I could not yet answer. The last message from him read, "What the Holder offers us, anything's worth doing for that." Elliott still had that quiet, strange demeanor, and I was still okay with it. The things he'd said about that leader, the Holder, though—something about it made me uneasy. The fantasy world... what did Elliott call it? Edannair? He sounded like an explorer on a new frontier—or maybe a survivor—in what had turned out to be one of the biggest online role-playing games in the world.

Groaning, I shut off my alarm, made my bed, and selected clothes for a run. Today was Sunday. It was nearing March, and though the day would get warmer, Austin mornings were chilly. I gathered my dark-blonde hair into a ponytail and looked into the mirror. Sunlight peeked through my windowpane, highlighting the pale yellow walls of my room and making the sandy carpet look white in the brightness. I lived with two flatmates, Sabrina and Marco, in a three-bedroom close to the university in downtown Austin. It was one of the older complexes around campus, in need of a new paint job, with those wood stairs and railings you wished had a little more support. But it was far from Washington, which was all I cared about.

Slipping into socks and tennis shoes, I stopped by the kitchen and gulped some strawberry-banana protein drink before heading off. Mrs. Pillai looked up from the folding chair outside her flat as my footsteps creaked our old stairs. The smell of curry and spices drenched the air from her open doorway.

"Running today, Kaylie?"

"Yes. How are you, Mrs. Pillai?"

"Fine, fine. Have a lovely time," she said, wrapping her coral-colored shawl more tightly around her shoulders.

The sidewalk was slick with soft morning mist, extending the night's dampness. *My running shoes are worn out*, I thought. *The soles feel too thin.* Houses, businesses, and apartments scrunched together on Duval Street, fighting for the closest proximity to the university. The congestion kept me hopscotching, gauging at every intersection a safe space to cross, dodging bicycles as well as cars. A local bakery hugged the corner of a one-way and saturated the air with aromas of banana bread and cinnamon rolls.

Thirty minutes of jogging and my legs ached. "I can't afford to be shy," Elliott had said. "The Holder will make sure of that." Traces of fear had laced his voice. "There are these morphis trials. It's something I have to do. Not *have to*, something I want to do. But honestly, I don't think I am going to make it through them."

The frown on his face—it stayed with me. What was Elliott mixed up in? He had said the Holder was an online icon, but also what the players called a Sewer King—a fellow gamer who manipulated others into following his rules—and he coerced them into real-world assignments called morphises. Those assignments seemed designed to humiliate them, and yet Elliott said that people competed for the chance to try.

Almost subconsciously, I took my usual turn at Red River Street, a path planned to include downtown's one steep hill. There were five and a half million hits on You-Tube when Elliott had typed in "Who is the Holder?" on his phone. Thousands upon thousands of people had joined online forums revolving around the game world called *Edannair*. Even video feeds of people's experiences there prompted lengthy discussions on message boards. I shook my head. That's a lot of interest. Players and spectators from all over the world either had an *alias*—a character in the game—or were fans of one. They lived Edannair, and most seemed obsessed with the Holder and his group, Sarkmarr. But why? I'd scrolled through hundreds of posts on Elliott's phone. Others were asking similar questions: "Who really leads Sarkmarr?" "Have You Seen the Holder?" "Will I Survive My Morphis?" "Is the Holder a Shade Gone Rogue?" Recruitment mixed with resistance: "Apply to Sarkmarr!" "MMOs Can Change Your

Life!" "How to Shut Down the Holder." "Sarkmarr's Elite." "Hate the Holder!" "The Holder's My Hero!" It was mayhem, all for a place that didn't really exist.

As I neared my flat, I slowed to a walk, hands on hips, stretching my legs with each stride, and I felt better. Runner's high, the cocktail of adrenaline and endorphins. *Gotta love it.*

The Pillais' door was closed, and I couldn't smell the food anymore—probably a good thing. I couldn't remember my last good meal, and my empty stomach ached. A shower, toast, and orange juice would do for now. As I made my food, my brother crossed my mind. Elliott had wondered how he was doing. Hunter was seventeen now, and skateboarding for all his young years had made him lean and strong. The two-and-a-half-year age difference between us kept our lives entwined, pursuing different activities but always sharing in each other's experiences. But since our father—well, he seemed more than a little resentful. We used to be good at sharing things, even painful things. It was different now. We seldom talked except to argue.

I pushed Hunter from my thoughts. I couldn't let myself drown in that topic. I already did that too often.

After breakfast, using my bed as a work-study station, I started on the history timeline due at midterms for Professor Haddox. I had chosen the *Bushi* movement in Japan—the shift from the age of aristocracy to the age of shoguns—and was just getting into page three hundred-and-something of the textbook when my cell trilled a familiar ringtone.

Hunter.

"Hey." His usual emotionless greeting.

Automatic conversation about my classes and the weather drifted into how second year was going, living in a flat with two roommates compared to last year's dorm. I almost went into the intrigue concerning Elliott and the Holder but stopped myself. I didn't know enough about it yet.

"Did you get my letter?" Hunter asked.

I looked at the nightstand drawer that had become his letter's home.

"Yes. I was going to call. School's just been a bit crazy."

"You didn't say anything about it, so I wasn't sure— not that hard to dial some numbers."

"I can't call if I'm in class, now can I? Stop making me do all the talking. How are you?" I paused before asking the harder question. "How's Mum?"

He didn't answer for a few breaths. "Mum's still cleaning obsessively. How do you think she is?"

"I wish I could be there to help, to—"

"You can. You just won't."

"Hunter. I can't."

"I'm here. But oh, that's right, I don't have a choice."

"You'll graduate eventually," I said.

7

"And then what? Off to university? What's the point?"

Pain flinted my ribs. "I don't think anyone would want me to drop out."

"I would. Come back. Go to college here."

"Hunt, I—"

The sound of Mum's voice rang out in the background of the call. "Hunter!"

He sighed. "I gotta go."

"Tell her I love—her." I finished the sentence to the air.

I threw the phone on the bed and ignored the emotion tightening my throat. Thankfully, both flatmates were MIA.

Mum and Hunt refused to understand my move for college the same year we lost Dad—the most horrible year. I can't explain it myself. But in that moment, existing had only seemed possible someplace else. Some days I wanted to tell them both to piss off for holding it against me. Others, part of me agreed with them.

My fingers found the letter and traced its envelope in the drawer.

Never mind. It's better as a bookmark, I thought, placing it in my textbook.

I looked for solace in the living room, submerging myself in our huge, overstuffed couch. My mind was mud. Channel-flipping through tedious daytime television did nothing but add more gunk. Trying to fill my mind with something else was a habit, like meds to cover up the side effects of other meds. Studying had worked at first, but not for long, and the parties, friends, and university romances were all too emotional. I needed a break, an escape. But risk-free. No substances. Just a secluded place where I could be unknown, where for one day I could be free from my family and my memories. Where I could be someone else.

Sabrina interrupted the monotony with a Tasmanian-Devil entrance, flinging out every detail of her day along with her jacket, purse, and hair clips—all of her, spilling out everywhere. "Kaylie, you would not believe this waitress. A spitting image of, of" —she snapped her fingers— "Twist! Ya know? From that show Marco loves. So, this Twist-twin waitress spills water in the booth, in my lap! Three times! You'd think pouring from a pitcher would be a fundamental foundation for waitressing." Her eyes widened and her brown ringlets bounced in their ponytail. "Oh my god, I sound like Marco, don't I?" She looked pleased. "Anyway, during this booth-spilling fiasco my cell rings. It was Eve. And Kay, you are not going to believe this. Danny proposed!"

By now she was in the next room. I sat up and called, "What? Really?"

"Yep. Uh huh. All of my mother's tarot cards could not have seen this coming! Get this, Danny called Eve's parents and invited them to fly out for a celebration dinner. Talk about a spring break to remember!"

"That Danny," I said. "Eve's parents are going to flip. All those tattoos. I hope they see how sweet he is, though."

"Eve's parents are actually going to come!" Saby returned to the living room. "Think of the bets my mother would have made if she'd seen this prophecy. And I think I got Marco to go." She paused, noticing the envelope in my open textbook, and picked it up. "What's this?"

"Oh, it's nothing," I said, reaching for it.

"From your brother. Oooh, he is such a cutie. You two could be models, you know that?" She pulled the paper from the envelope, and a fog-colored marble dropped to our wood floor and rolled toward the couch. I scooped it up with a frantic grab and shoved it down into my jeans pocket just as Saby started to read the note aloud. I was already cringing.

"'Here's the last marble Dad gave you. I know it was the last because I helped him pick it out. Nice to see you brought what's most important to you....'"

CHAPTER TWO

THERE IS SOMETHING ABOUT A MOTHER'S VOICE, a voice you've heard all your life. It's familiar and comforting, and it can surround you like a warm blanket. I had just left the library when my phone rang and displayed Mum's number. I answered, expecting the voice from when I was young.

"Kaylie, hello?" Her voice wasn't recognizable any-more. A pseudo-Mum had taken my real mother's place. I pressed my hand to my forehead and sighed. "Kaylie. Are you there? Can you hear me?"

"I'm here, Mum."

"It's about your brother. He's gone!"

My hand flew to my jeans pocket. I felt the marble beneath the fabric. It was there, but Hunter was gone.

"That's just Hunter now." I tried to sound convincing. "He'll be back."

"This time is different. He wasn't talking."

"What do you mean?"

"I'd ask him what he wanted for dinner, where he had

been, he wouldn't answer anything. And now he's been gone almost a week."

I stopped myself from gasping. *Almost a week? That's too long, even for Hunter.* I didn't want to encourage more panic; I steeled my voice. "Mum. He doesn't talk to anyone."

"He talks to you."

"Maybe when we were younger. Not that much anymore."

"Kaylie." There were several long seconds of silence. "He was different this time. At least when I would ask my son a question before, I would get a response. It might have been yes or no, but at least I knew what he sounded like. I don't remember anymore."

Was it really him she was speaking about right then? I wondered. She never mentioned Dad, but sometimes she seemed to talk about him in other ways.

"He looked weak, Kaylie. And so silent."

"He's almost eighteen. He'll be fine. What do you want me to do?"

"Come home. Talk to him."

"What am I going to say? He's not even there. We just spoke last Sun—"

"He called you?"

My hand went limp around the phone. I retraced the days, realizing it was the Sunday before last when he had called.

"Kaylie, answer me."

"No. No, I haven't talked to him."

"Come home."

"What can I do? I tell him the same things, Mum. To quit disappearing, quit hurting himself and you, and focus on school."

"You two have always talked; growing up, you two could talk for hours."

It was like that with her now. She could continue the conversation without acknowledging anything I said.

"Mum."

"You could have been twins, you two."

"Mum."

"You even had the same favorite games."

I sighed. "Check plane tickets. I could make a long weekend."

FLYING NORTH. Visiting home midsemester or for holidays can seem strange. Like you've stepped back into old tennis shoes that feel familiar, but have a weird stiffness and dusty feeling from disuse. I was uncomfortable in Tacoma. There was still too much pain associated with it. Even though I was older now, I couldn't bring up memories at home and, therefore, couldn't feel, well, at home. We never spoke about Dad. Mum wouldn't allow it. So this trip would be the same as the last. Hunter had disappeared again, run away from home for the umpteenth time, and Mum would still refuse to call any neighbors

13

or authorities to help find him. I knew why. It would be too painful, considering the last time the authorities had showed up on our doorstep.

Mum and I searched all the usual places, his Dome and Hilltop District hangouts. And then the unusual ones, the cobblestone streets of Old Town and the ferry docks and quarry ports along the waterfront. When we gave up and headed back home, the thought was an anvil. *What if something really did happen to him?*

MUM AND I STOOD IN THE KITCHEN, unsure of how to act. Hunter's disappearance resurrected a deep pain that neither of us could handle well. It wasn't long before Mum began fussing around the kitchen.

"Kaylie. Hand me a place mat."

"Sure." I opened the cupboard left of the sink, second shelf, and found three rows of colored vases. "Did you move the place mats, Mum?"

"Yes, yes. They're in the pantry by the table. There."

I found the place mats next to the cutlery. Mum had become compulsive about overcleaning and reorganizing. I hoped it was a temporary coping thing and nothing permanent. "Rearranged again, then?" I said as I handed it to her.

"You know how the clutter does. Everything gets out of order."

"S'pose so."

"Tell me. How are your professors, Kaylie? For what that university costs, would you recommend it for your brother?"

"It's good," I said, flipping my thumbs together. I couldn't sit still. I perused the pantry again and then moved into the living room.

"Are you still planning on the study visa in Cambridge? If you want to work abroad in business, it'd be wise to look into it sooner than later. And we could visit you. I think it'd be lovely to see Britain again.

"I don't know."

Mum prattled on about tuition versus education. I touched the mantel above the fireplace. It was uncanny seeing one again. In Austin, there weren't many fireplaces. Mum's mantel still had a few pictures on it. I lifted one of the frames and interrupted her sentence. "I love this picture of us in Brazil." The space got uncomfortable and shrank. "My first time in the ocean."

"Your brother wouldn't go an inch toward the shore." She laughed with a high-pitched sound I'd never heard in her voice before.

"Dad took this picture, didn't he?" Quiet filled the space instead of an answer. "I think he would have been a photographer in his second profession, if he'd had the time, huh, Mum?" She didn't answer. Memory ached. Setting the frame down, I spoke through it. "We have to call the police about Hunter. It's been too long. We have to report him missing."

"He'll be back. You said so yourself."

She reached up to put away the pound of sugar she held. I placed my hand on hers. "We have to, Mum."

THE OFFICERS WERE TAKING REPORTS and asking Mum about relatives. We both stood like statues on the veranda, trying to ignore what we'd rather not remember.

The teapot began to shriek.

"Kaylie. Tend to it."

In that moment, we heard a stumbling sound, then saw Hunter looking shrunken in the doorway. His frame had always been small, but his skateboarding muscles had disappeared. He looked weak and tattered. His khakis were dirt-stained and full of holes.

Mum put her hand to her mouth and almost pushed the officer aside to go to him. Hunter's surfer-dude hair was not combed with the usual sideswept charm; instead it clung to his skull like seaweed.

"Hunter!" Mum grabbed him. "What happened to you?"

He looked from the police to Mum and me. "You called them?"

"It was your sister's idea. She was worried about you."

Mother ushered him down the hallway, insisting on running a hot bath, and promised to have chicken soup and biscuits ready when he got out. He resisted, but her affection eventually suffocated his protestations. I apologized to the officers and showed them out.

THE NEXT DAY, Mum sent us to spend some time together. We obliged. Hunter and I had lunch at a local place and stopped afterward in Wright Park, finding a bench shaded by giant sequoias.

"So what's up with you?"

"I'm doing this for Mum. You called the cops on me. Don't think I'm just going to ignore that."

"It had been almost a week, Hunter. A *week*."

He shrugged.

"And Mum was right, y'know. I am really worried about you. You're looking terrible. And skinny."

"Or maybe I grew. I do feel taller. Maybe that's just the weightloss talking," he said, smirking.

"All joking aside, come on, your weight does affect your health."

"Ohhh, *Doctor Ames* now, are we?"

"I can be concerned. You're my brother."

"Yeah, right. Where was this concern when you moved away?"

"I moved away to college. People do that. Doesn't mean I don't care about you."

"It does to me."

We both looked up as a loose dog bounded across

the park, its complacent owner trailing behind. We sat for a long while, listening to the wind in the trees. Finally, Hunter began to speak. He sounded as if he was speaking to nature at first, rather than to me.

"Inconsiderate people. That has to be the human flaw I hate most. They're oblivious. They carry out their day, plaguing others' lives with their chaos, forcing their obnoxiousness on everyone. Inconsiderate people don't live by an honorable code. They spoil and rot everything. Johnny Winters was like that, the epitome of everything I despise."

"Who?"

"Big guy. Flunked freshman year twice; it put his height and weight up to double that of the rest of us. He was one of four brothers, all high-school football types. I'm sure he was intimidated by us skater boys." Hunter ran his fingers through his hair and pursed his lips.

I nodded, smiling at him.

"His favorite habit was holding you down, pouring superglue on your legs and arms, and ripping it back off. I held my own some days. Tried to punch his face every chance I got. Of course, the only day it mattered was when I finally got to talk to Renee."

"Renee?"

"This girl I liked for a while. I finally got up the nerve to talk to her. He saw us together, went on a rampage. He stretched me out like a pencil above his head, propellered me, and then hurled me onto the basketball court for a nice, rough landing. Renee started laughing. I thought I loved her laugh. I hated it right then. And her." Hunter shook his head and looked at me. "Never understood why I couldn't fit into your most-popular club, Kay."

"It's not as good as it sounds."

"I came home black and blue and more pissed off about my size than ever. And Dad. Remember? He had brought home a black-and-silver skateboard. No birthday, no reason, he just knew I wanted one so badly. He just happened to bring it home on the worst day of my life. Flying on my board never felt so free. Above and beyond everyone. Skating's freedom. I'll never have that feeling again."

Long seconds of silence stretched out between us, both of us feeling the same asphyxiation at the thought of Dad.

After a long while, we walked home. I tried to speak, but the words didn't come easily. Mum was right. Hunter and I had always talked and gotten along when we were younger, but the guilt of knowing that I hadn't been there for him, and didn't know how to be there for him now, nipped at me with sharp teeth. Our dad had always known what we needed somehow, and now he was gone. I was never going to be able to help the way he had. And I walked in the sickening recognition of that reality.

When the day came for me to return to school, Mum was openly upset about it. She paced around the house all morning, and when I looked at her, she looked away. "You can stay awhile longer. Why don't you stay?"

"I'll be back."

Tension rolled through Mum's shoulders as she moved away from me. "Hunter." Mum sipped her tea, looking out the parlor window. "Say good-bye to your sister."

I looked at Hunter and then at Mum. Neither one was looking at me. They both stared at their side of the room as if I'd already departed. I wasn't strong enough to stay one more minute. I was never strong enough to compete or pucker up and do what needed to be done when conflict was involved. And my father's absence amplified my weakness. I had to get out.

As I stepped onto the plane, it wasn't grief and emptiness that dogged me—it was a bitter hardening, icing the pain inside. I double-checked the marble in my pocket. And sighed a tiny breath of relief. It was proof of Dad, proof of a time when I had been a better sister.

My phone chimed an alert. It was a message from Elliott. "I have more updates on the Holder. Want to come by? I'm staying at Gage's place. Remember him?"

"Yeah. I think so. I can come by when I get back in town. How about Friday? Text me directions."

CHAPTER THREE

THE NOISE OF THE CROWDED RESTAURANT ricocheted in my head. Friday night, and the place was packed. Danny and Eve's celebration dinner filled several tables pulled together—the happy couple was at the center, their parents to their left and right, then other close friends, and Sabrina and I sat at the end. Saby twitched in her seat, watching all doors and exits for a sign of our Latin flatmate.

Eve's parents were driving her mental, asking Danny all kinds of questions about his background. When they asked about his belief in the Almighty, Eve's face turned apple-red. Danny's father wore a frown—a statement, or just his normal expression? Intimidating and military, just as I had imagined he would be.

I chuckled. My friends would get through this night. They were that couple—made for each other. They both came from linear childhoods, but each found refuge in the other's decision to go lateral. Danny's sleeve tattoos and jet-black anime hair had made him the most unforgettable angel last Halloween. His father had wanted him to join the Marines at eighteen. He refused and was getting a sound engineering degree. Eve grew up in a Mormon family who wanted her to stay in Prescott, marry a childhood friend, and have kids. Eve and Sabrina had been high school BFFs—I think that's what they called each other—and after Sabrina got into UT, Eve applied. When I asked her how she found the gumption to follow Sabrina to an out-of-state college, she gave all the credit to the palm reading she had received from Sabrina's mother: "Follow the way of twos, follow the way of twins, follow the way of the pair." Although I think Eve would have followed a fortune cookie slip if it meant getting out of Arizona. She met Danny during her freshman year, and they had been inseparable since. When Eve and Danny decided to move in together, Sabrina found me to room with and then met Marco, who ended up as our third flatmate.

I felt vibrations on my hip and reached in my jeans for my phone. It was Mum.

"Saby," I said, "I've got to take this."

"Danny's about to make his speech Kay, to the *parents,* you can't miss this—"

My expression must have been intense, because Saby just stopped and nodded.

I ushered myself out the front door and answered.

"Kaylie?" Her voice was slow and frail.

I huddled next to a pillar along the sidewalk. "Mum. Hi. How are you?"

"I don't know where he is. He's gone, again."

I slumped against the pillar in utter defeat. Her tone,

Hunt leaving—both reinforced the bitterness of more than one memory. How could Hunter disappear again, so soon after the last time? *Doesn't he know what this does to Mum? What it does to us all?*

Stay calm, I told myself. *Be a big sister.* "How long ago? What happened?"

MY FOCUS WENT IN AND OUT as I sat back down at the table. Everything around me seemed to be moving in slow motion. I felt sick to my stomach. Where was Hunt? How could Mum act as if it was the first time, every time it happened? We've done this waltz before. *He's never been gone so often, though, or for so long.* The way she said it made me feel guilty on top of helpless. I tried shrugging the feelings off. *What could I do anyway?* My visit had done nothing to help. Hunter was gone. The people, the food, the clatter in the restaurant all began to fade. My head was throbbing with memories. It didn't matter that I wanted to move on with my life: knowing that my family was still in chaos jammed me to a halt.

I found an exit. I couldn't remember if I had said good-bye, but I was driving. I stepped on the gas and shifted into fifth. Hugging curves and weaving through traffic, I raced to Gage's house.

It was an older, sagging home with a yard overgrown with weeds, but the porch wall had been decorated in a cute sort of way with several clocks—no, wait—as I walked

23

up the front steps, I saw words as well as numerals. They were barometers. My fist hit the door, and the impact sent a twinge of pain through my wrist. I slumped against the wood almost involuntarily just as it swung open. I lost my balance, but a freckle-faced boy steadied me.

"Whoa, easy there. Are you okay? Hey! Kaylie Ames! Good to see you!"

I struggled to make a half-decent impression. "Hi. Gage, right?" He nodded. "Elliott said I could come by. Is it all right?"

"Of course, yeah. Come on in."

Elliott had met Gage that year we were in middle school together. I vaguely remembered that. But Elliott said they'd remained friends ever since. After high school, Gage had invited Elliott to tour as a techie with the band he'd started. It sounded like he had helped Elliott feel not so out of place in the world, and that made me smile. Gage introduced me to his housemates who were also his band members. Just now, the three of them were watching the Weather Channel. Vehement weather seemed to be an obsession in this house.

"That's a lot of barometers you got on your porch," I said.

Gage chuckled. "We're musicians first, I swear. But without the band we'd all have been tornado chasers for sure." Ben, the bassist, grinned.

The drummer, Ashaad, waved, but then snapped at Gage, "Shhh. They're talking about an F-five."

"Come on," Gage said. We moved into the dining room, where Elliott shot up out of his chair as we entered.

"Hey, Elliott," I said.

"Hi."

"I like the house, Gage. It's nice. Spacious."

"Thanks." Gage poured a glass of iced tea from a pitcher on the table. "This place is my mom's. Well, one of hers." He handed me the drink as we sat down. "She held off on renting it 'cause the band needed a place."

"That's great."

"It's good to see you, Kay," Gage said. "Besides, good thing you came over. Elliott's been talking about you nonstop—"

"No I haven't!"

"—and we were beginning to think his whole 'I ran into her; we talked for hours' story was made up." Gage clapped his hands together. "I'm just joshin', man."

Elliott glared.

"Glad I could purge the rumor, then," I said and took a sip.

"That you did. Oh. Kay. Elliott told me about your dad—"

"Don't. Gage. Please." The coldness in my voice made me pause for a moment. I almost didn't recognize it. "I'm sorry—just a rough night."

Gage and Elliott looked away and then at each other. They must have had the same thought, because they both stood up.

"Come on," Gage said to me.

"Where're we going?"

"Elliott told you about Edannair, right? But he didn't get to show you. And now's the perfect time."

"Why's that?"

"Anytime we need a break or need to get away, this is how we get our minds off things and just have some fun."

"Thanks for the thought, really, but, I don't think I'm up for much anything right now. And I'm not really into—"

"It's not what you think. It's even better than what you've heard." Gage jabbed an elbow at Elliott's ribs. "Right, Elliott? Weren't you just talking about how you wanted Kaylie to try the game?"

Elliott gaped at Gage before glancing at me. He looked paralyzed.

"Come on, what do you say?" Gage said. He pointed to Elliott. "Could you really say no to that face, Kay?"

"Well. I could just watch?" I asked.

Gage looked to Elliott for confirmation, but Elliott didn't move. "Of course that'd be fine," Gage said. "You don't have to do a thing. We'll show you everything."

"Okay. Let's see it."

Following the two of them through a hallway, I watched as Gage pointed out bedrooms and washrooms like a tour guide. Elliott stayed quiet. We ended up in a stark white sitting room. There seemed to be way too many office chairs tucked under two long desks against one wall and a tan futon sat against the other. Four computers were hooked up on the desks—Gage directed me into a seat facing one, while Elliott sank into the futon. It all looked pretty advanced, as if a computer store had set up a display of top-end hardware on the guys' cheap furniture: keyboards, mice, monitors big enough to be flat-screen televisions, towers with see-through panels showing fans and fluorescent lights tucked in between video cards and wiring, and headsets that would have looked at home on an aircraft pilot.

"All right, try to forget about your bad day and watch this." Gage turned on the monitor and punched a key. The screen went black, then irised open on a frozen wasteland rolling out to a distant horizon. Soft, hollow music—the kind that makes your soul feel empty—rose in the background. The colors were clear and the images lifelike—an impressive work of art. Huge ice cliffs loomed over bare trees and rolling snowdrifts. As the view zoomed in, a shape evolved out of the snow. It looked human at first, but as it came into focus I saw differences. It had long claws instead of fingers and toes. Its face was shadowed by its hair, its expression hidden, but I spotted a masculine jawline beneath the sharp nose and mouth. His peculiarity did not bother me until I saw his eyes—an abyss of black: depthless, alien.

A hint of a smoke encircled him—an aura, rising ever so slightly from his naked shoulders and waist. Despite his one piece of clothing, he stood like a king, omnipotent in the wasteland surrounding him. The freezing air made a fog of his breath, a silent barrier in front of him. I shivered as if I could feel the cold. He looked so alone, so abandoned, and yet so powerful. Even though I had never thought of myself as bookish or as a fantasy-genre fan, this was intriguing.

The alien king knelt and recited a prayer or curse. He touched the ice, and immediately it cracked. Something moaned from the schism, which shattered along jagged lines that sprayed ice in all directions. The figure's footing remained solid, as if the land was mindful of him.

Out of the frozen shards, a creature rose—a female form encased by ice, her legs curled to her chest. She awoke and, like a hatchling trying to break free of an invisible shell, fought to move her long, muscular limbs. Black wings loosened themselves and stretched open. Her moan rose to a scream, and this eerie, fairylike woman lifted into the air. Strings of pearls wrapped her body like clothing and wove through her dark tresses. She hovered over the alien king, looking as cold as the icy mountains. The king produced a breathtaking object. It looked like a pearl, but oversized, large enough to fill both palms. The fairy's expression changed when she saw it. Her eyes turned green and her mouth opened, exposing hundreds of fangs. She darted down to skim the frozen ground. Wherever her fingertip touched, the ice cracked away and another of her kind rose from the ice.

The view hurtled southward, leaving the alien king

and the strange fairies behind. The ice gave way to a new landscape. Winter's grip was looser here, and the land showed signs of habitation. Wheat fields rolled along next to rivers, and then the plains expanded into forests cut by roads between forts. The camera closed in on creatures that looked almost familiar, like the denizens of fairytales and childhood stories. Graceful sentient beings ("Zanas," Elliott murmured) moved swiftly along the roadways. Their faces were human except for feline eyes and ears, and their fingers were tipped with claws. In one market-place, they stacked baskets of herbs and unrolled knives from cloth satchels. Towering zebra-striped humanoids ("Those ones are called Quarlins," he added) weighed bludgeons and sharpened swords.

A trail worn among scattered leaves and forest under-growth led to a communal pot of liquid brew. Child-sized, mousy-faced creatures ("The Elowfons," Gage said) drew glinting dust from the pockets of their robes and sprin-kled it into the brew and drizzled patterns with it on the earth. The boiling liquid thickened into a sticky honey, and the ground burst into a shower of floating sparks as the small creatures struck patterns with staves and wands.

In the further reaches of the forest, sea-elves tested bows on gold and red willow-tree targets. Deeper in, dwarves huddled around maps and puffed on stout tobacco pipes.

A drum thundered to life, and all of the creatures looked to the skies. Then a frenzy of activity burst over every settlement. Golden-striped phoenixes rainbowed the sky, bearing messengers headed north. The beings below hustled to pack bags and weapons, and within moments they had set off, trekking to the frozen wastelands and the alien king's encampment of black-winged fairies.

Without knowing exactly why, I felt drawn into the storyline—captured by it. I empathized with the characters, imagining my own home under threat of attack, and thought of what I would be willing to do to protect it.

The many species of creatures marched north with their bows, guns, swords, and magical spells, leaving behind their families and their land, united to fight. They arrived in the frozen lands that shimmered even in the dim light of a veiled sun. The alien king detected their presence and began circling his encampment. His growl of laughter echoed along the iced walls.

The defenders tensed as they watched the strange fairies rise above them, and their eyes widened when they looked upon the leader's strange, kingly silhouette. The king raised the pearl and threw it down toward the new arrivals. As his palms dropped, thousands of the hovering winged things raged forward. Quarlins and dwarves aimed their guns, bows, and spells at the creatures bearing down on them. Norsemen charged, Zanas shot knives from one-handed crossbows, and Elowfons threw arcs of fire from their palms.

Then it all disappeared as the flat-screen monitor

went dark. A few glowing words appeared: *Fdannair* by Deluvian Games.

I sat still for a moment. The creatures seemed so vulnerable and human as they rallied to defend their homeland—it was light-years beyond any game I'd ever seen before. "There's no more?" I asked.

"What do you mean?" Gage was coy.

"They totally left us hanging, is what I mean."

I had completely forgotten how I had ended up here—the crowded restaurant, Hunter and memories of Dad, the anxiety of failing my family. After the vivid drama of the game's prologue, they seemed comfortably distant and dull.

Gage looked at Elliott. They both grinned.

"What happens?"

"Well," Gage said. "First of all, glad you liked it. And second, that event was what sparked the search for Orexia in the first place."

"Orexia?"

"Well, never mind that for now."

"But what were those winged things?"

"Asrai—they are obsessed with and controlled by Orexia pearls."

"How do I see what happens?"

"Well, that depends."

I looked at them, baffled.

Gage smiled at my puzzlement. "If you were to train

and go through some growing pains, you see what happens. No. Actually, you help create what happens."

"Create?"

Elliott spoke up. "Yeah, that's what Edannair is. It's the main continent on the world of Ylora, where you—well, your *alias*—searches, investigates, explores, and if you're lucky, gets a sneak peek of the really cool stuff." He gave me a shy, knowing smirk. "Well, that's unless you think this sort of stuff is really uncool."

"It's hard to explain," Gage said. "It's easier if you learn by doing. Like, you can't understand why it's cool unless you see it, right?"

"Yeah. I mean, it sounds interesting. And where does the Holder fit into all this?"

Gage shot Elliott a confused, furious look. "You told her about the *Holder*?"

"No!" Elliott looked at me. "Well, yes. Barely. I didn't exactly mean to, it just happened. It's fine, anyhow. Kaylie gets it."

"I wouldn't say I exactly get it, but what's wrong? Why can't we talk about him?"

Gage looked at me. "Look, not everyone has the capability to understand, even if we explain. People jump to conclusions and make trouble. Unless you already have an alias, you most likely won't grasp it."

"Well, I'm not everyone. Elliott confided in me for a reason. And I didn't misjudge him. Tell me more, please."

Gage looked at Elliott. "It's true," Elliott said.

"All right. Considering Elliott never feels comfortable talking or trusting anyone, you must be really freaking special."

Elliott's expression softened into a smile. "Let's show her more."

CHAPTER FOUR

I WATCHED THEM PLAY. Gage's alias was a sea-elf called Svar, and Elliott's was a dwarf called Asillus. They moved their characters using keyboards and computer mice. Both currently sat astride giant flying creatures, plunging a thousand feet through diamond dust and funneled rain twisters while hurling charmed pouches and yelling commands to sky allies. I liked that no one used real names in Edannair. Once inside, you are your alias. "Svar" and "Asillus" were strange and foreign code names to me at first, but within moments they seemed normal. And I sensed that the masses of new rules and facts about Edannair would soon grow just as familiar.

Svar and Asillus moved like gods in the sky, one on an alabaster griffin and the other on a crimson phoenix. Within a few moments, they had landed and hailed new mounts for ground travel—a mammoth and an alligator—and then together passed into a city of undulating stone streets and precise masonry.

Inns and shops advertised their wares through foreign-language labels identifiable by pictograms, offering skill training, potions, weapons, and animal trading. After they dismissed their mounts, Svar and Asillus toured the city on foot. Farriers and blacksmiths worked in stone corners, while castle towers and cathedral spires jutted up against an indigo sky. Even in broad daylight, the bright white and yellow streaks of distant galaxies glowed there.

Representatives from no fewer than two dozen species bustled around us, each with a purpose: preparing or moving something, working heartily with one another. Even the younglings made themselves useful by towing food or weapons between elders.

So this is what a tightly packed strip mall would look like in another universe. Can't say I miss the bratty, screaming children at the Cedarcreek Mall.

I caught flashes and sparks of white and red in the corner of my eye. I looked, but I couldn't name the type of beings I saw. They were tall and lean-bodied, but had wide shoulders and thighs. They had deathly white skin, hard like a beetle's carapace, but the bones in their faces looked sharp enough to pierce it. Their hollow cheekbones sunk into violet mouths, and their hair was tube-shaped, like dreadlocks, but hard.

"They're Murinkai," Asillus whispered to me.

Colors flowed from their hands—spells. In an almost silent trilling, they conjured sparks that flew in every direction before forming perfect blue circles above their palms. Mesmerized, I watched them flick their wrists and produce solid blocks of ice that towered over them.

"Did you see that?" Gage asked. "Eludan guys are showing off again."

Before I could answer, I heard a stranger's voice through Gage's speakers. "They're still there?" The voice had an accent. Sounded Irish. "Let me guess. They're throwing blocks of ice in the middle of the square?"

"That's exactly what they're doing," Gage said.

"Who are you talking to?" I whispered. "Whose voice was that?"

"Modaga. A friend of ours," Gage said. "Why are you whispering?"

"Can other people hear me?"

Elliott and Gage couldn't help but laugh at the question. "No. No one can hear you unless I push this button for public chat." He showed me a separate numeric keypad that sat alongside his mouse. "And these keys, here—" He pointed to the F1 through F12 keys on the keyboard. "are used for private conversations to individual people. Or for private groups, either one."

"That's incredible. You can just talk to anybody like they're right here?"

"Anyone from anywhere in the world."

"That's cool. And this city is where everyone plays together?"

"This is only Ruinnlark. Granted, it is one of the largest cities in Edannair, but there are hundreds of cities and thousands of miles of land in this game. Designed so that if you want to take your alias from one continent to another, around all of Ylora, it would take forever, just like in real life."

"Wow."

"But let's show you the rest of this city before thinking about all that."

The flat screen's resolution was mind-boggling. I could detect even tiny crystalline shards that swirled up in clouds of vapor before the catlike Zanas who controlled them. I studied the species in the game, each more fascinating than the next. Elowfons conducted their business of taming animals. Tigers uncaged and unleashed growled at passersby, and ratites pecked and sucked at the air. The first sighting of an earth-troll made me gape: a sickly, yellow-skinned, hunching thing with scowling eyes and a large gorilla mouth. The sea-elves were statuesque and athletic and had long eyebrows above alert round eyes, gills behind narrow cheekbones, faint scales for skin, and small, pouty lips. Tan, broad-bodied orcs exposed their fangs to challenge Norsemen and dwarves to a duel. Helmets, chestplates, and swords were displayed in shop windows, and—thanks to the surround-sound speakers—the sound of shouts and bids for items filled the streets. Bells rang in the distance, guards in silvery armor paced the streets, and emissaries rattled speeches to the large crowds gathered around them. It was a marketplace and armory in one.

And then I saw something that stood out even more in the foreign crowd. The thing moved slowly. Gracefully.

A tall black wisp with even less essence than a shadow. It floated above the ground and exhaled a deep, cursed-sounding whisper. Just a glance and I felt colder. It followed a hooded figure that wore shoulder armor over a cloth robe. Deep gashes marred the protective plates, a kind of writing that was itself scarred and distorted. Welded spikes reached above the hooded head, and small white objects—little skulls, as I looked closer—were impaled on them. The hidden-faced figure moved as if stalking someone, and everywhere it went, the black ghost followed.

"Who are those guys?" I asked.

"Hmm?" Gage looked to where I was pointing. "Whoa! Is that Ilusas?" Gage leaned closer to the screen. "Did he get his Demon-wisp back, Elliott?"

"Not that I know of."

"Never mind. That's Leo. But I thought he stopped playing?"

"He might've logged on just to check something," Elliott said.

"Wait, what happened?" I asked. "I'm getting lost."

"Kaylie, there are only two aliases on this continent who've obtained one of those." Gage motioned to the black ghost. "That's a Demon-wisp. They are nearly impossible to get. Ilusas and Leo, and only like three others from other continents, are the only ones out of all the millions of players in Ylora to have gotten one. It's a huge deal." Gage motioned to the hooded figure ahead of the Demon-wisp. "See him? That's Leo, the shadowlock who

38

conquered it. You see how it follows him? The Demon-wisp is bound to serve him."

"What is a shadowlock?"

"A classification. It defines your alias's specialty. The shadowlock class can manipulate elements like fire. A rogue is skilled with daggers while a ranger is skilled with a bow. A shaman uses hexes and charms. I can't believe you're seeing this. I can't believe I'm seeing this. This is so rare."

"It's beautiful, in a dark sort of way."

"Think that could be you someday?"

I gulped. A swirling aura wrapped the hooded shadowlock, emanating dominance. He ignored other aliases, who were calling out, "Demon-wisp!"

"He's probably trying to log off and...." The roar of a growing crowd surged around us in the opposite direction of the shadowlock and Demon-wisp. With a swipe of the mouse, Gage panned the screen view around so we could see the commotion.

"Asi, look, look, that's him, isn't it?" Gage's voice was strange.

"Who?" I asked.

"The ... Holder." Gage almost choked on the name.

"What's the Holder doing here?" Elliott said.

Gage whirled his chair to look at Elliott. "That is him! That's Lorgen!"

"Shhh! Svar. Don't draw attention."

It was so different hearing the guys call each other "Svar" and "Asi." It was as if my friends had stepped into this weird, fantastical movie and were playing their parts, right there in their office chairs.

"Asillus. Grow a pair. Come on, man. *The* Holder. He's right *here!*"

I swayed, searching the monitor, but I couldn't get a good view. The crowd had formed and thickened quickly. The mystery man was walking in the opposite direction. I glimpsed a high-collared black coat. He looked similar to the sea-elves, with lean height and long hair that fell around his face. His ears were hidden, but I didn't see a trace of scales on what little skin I could view. I guessed he was his own species.

Elliott breathed, "Hho my god, hhho my god, it's him, I cannot believe it's him."

On-screen, Svar took a few steps left, then right. "Let's go up to him."

"What? No. He's busy. Look at the crowd."

"He's always busy. Do you want to move up the ranks or not? Come on. Always time to make a good impression."

Svar plunged into the crowd. Asillus followed.

"We're seeing the Holder. That never happens outside a meeting or assignment. Major props man, major." Svar's alias suddenly became a cloud of smoke. He shifted shape into a cheetah and thwacked Asi across his hunching shoulders.

They reached the dense cluster surrounding the Holder, and Svar reappeared in his sea-elven form. Asillus caught up with him, the metal on his armor reflecting blinding red-yellow sunlight. They jumped and tiptoed to see over the packed crowd. Then Svar signaled something to Asi. He pointed at a symbol on a medallion hanging around his neck. The Sarkmarr lynx. Svar had mentioned this—something given to the Holder's members. My friends waved their medallions in the air, shouting, "May Sarkmarr live!"

The Holder must have heard their chant. He turned and cut through the throngs like a prophet. Everyone scurried out of his way, and when he waved his hand and said something, the crowd reluctantly dissipated. As he came closer, I saw the same lynx symbol hanging between the lapels of his coat.

"Svar." The Holder nodded. "Asillus." His voice was deep and assertive. He continued walking, and Svar and Asillus instinctively turned and matched his pace. The high collar of his cloak and an umber bandana tied low around his forehead hid everything not obscured by long untidy hair, leaving only the suggestion of a straight nose and sharp mouth.

An earth-troll lumbered by on foot, others on horseback, and Elowfons passed by astride tigers and ostriches. I looked twice when a Zana, female by her figure, strapped a pair of axes to her back and leapt astride an elephant.

"You are two of my newest recruits." The Holder paused. "Just joined Sarkmarr, is that correct?"

"Well, not *just*—"

"Yes. Yep," Svar interrupted Asillus, almost stuttering. "Just a few months ago."

"Svar, your shapeshifting has caught the attention of quite a few," the Holder continued. "And, to my understanding, you've progressed rather quickly for your rank. Good work." The Holder's voice was controlled. I had never heard anyone pause so frequently between statements.

"Thank you, sir." Gage sounded astonished. "I wouldn't be here, though, if it wasn't for this guy right here. Asi's my mentor. Got me to Edannair, taught me everything I know."

"Ah. Asillus?"

"Yes," Asi answered slowly.

The Holder stopped. Turned. Squared his shoulders, facing Asillus. My friends stopped as well and turned to face him. "How many times did you end up applying?" the Holder asked, an edge in his voice.

Several seconds elapsed.

The Holder let the silence build before he spoke again. "I wouldn't give too much credit, Svar, to someone who can hardly speak for himself. After all, you're almost done with tier two. Where does your mentor stand?"

"It's—I've been ..." Asillus struggled and glanced from the ground to his friend.

"He gets a little tongue-tied, sir. That's all." Svar patted Asi's chest. "He has been looking for a cure, though."

The Holder snickered. "I would think carefully on

who you choose to make a mentor, then, especially ones who cannot pass their first rank of tier two properly."

My own ears burned at the acrid provocation. It reminded me of how the bullies had provoked Hunter in middle school. Right in front of me, Elliott was bright red and blank-eyed, as uncomfortable as if the Holder were in this very room.

Asi attempted to answer. "I did. I—I almost finished."

"Interesting. You speak so rarely, and when you do, you lie. Should we ask Svar what tier two's first rule is? At this point, should you even call yourself a Sarkmarr? What have you done to separate yourself from the average player, the commoners?"

I looked from Elliott to the Holder's animated figure disbelievingly.

"Well—I have tr-tried to do more," Asi said. "But I just need more time."

"You're sounding more and more like an Isolit."

Svar flinched, and Asi hung his head in shame.

Isolit? The Holder seemed to be thoroughly enjoying the insult.

"If you do not stop disgracing my organization, Asillus, you will find yourself not only expelled from my sight, but also shunned by every single person on this continent. You will have no choice but to leave the game."

Both of my friends stood frozen and silent. The Holder waited a few moments, then turned on his heel and walked away. Flocks of aliases poured forth around him as if on cue. He shooed them and disappeared behind a large, virescent ogre—no, it was a broad-bodied orc, and he was juggling three shaman totems for a group of zebra-striped Quarlin.

"Where does that guy get the nerve?" I heard the protective note in my voice and realized I meant it. "He was being outrageous. Don't listen to him. He had no right—"

"He does have the right." Elliott interrupted me softly. "We want to be a part of Sarkmarr. It's prestigious. And if we have to endure a little scolding or humiliation along the way, okay."

"But—"

"But nothing. You're not a part of this world. Not yet, anyway."

"Elliott, listen. If he had any tact at all he would wait and see that you're a good person, and you work hard—"

"That doesn't matter—none of that matters. He's right. I've been tier two for weeks and what? I can't even complete my new rank's challenge. I should be humiliated."

Frustrated, I struggled to understand how the Holder, with his disregard and his coldness, was tolerated—even revered.

Gage broke the silence with bright-idea eyes. "Want to go dragon-plunging?"

CHAPTER FIVE

TUESDAY'S CLASSES WERE MY FAVORITES. I almost forgot about the Holder, and only when I overheard some typical college trash-talking between friends in the hallway did I remember what a jerk the Holder had been to Elliott. The Holder neither argued nor agreed, and yet he had said enough to make me wrestle with the interaction days later.

As I followed Professor Suis and a dozen other classmates around the north side of campus, I couldn't stop wondering. Why did the Holder taunt Elliott, spotlighting his failures? Where did he get off talking to my friend that way? And how could Elliott welcome it? The professor picked up a cluster of epiphytes. He peered out from behind the plant in his hands, its wiry stems shooting out like antennas, and said something about our next botany exam.

Class ended and I hurried to my next one. Professor Gorgoux's classroom brimmed to overflowing, and I tried to listen fully as she lectured at warp speed, but I was distracted. Elliott didn't deserve that treatment, and for some reason I felt concerened about him like I'd be for Hunter. I promised myself I would find out more. If the Holder ever tried again to hurt Elliott's feelings over something as minor as a computer game, I would be there to defend him. *Damn*, I thought, *give the kid a break*.

The afternoon passed, and after classes, I finished the next day's assignments and collapsed onto my comfy bed. A Will Smith movie played from the living room, and I tried to use it as a lullaby. Sleep scoffed. Elliott, then Hunter, filled my thoughts. I called Hunter's cell phone with the remote hope he'd answer. It rang and rang. The message I finally left begged him to call me back, to go home, or to come visit Austin. Anything but disappear.

AFTER CLASSES THE NEXT DAY, Saby cooked in the kitchen while Marco hovered over architectural blueprints on the table. The phone rang, and Sabrina looked remarkably kittenlike as she bounded from couch to kitchen after the jangling string. Sabrina twisted the cord of our old phone while giving Marco the play-by-play in staccato whispers.

"Have fun tonight, you guys," I said on my way to my room.

They nodded and waved. And even after I had shut my door, I could hear Sabrina's coquettish voice through the thin walls. She was going on about directions and parking options for the night's plans. She liked Marco so much. Problem was, he was either blind to it, or else acting ignorant because he didn't fancy her the same way. Hopefully it wasn't the latter.

I cranked up the showerhead. Hot water poured over me. Evening showers—one of my favorite things. The hope of a restorative long night's sleep still tempted me; maybe tonight was the night. Usually, I stayed up to read or watch a movie until my eyes ached and my body had no choice but to pass out for at least a few hours. But every once in a while, like tonight, I tried to sleep at a decent hour, coaxing my body to fall asleep naturally with a hot shower and the reward of a good night's rest.

I stared up into the blackness. Who was I kidding? If only I had those glow-in-the-dark stars on the ceiling.

Hours passed.

My head felt hazy, drifting mockingly close to unconsciousness. One thing about not sleeping, it's hard to lose track of anything: yourself, your happiness, your unhappiness, and especially the number of good sleeping hours you are losing. You feel like a giant clock screaming every minute of every hour ticking by. I put both hands to my temples and pressed.

School has the ability to separate us from family problems.

Old hope. School was no substitute for family.

The letter surfaced in my thoughts. *How long before Hunter will come home this time?* He had not responded to my message, but I waited in the stillness as if my phone would ring any minute, as if I'd hear an answer. The doubting game is addictive: a part of your mind is so sure about a thing, but the other parts, like an unraveling braid, compete to convince you that you know nothing. That must have been how Mum felt when they told her about Dad's disappearance.

I reached out into the darkness until I felt the lamp switch. The dim light shone through the shade's colored glass, transforming the yellow and blue panes. *3:00 a.m. That feels about right.* I paused, imagining my dad. The hollowness—you can hide for a while. But sometimes it awoke and raged. *I miss him so much.*

BRUCE WAS MY FATHER'S NAME. He was one of those big, tough guys who could bulldoze a wall, but oddly enough, he never showed that side. He smiled a lot. And had one of those goofy dimple smiles—like he had a secret but was too excited to share it just yet. He always told us smiling was the gateway to learning and bettering your-self through others. If you smiled at people, they would instinctively feel comfortable with you and would want to share their lives, discoveries, and experiences. And you'd get more out of your day than you'd ever expected.

He married my mum, Emma, when they were both twenty. They had met in Seattle. She had just moved from London and he from Wisconsin, and they both hoped Seattle was it for them—it was, and the rest is history.

They told their story just like that to everyone.

We moved from Seattle when I was twelve and Hunt

only ten. The Tacoma Firefighters had offered Dad a job too good to resist. He worked four days on and three days off and loved it. We had plenty of time for our favorite things. We'd play marbles with him every weekend unless Mum called for a night at the theatre. But games were where Dad shined. He loved playing with anyone. Cards, board games, video games, dominoes, dice—they were all there, stacked under the coffee table, with a few even hanging off the edges. I think because he spent so much time away from home, it was nice for him to stay in and play.

Some weekends, usually one a month, he also volunteered to be on call for search-and-rescue missions. In between those, he and I would scout a map for a new ski trail or he and Hunt would find a new skate park to ride.

Mum always said she didn't like Dad's line of work. She was always so worried about his fighting fires, told him she was afraid he wouldn't come home from one of them. She would listen to the scanner every day while she cooked or cleaned. She worried, but she never really expected him to get hurt. Neither did we.

Two winters ago, a cross-country skier didn't show up at his party's rendezvous point on Mount Rainier. Dad was on the rescue team. A blizzard moved in after dusk, and my dad and the skier never came back.

After six weeks and not a day without snowfall, they suspended the searches. Hunter never forgave Mum for not finding a way to continue them.

All I could picture for a long time after he disappeared was my dad's hands. He was animated when he talked, his hands always moving and miming his words. "Get out and live like a tornado," he'd say, moving his hand like a twister. "Suck up everything in your path. Enjoy everything. Enjoy everyone. Those funnels spin fast and scatter everything. So choose your tornado's path carefully, little ones."

Since he disappeared, Hunter's skateboard hadn't left its wall hook, and I hadn't touched a game.

MY FINGERS MOVED; I wanted to hold the marble. Somehow it connected me with my father now. I crawled to the edge of the bed where I had left my clothes. I took the marble from the pocket and pressed it against my chest. My eyes shut hard, I tried to fall asleep that way. But tonight was the same as every night. Insomnia.

Chapter Six

It was getting warmer out. Spring was in end-bloom, and classes were not remotely distracting enough. I found myself going over to Elliott and Gage's place on week-nights. If my flatmates had cared enough to ask why, I would have said that Edannair was a hybrid between the dream world and the real world—a place where I could be myself, but better. And I had a hunch about something, even if I could not find the words for it yet.

I finished my homework, checked the calendar for study groups or alliance meetings, and finding nothing much on the agenda, I headed to the gang's abode.

"Back for more, huh?" Gage asked when he opened the door.

I followed him on the now familiar route, waving at Ashaad and Ben, who were watching the Weather Channel.

"Welcome back, Kay." Elliott spun around in his chair to greet me.

"Thanks, Elliott. How's it going?"

I watched for hours, asked a few questions, and filled everyone's cups with fizzy drinks.

"You don't have to do that, Kay," Elliott said.

"I don't mind."

"If you don't make an alias yourself soon, you're going to have a permanent position on the drink staff," Gage said.

"Yeah. You don't want to watch forever." A smile slipped to Elliott's lips. *He should smile more often*, I thought.

"Maybe sometime," I said.

Something in the game caused Elliott to panic. "Black drakes! Svar!" Elliott's voice turned confident and stern. "They're circling back!"

"What? How? Tell Ilusas. We need those griffins back at Volstrim Tower!"

"Svar, they're past Tempest's Gate. There's no way—"

"Watch that death cloud! Asillus drop! Drop! Stop them!"

I watched Asillus whirl his weapon overhead and slam it against another paladin's—axe to sword, the dance of metal and sparks echoed. Warriors charged at Svar. Out of puffs of smoke, he shapeshifted, dodging bludgeons and blades, morphing from sea-elf to cheetah to gorilla, missing blows and hurling his attackers into walls at any opportunity.

I was getting a feel for how it worked. You signed up, and you picked one of the species as your alias. Then you picked the kind of skills you wanted to play with. There were damage dealers that fought up close and personal with daggers and axes, and there were casters who, from afar, used bursts of magic to hit a wide range of enemies at once. Healers kept everyone alive, and protectors lured the attention or *hate* from the masters—the biggest bad guys. Each specialist was needed if a team was trying to defeat complex or long-lived enemies, be it a quietus-angel, beast, or elemental lord. And if it was a master? Forget it. The night was going to be long and intense.

Everything was individualized and unique. Every alias had different qualities and roles. I could barely keep up; there was so much detail. It was like being in a foreign country where you didn't speak the language, but it was worth enduring the embarrassment and mispronunciation of words as long as it meant reaching the next destination. The texture and detail of the landscapes and cities—absolutely breathtaking. It was like being in a fairytale.

AFTER NIGHTS WITH THE GANG, I couldn't keep Edannair from my mind. I lay awake in my dark bedroom watching afterimages of golden banners fluttering from watchtowers and marble city gates touching the skies. Ylora felt alive. It was so real that I—well, my alias—could skip down cobblestone paths twisting and rippling through kingdoms and fly astride dragon turtles and pegasi patrolling blush skies. And most importantly, it offered protection from the real world somehow, as if something as fantastic as live gargoyles roosting on parapets could save me from wakefulness. Instead of obsessing over the spectres of my family, I could revel in this new world…and, hopefully, follow it into dreams.

It would be easy to lose myself in the game elements alone. But I wanted to know something. *Who is the Holder? What does he want from Elliott?* When I spotted Elliott on the floor in that grocery store, overpowered with anxiety, protectiveness had ignited in me, even if Elliott would still only say it had to do with his morphis assignment.

I shaded shapes with my pen in my notebook, idly listening to the Chef's Channel. It was Saby's standard channel, and I left it on because there was nothing else I wanted to watch. But my mind was with Gage and Elliott. I hadn't realized that my open-ended response to their invitation would ignite a spark to actually sign me up. It had been a week or two since they had set me up with an Edannair network of my own, and now I too had a top-notch display and an upgraded computer, new keyboard and mouse with more buttons than I knew what to do with, and one of those aircraft-pilot headsets. This way, they had said, if I ever wanted to, I could link to the game from home.

I fiddled around the apartment, cleaning dishes and listening to the TV foodies.

After what could have been an hour or two, I made my way to the computer and sat down. I stared at the screen for a few minutes, then got up and went back to the kitchen to make some food.

I tried to tell myself I was hungry but knew it was an attempt to not reflect. After my inspiring meal of peanut butter and jelly toast that for some reason took fifteen minutes to make, I sat back down at my computer with the login screen staring back at me.

What am I doing here? Why do I think this is going to help? Where is he?

My eyes started to water as I thought of the last time I played marbles with Dad—his passion, his excitement, my love for him, and the inclusiveness of game night.

I searched for a tissue. I couldn't stop thinking about how much I missed him. How sad I was for Hunter. How much Hunter and I got along in those moments. Life had been so much better.

As my throat tightened, I sat staring, wanting to bring him back. Because I couldn't exit those thoughts in any other way, I entered Edannair.

Chapter Seven

I maneuvered through golden grass, surrounded by mauve-colored trees. The branches swayed, and their movement seemed to match the ambient song in the background. A bushy-tailed red squirrel paid no mind to the tranquil music, leaping and scurrying from branch to branch.

I had picked a Zana for my character. Loxy—a good alias name, I thought, feminine and strong, and it didn't end in *a* like so many other female names here. The hybrid of cat and human genes made my alias's movements stoic and polished, and there was a slight dark aura pulsing around my silhouette, a symbol of my shadowlock class. It was difficult at first, transferring my knowledge of the game from watching Gage and Elliott—that is, Svar and Asi—to doing it myself. But the interface and functions were not as complicated as I thought they'd be, and I was soon feeling as fluid and comfortable at my console as they were at theirs.

I found Quartermaster Jingith stationed in Gavion Gully, exactly where the shadowlock trainer had said he'd be.

"Loxy!" A baritone voice rang out through my computer speakers. "We're glad you've come!" Jingith greeted me and immediately began a diatribe. "Beyond the Delfkut Swamps, my people are weakened by plague and famine and are in desperate need of your help. Would you clear the swamps, Loxy? The herg beasts. They are destroying our crops, our livestock, even the children—they are feeding on our children! They live in the swamps but have overtaken Coros Valley. You will know them by their fat faces, wide paws, long claws, pig snouts, and ridged backsides. They are horrible! They are surely going to be the end of us!"

"I'll do my best to help, Jingith."

"Oh, gracious Zana. We will not only enshrine your name for this favor, but you will also be rewarded." I hadn't expected to get a reasonable answer to that statement from an algorithm like Jingith, but he and my shadowlock trainer responded realistically even to vague questions and slang. *They could pass for actual players*, I thought. Yet another impressive element in the game. Kudos to the designers.

THUNDER DUELED LIGHTNING, making music in Edannair's sky. Thick virga hung over the marshes of Delfkut Swamp. Hummingbirds with rainbow butterfly wings fluttered past my shoulders and disappeared into the canopy. My boots splashed and sank into the earth, leaving a path of deep, water-filled footprints. The rain and mud darkened my maroon and auburn robe and threatened to leak into the two leather cases strapped to my back. One held a mace and the other a spell book and potions. The shadowlock trainer had explained that the weapon was a precautionary measure. If I were to forget an essential part of the spell, I had not only a reference, but a weapon as well.

Spellcasting is all about focus. I was nervous and tried to remember the trainer's instructions. *Breath deeply. Pick the spell. Picture its name. Then think it. DemonCoil. Repeat its name. Bring the power from within you, feel it flowing from the core of you, then through your hands. Know the tool; harness it.* I kept repeating the instructions as I trudged farther and farther into the soggy swamp. Like my science classes, the spells required understanding as well as rote.

A rustling sound froze me in my tracks. From somewhere ahead in the thicket came a hyena-like squeal. A herg emerged from the bushes, tossing its powerful head from side to side. As the animal came into full view, I spotted something dangling from its mouth—a poor mangled meal. I couldn't do this. I needed more practice—but not on this creature! It was almost as big as my alias. Maybe I could start somewhere safer.

Wait, what was I talking about? The Holder would have his laugh if he knew I was shaking in my boots—and he'd treat me like the rest of his players.

When I meet the Holder, he needs to take me seriously. I have to do this.

I took a step forward, then back, widening and shortening my stance and trying to remember the perfect position for spellcasting. A more watchful eye to the ground would have been helpful—my boots sloshed in a puddle, and the herg tensed. It dropped the kill from its mouth and made a heinous snort that ended in a growl. In a moment, it pawed the ground twice and charged. Twigs snapped. Leaves flew into the air.

Look at your target. Concentrate. Focus on the target. Form the spell!

The herg barreled down on me.

Let the fire build in your palms. Watch your target.

A dark flame coiled in my hands. It grew, widening and lengthening until it reached from my waist to my chin. With a thrust of my hands, the spell flew from my palms and smashed against a tree three feet away from the angry beast. The herg's course wavered, but in a second, it caught its footing and charged again.

I cast another, then another, but each time I missed my target. *Focus!* My hands moved over and under each other as I formed the dark flame again. I stared at the herg and held its gaze as I released the coiling fire. The swirling black flame hit it square in the mouth. Inertia somersaulted it into the mud, squealing. It rolled to a halt a few feet from me and lay silent and still.

What a rush!

I glanced down at my hands, turning them over as if regarding a new instrument—an instrument of power with the ability to wield and beckon fire.

So this is what a superhero must feel like. Cool.

Another herg stomped out of the brush. *Here for revenge, I bet.* Beaming with pride and confidence, I took up my casting stance. The herg tipped its head back and lunged toward me. I conjured the fire again. *Bring it on, beastie.* A billowing, golden masterpiece of fire blazed in my hands. I moved to release the spell, but before a flicker of flame left my hand, a hard smack sent me flying backward through the air. As I landed flat on my back, the screen changed. It began pulsing red. I knew what this meant. My health was dropping. I was dying!

I watched the herg prepare to ram me again. I scrambled to get to my feet. The herg was already on its way. I tried throwing every spell I knew, anything to keep the herg off me. My sporadic and unfocused attempts only sullied my chances. The herg hit me head-on, and red washed over the screen as my alias collapsed to the ground.

I thought it was game over. My alias's spirit wisped out above my body; the game world lost all color, and a hazy vignette framed the screen. Panic hit me. I didn't remember what to do. How did Gage and Elliott resurrect themselves? I grabbed my phone and called Elliott.

"Elliott! Hello. I need your help. I died! And I don't know how to resurrect."

"Who is this?"

"Elliott!"

"I'm just kidding. What zone are you in?"

"I was fighting the hergs—"

"By yourself? Without a healer with you?"

"Well, yeah."

Elliott chuckled. "You need to find a life guardian. Look at the map of your zone. There will be icons that look like doves. Take your spirit there, talk to the guardian, and you'll get a res."

"Thank you!"

Finding the nearest life guardian took me nearly an hour, I got so lost. I didn't realize finding a spirit dove would mean so much to me, but as soon as I saw the dove, I ran to it! The guardian revived my alias with a ritual chant.

I got back on the proverbial horse and practiced some more. After a while, spell-conjuring grew easier. The control, the stillness, the sustained focus, the explosions when the magic hit its mark, and the strength I felt afterward—it was all empowering. Though, exhilarating as it was becoming better at the game mechanics, I felt a pang of remorse each time a herg fell. The game was so realistic that I felt like I was killing flesh-and-bone creatures—their last breaths misted in the damp air, and mud and blood matted their hides. But I focused on the help and safety I was providing for Jingith and his people.

I returned to the quartermaster feeling more like a warrior princess than a student.

"You've done it!" Jingith said, raising his arms to the sky. "You have saved us! All of Coros Valley thanks you." He bowed. I returned the gesture.

Jingith picked up the shaman staff that rested against

the stool at his side. He waived it and then held it before me. A bright aura fell around my alias, as if winter had engineered a flurry of golden snowflakes. They swirled around slowly, then faster and faster, before disappearing with a snap. The tail end of the flurry inscribed a crest of honor on my belt.

I smiled. I was getting the hang of this.

Jingith thanked me again and asked for assistance with one thing more. "The Caraf Mines," he said. "One of our shamans is waiting there. Will you deliver this message to him?" I nodded, and he handed me a scroll.

Jingith uttered a series of clacks and whistles, and a large animal appeared from behind him. It had a horse's face, neck, and mane, but its muscular flanks, legs, paws, and tail were those of a lion.

"This leonim is swift and strong," Jingith said. "He will take you all the way to the mines."

The leonim and I departed Coros Valley. The beast maneuvered effortlessly through the slough, and as we crossed out of the swampland, the top of a canyon became just visible on the horizon. The leonim halted at the edge of the plateau and seemed to ponder how he would descend. Tree roots snaked in and out of the canyon wall. The leonim leaped off the edge to perch on a sturdy root, and from there we skipped down from root to root until we reached the bottom. I said good-bye to the powerful beast, patting him gratefully; he turned and scaled the canyon wall the same way we'd come.

An unfamiliar voice called out, "Hey!"

Lithe and light-skinned, a sea-elf emerged from the mines. As he approached, I could see faint traces of scales gleaming in his skin. His species fascinated me. I'd learned that the sea-elves could breathe underwater as easily as a fish and moved very gracefully on foot. With no tolerance for disloyalty or injustice, they were the first to aid the Elowfons during the invasion in the Elder Wars. Without that help, the dominion of Ylora would have been completely overrun by the undead Murinkai—and for that service, sea-elves were universally respected.

"You're Asillus's and Svar's little experiment, aren't you?" The sea-elf wore a haughty grin. He was tall, more than a head higher than my Zana. Slender and strong like most of the warriors in Edannair, he wore metal shoulder armor and a breastplate, and he carried two daggers on his hips. "It's Loxy, am I right?"

"How would you know that?"

"You are female. That news gets around," said the stranger.

"And you are?"

Before he could answer, something thudded behind me. I turned. It was Asillus. He had dismounted and was standing beside his alligator. "Hey, Loxy. Everything okay?"

"Hey, Elli … um, Asi." I nodded, bewildered at his sudden appearance.

"Rowley," Asi said, acknowledging the stranger.

"Asillus. What's happening? How are your morphises going these days, buddy?"

"Fine. Thanks." Asi's tone was guarded. "What about you, Rowley? Up to no good, as usual?"

"I'm tier four now. That's as 'no good' as it gets. I'll be going before the Holder soon. I'm sure I'll become an officer after that. Imagine, Asi. Climbing the ranks this fast while others can't pass their first rank in tier two? Weakness can be a bitch."

The apple doesn't fall far from the Holder's ruthless tree, I thought.

"Leave it, Rowley," Asillus's tone was sharp.

"What would the Holder say if he saw you now? Wasting time helping an Isolit. And a female, too. Even more of a waste." Rowley laughed, a short low sound, like gravel under a boot.

"You see her here, don't you? She's not an Isolit anymore."

"Pfft, every female is. Show me one that can avoid a rattrap while crowd controlling and channeling Ingle Lightning."

"What is he talking about, Asi?" I asked.

"My point exactly," Rowley snapped.

"Shut up, Rowley," Asi said.

Rowley laughed again. "Why don't you enter a WAM, Loxy? My brother Xuvy could personally demonstrate it for you."

"Good-bye, Rowley," Asi said.

"That's W-A-M. I'll send you an invitation, Loxy."

We turned and walked away. Asillus's alligator followed.

I felt stung and confused, and in the privacy of my bedroom, I was angry enough to cry. But I didn't want Asi to see me lose it in the game, so I made my voice big-sister steady over the microphone and asked as neutrally as I could, "So, what was that about? What's an Isolit?"

He paused a moment before answering. "Someone who isn't good enough to be a part of Edannair. Some-one who fails."

"Why did Rowley say the Holder would be mad you're helping me?"

"Just ignore him, Loxy."

"He's not here. How would the Holder even know?"

Rowley must have overheard, because he yelled from the cave entrance, "He's everywhere!"

"Don't worry about it, Lox," Asillus said. He stopped and glared back at the sea-elf. "Row is just bored and likes scaring people."

Rowley started to laugh again.

Asi kept walking. His alligator yawned. I followed and lowered my voice. "How is the Holder ... everywhere?"

"The Holder always knows what's going on. His spies tell him everything."

I glanced over my shoulder and saw something huge and bristling above the mine's entrance, getting ready to pounce on Rowley. Spinning around, I wedged my feet and raised my hands. I twisted my wrists—swirling diamond shapes formed, and my palms glowed. I thrust the magic hard, and zipping above Rowley's shoulder, it knocked its target down cold. A snow leopard fell at Rowley's feet from the boulders above. He winced.

Asi burst out laughing. "You okay there, Row?"

"I'm fine."

"Nice Raven's Blast, Loxy." Asillus grinned. "Hey, Rowley! I'd say she's not bad. Just saved your hide, huh?"

"She's a novice," Rowley called back. He wiped his hands on his tunic. "That was just lucky. Let's see you do that in a Sarkmarr raid. You'd see nothing but the spells of others. Let's see then." He tore his daggers from their sheaths and disappeared behind the mines.

I stared after him a moment, his words echoing like bell chimes. *Let's see, indeed.*

CHAPTER EIGHT

"I CAN'T PICTURE HIM. I can't picture Dad, Kay—" Hunter's voice was strained, and he broke off, coughing. "What was it Dad said to me on your birthday? You would have loved it. It was nice." I felt outside myself, like a spectator taking notes. "Did we even go to the tour, sis? Did I compete? I don't know what I'm imagining or what I'm remembering. I feel so screwed up." His voice got tighter—higher. "I can't remember." His voice screeched. "I can't fucking remember!"

Walking blind figure eights around campus, my attention funneled into the phone, I had lost track of time. My body felt numb, my hands limp. I was lugging a stack of final exam study guides that had fallen to the sidewalk more than once. I didn't care. My brother needed me, and I had no idea how to comfort him.

"Hunt. Hunter. Stop a second. When you leave, where do you go?"

"I can't remember him, Kaylie. Listen to me."

"I am listening. Just tell—"

"What was his favorite song? Do you remember that?"

No matter what I tried, for the rest of the call he would only repeat questions about our father, about what we did together, what didn't exist anymore in our lives, and what barely existed in our memories.

We all deal with death in different ways. That's what our high school counselor told Hunter and me. Our mother didn't seem to *deal* in any way we could notice. That's what was tearing Hunter—well both of us—apart. She made Dad's death disappear. Within weeks, it was as if nothing had happened. Pretending to or not, she made it look, smell, and taste like our father had never lived in our home.

After they called off the search and assumed our father dead, he didn't just disappear somewhere on that mountain. He disappeared from us. She stripped the house of anything that was his, reminded us of him, or made us play like him. Hunter ran in front of our mother, frantic, filling his arms with cards, board games, and toys. I watched her pull the Monopoly box from his white, gripping fingers. Everything disappeared behind the rim of a garbage bag. Hiding in the hall closet, Hunter clutched the red marble pouch with Dad's prized shooters and target marbles. When she found him, my brother pleaded, "No! It's Dad's!"

She took it, her eyes glazed over, not even looking at him. "Everything has to go," she said, in a trance. "This is how we move on."

Even now, two years later, cleaning was still her preferred emotional outlet. Of course, it was more than keeping the dirt and dust away. She rearranges the house a few dozen times a year. She shuts the world out and herself off. No newspapers can be found in our house. No radio can hum its tune or television transmit its tales from the rabble. Hunter knows better than to wear headphones around her: she'll pull them out of his ears. "There's nothing productive that comes from being so plugged in," she'd say. "It's more important to be together, be in the moment with each other."

I might agree, but of the three of us, she is the most unreachable.

SABRINA AND MARCO WERE IN MID-DEBATE when I finally trudged in. I let my backpack fall on the couch. Dusk had settled, giving the windows a bleak, gray cast. Sabrina looked up from a recipe book on the island—she was wearing her rainbow apron, and Marco leaned his tan frame against the kitchen wall.

"All I'm saying is," he continued, "even if the woman had a sixty percent chance of survival facing the bear, compared to the ten percent chance she would have running away, she would still run away."

Saby pursed her lips. "How do you know what she would do?"

"Women's minds are like architectural columns. You tilt the foundation and the pillar will falter. It's physics."

"You're the future architect of America," Sabrina said. "Practicing his acceptance speeches."

Marco posed with both hands on his hips. "*¿Ah nena, no me conocés? ¡Soy Argentino!*"

"When are you going to teach me Spanish?" Saby crooned.

Meanwhile, I started a scavenger hunt around the house for my headphones. Finding them hanging over the bathroom doorknob, I shook my head. Of course— the last place I looked.

In the kitchen, Saby had descended into flirtatious giggles. "Kay! We're going to *something something* opening in a few, come with!" Sabrina was shouting in between her flirtatious giggles.

"What?"

She tried repeating it again to me; I got an even worse translation.

"What was that?" I said, entering the kitchen.

"We're going...." She giggled through her words. "Stop it, Marco." He was holding his hand over his mouth, also laughing at some inside joke. "We're going to Ni Che's grand opening tonight. I've got passes for me and three guests to speak with the chefs after the presentation. Free sake, too."

"Thanks. But you guys go ahead."

"I've already put your name on the list."

Since Hunter's call, my stomach had ached with empty sulkiness. It was sort of like the feeling after you've gone hours without eating, but even more hollow, more drab.

"Marco, don't you think she should go?"

Marco stroked his chin—enjoying his role as judge and jury. "I do. I do think you should go. It's been too long since either of you have seen me down twelve sakes. Then it won't be bears and percentages, but pyramids! On the foundation of a telephone poll."

Sabrina howled and looked to me to join in. "He's been cracking me up like this since lunch!"

"You guys go ahead. I've had a hard day. I wouldn't be much company."

"You need to go out more. You know I know what I'm talking about."

I inhaled, but my breath felt strained. I couldn't find appropriate words. I wanted to catalogue every detail of how shitty I felt in that moment. But I couldn't. "I'm sorry. I just don't feel well enough to go."

After a few muttled, terse comments, I heard the front door slam. I shut my eyes, squeezed the pillow in my arms, and tried to reassure myself. It'd be better to stay in tonight. I couldn't ride the night, meet people, and waste time in the same forced chitchat my mother demanded from me at home. It made me sick. *I've proven that already*, I thought, picturing Wes. *What a perfect example.* I let my chin fall into the feather cushion and fought back the tears. I didn't want to recount my steps, wondering how many mistakes I was making or how many friends I was hurting.

Wes had been my first college love, and he had meant

a great deal to me, but I ended it. We met during a study group at the library. Weston Ryan Caine had introduced himself by passing out Pez candy dispensers to everyone. Weston Caine. It sounded like a superhero name. He made me laugh—he poked fun at the group's halfhearted attempts to focus on studying, and he joked that I was attending college in the wrong country because I spoke with a hint of Mum's BBC English. Dating came naturally. We fit together. Whether we were walking and talking between classes or leaning into each other while studying, it was effortless. He was confident, yet down-to-earth, and he loved to laugh. Like my dad, I guess. But then his interest in my family and background grew. Avoiding questions worked for a little while, but I knew the connection between us was getting stronger. So, I shut the door.

It had been a Tuesday. I waited by the tower, our usual meetup spot. When he walked around the corner, I swallowed hard, as if it was the first time I had seen him. He was so attractive—it was the quiet confidence he had that made him more attractive than other handsome guys. I watched his perfect smile light up his face when he saw me. His hat tilted a fraction to one side, and his clothes were immaculate and fashionable. He kissed my cheek and said, "Hi, beautiful."

I tried to respond. But it was the first day of my brother's first disappearance. I'd spent the morning crying and thinking about Dad. Weary and feeling torn apart, I let my gaze fall to the sidewalk. "Wes, I'm sorry. I can't... I can't do this."

Thinking about that day only made me feel worse. Grabbing my running shoes, I ignored the dusk and dangers of jogging alone. I had to get out. I had to run the pain out of my life. The emotions were closing in—hovering like demons.

I ran hard on the hills. Every step had to mean something, had to get me away from everything and everyone. I tried to ignore how lonely it felt—living without the warmth of family and the intimacy of strong friendships. Clenching my teeth, I ran faster.

After what could have been minutes or an hour— I couldn't pay attention to time—I realized that the buildings and street signs around me were unfamiliar. I slowed down. I was very far from campus. Fear struck a chord somewhere deep inside my abdomen, and I shivered even though my body was hot from the exercise. I gave in to the biting panic, turned around, and ran harder than before, desperate to see a business or street corner I recognized. Finally, in the dim light ahead, I spotted the familiar corner bakery.

A hot shower did nothing to comfort me. I didn't want to sleep, but awake I felt trapped. "Can I just disappear for a while?" I asked the stillness.

Who would answer?

CHAPTER NINE

My dad kneeled beside Hunter. Hunter only had moments to tuck the excess shoelace inside his skater shoes—he was up next. Tipping his skateboard up with his foot, he balanced it with the tips of his fingers, snickered, and said something inaudible to Dad.

The crowd screamed and cheered while the current contender did ollies and grinds over ledges and rails. Thousands of fans had come from everywhere to watch the Tour Cup National Skateboarding Finals. I couldn't believe my younger brother had qualified; he was now considered one of the best competitive skaters in the country. Hunter had worked tireless hours preparing for this moment. He and Dad had exhausted every skate park they could find, and when those were overworked, they built new challenges in the yard or garage. Pride washed over me—it was such an accomplishment for Hunter.

I exhaled heavily. *I'm glad it's not me having to compete under this kind of pressure.*

I never wanted the spotlight. Though I loved the art of competition, it was difficult for me to believe in myself enough to see it through to the finish. Mum always asked me how that was possible. As the elder sister, how could I not want to compete and win for Hunter, for the family, and for my own success? I couldn't really answer her. I did all those things for Hunter already—just in small, everyday ways. I made sure he remembered his lunch, and when he dented the side of Dad's car with his skateboard, I lied for him and said I'd done it with my bicycle. Formal competition was irrelevant to the daily fact of being Hunter's big sister.

I looked to the section where Mum was sitting. I could see her, but barely. She held a camera in one hand and with the other waved a pennant with my brother's competitor number. Dad and I stood just behind the skaters' box on the backside of the stage.

"Hunter Ames," the announcer called. Hunter threw his board in front of him and, in one fluid motion, hopped aboard and sailed toward a bench with a rail above it. His board flipped and turned in the air onto the first bench, and the announcer shouted, "A nollie flip crook at the bench, and Hunter Ames is on his way!"

I watched Hunter's expression—solemn in concentration. He kicked for more speed and bent his knees. He ollied over a ledge and kick-flipped over another. Hunter skated like he was born for wheels. He zigzagged around the arena, flipping tricks of all technical levels with ease.

In the far corner of the ring, there were two larger ramps. On one side, there was a handrail and on the other a gap between the two ramps. A skater had the choice to either ollie over the ramps or grind the handrail. Earlier, I had overheard Hunter talking about one trick he wanted to do specifically for that end ramp. Dad said something close to, "Well, risk is what gets reward."

The announcer shouted again. "A kick flip back-side-fifty-fifty, and Hunter has taken that directly into a switch-crooked grind! He is on fire, folks!"

I couldn't follow all the tricks, but I saw my brother airborne and immune to gravity. The crowd was already on their feet. Hunter was nearing the larger ramps for the ending. I watched as he ollied high into the air. He flipped his board at the peak of his ascent—as if it was an extension of himself—and going backward on the tip of his board, he sailed along the handrail. The crowd ignited. But as Hunter and his board left the rail, they came down in an awkward slant. He lost his balance, and as he landed, his ankle twisted off his board. As he hit the concrete, Hunter went rigid and his face screwed up in pain. He rolled to his side and rocked in slow motion, reaching for his ankle.

Two medics rushed to Hunter's side. They tried to lay him on a gurney, but Hunter shrugged them off and stood up. He took a step, then another on his bad ankle, and almost fell. The medics placed Hunter's arms over their shoulders and helped him to the skaters' area, where they began wrapping his ankle.

Hunter was holding second place after four rounds of

technical and freestyle attempts, but if he didn't finish the fifth and final round, he would be disqualified. I watched as Hunter pleaded with my father about something. Dad was watching Hunter carefully.

He's not trying to go back out and skate, is he?

I watched, baffled, as my father nodded to Hunter. My brother grabbed his skateboard and got back in line behind the other competitors. My father spoke with the medics. I glanced to the audience, knowing Mum must have felt as confused as I was. Before I could protest, it was Hunter's turn again; he was back on his board, skating across the floor for another freestyle routine. He cut out the big tricks because his ankle was visibly giving out on him, and the immense pain was evident in his face. But he wouldn't give up. He had to skate. He forced himself to skate. It was his moment. He seized it beyond any pain or logic for health or safety.

The crowd roared as Hunter finished. He collapsed onto the concrete and threw his arms in the air. Mum was clapping and twisting her hips in a victory dance. I cheered, and Dad was beaming. My brother had done it. Risk for reward. He had held on and somehow managed to finish. Hunter looked up at the scoreboard, waiting as his scores were tallied. His name appeared after several others, placing him in sixth. He threw his fist in the air and waved to the crowd. Sixth may not have been high enough for the winner's circle, but he wasn't disqualified and could return to the tour next year.

During the awards ceremony, the judges asked Hunter to stand next to the winner in recognition of his profound tenacity. Hunter stood on stage, smiling brightly and balancing on his good ankle.

My father couldn't stop whooping and calling out, "You did it, son! You did it!" Mum waved the pennant high overhead, and I clapped and cheered.

As I called out to him, the stage, my parents, the skaters, and everything else disappeared. I awoke. I sat up, unsure if it had been a dream or if the room and flat silent around me now were unreal. The air was cold, but a deeper frigidity bothered me. I could feel it in my heart, heavy and aching like a block of dry ice. I sank back down beneath the covers, accepting that I was still here, trapped.

Hunter's words echoed in my mind—his tortured voice on the telephone. The way he asked what was real and what was imagination, trying to place the foggy memories. I knew all too well how he felt. That day at the Tour Cup, though—Hunter had made our family so proud. I looked up to *him* that day, as if he was the elder sibling. The four of us were happy and real and perfect, just for a day. *I'm failing as a big sister*, I thought. The image of Elliott in the grocery store struck me again. I felt sick thinking about the humiliation and bullying he was enduring. *Well, I won't fail with Elliott. I won't lose all my friends.*

The Holder investigation wasn't progressing fast enough. How could I learn what really goes on in Sarkmarr and how morphises were assigned? Did the Holder know about Elliott's difficulties trusting people?

Only Sarkmarr members know the answers.

And in that moment, I knew what to do.

CHAPTER TEN

"THAT'S IT. After that he sent me on my way." Camadro was describing the previous day's interaction with a Sarkmarr officer to Asillus. His large mouth and yellow earthtroll skin would have made him hideous, except for the teddy-bear softness to his voice.

I had come late to the story, but from what I could tell, the officer's name was Ilusas. He was checking on Camadro's recent morphis mission but wouldn't promise that Camadro would move to the next tier: "Relax, Camadro," he'd said. "If you did the mission correctly, you'll move ahead. No need to get abrupt." I didn't believe that Camadro was presumptuous enough to push a Sarkmarr officer—it sounded like Ilusas just loved to hear himself talk.

Ilusas had continued, "You wrote the e-mails to each woman on your floor explaining your handicap? That your lisp is genetic—there is nothing you can do about it—and that, no, you are not drunk and you hope it is not offensive?"

Camadro agreed and gave Ilusas copies of the women's responses. He reminded Ilusas that he had no such impediment and tried to broach the issue of the morphis missions getting out of hand. "For venting's sake, can I just say, the Holder is such a bastard."

Ilusas laughed and said it would be the Holder's decision to promote Camadro to tier three. "So be nice to him."

Camadro sat back on his heels. "Well? What do you think, Asillus?"

Asi shrugged as he picked up another emerald from the sack at his feet. Of the many things Asillus took up in Edannair, jewelcrafting was his most advanced skill. "That's how these trials go, I guess."

"It's ridiculous," Camadro said, now pacing back and forth. Asillus nodded. It was an absurd sight: a dwarf of Asi's height only reached Camadro's waist. "How long have you known me?"

Asi paused in thought.

"Exactly. Way too long. You know I'm a good guy. But patience is not my virtue."

I listened to the two of them from a few yards away, where the shadowlock trainer had set up his shop, offering in-game learning with simulation examples. He had outfitted me with weapons and spell ingredients, too. Though I was supposed to be practicing, it was hard not to overhear Camadro and Asi.

"Gotta keep my eye on the prize, Asillus, or I'm going to go out of my mind on all their asses," Camadro said.

The easy communication in Edannair still fascinated

me. I could speak and listen to conversations as if they were happening in my own room, even though the people "around" me actually resided in other cities, states, or countries.

The three of us were in Quillinthos. The massive city was busy, like most in Edannair, but it exuded a prestigious strength and decadence. It was built underground, on a triangular plan, and was one of Edannair's leading production sites for coal, iron, and steel. The architecture was almost ancient Egyptian. The walls reminded me of a pyramid's, with red and tan rocks stacked to dizzying heights. There were no ceilings that reached less than forty yards above me. Clearly, claustrophobia was not going to be an issue.

Camadro looked toward me; I kept my alias's body aimed toward the trainer. "What about Lady Loxy? How's she getting along?"

I froze and then pretended not to have heard.

"Going well," Asi said. "She works hard and practices a lot; she's actually picking it up really fast. And always in a hurry."

"Newbies. Always think they can one-shot this place, don't they? Has she seen any WAMs?"

"No, not yet."

"Don't tell me all she's done are missions, Asillus. You prude. What the hell, man? Take her into some WAMs."

"She's not allowed yet."

"Oh, right, eh. Well, when she hits Highmark, get her in."

"Until then, I'd like to *keep* her in Edannair, remember, not scare her away."

"I'm sure you do."

"She's really good in dungeons. Quick to cast. Pretty impressive. She hasn't been here that long."

They lowered their voices. I tried to focus on the trainer's lecture and to drown out the general trading chatter, but it was hard to ignore.

"Looking for jewelcrafter to cut Dirambic ruby!"

"Healers looking for group. Anything going on?"

"Want to trade furwoven cloth for Crusable orbs!"

It never stopped.

"Hey, Camadro," I said, approaching the two. "I overheard a little bit about your trials. You sounded upset."

"It's ridiculous. You don't want to get me started again. Sarkmarr's unbelievable. By the way, Asillus—did you hear about Zulu?"

"Who?"

"Zulu. Remember the druid that went up against Xuvy—last year's WAMs. He beat him, remember?" Laughter bellowed from his almost simian alias. "Well, he's gone! A tier four! Supposedly one of the best conjurers on the continent."

"What happened?" I asked.

"He was brought before the Holder, normal protocol, had just been promoted to tier four, *tier four*, after how many missions in Edannair and out? And he said some wrong f'ing thing and got tossed."

"Do you know what he said?"

"Acted like a pig is what I heard. And before he knew it, the Holder had grabbed his ankle, flew him up above Ruinnlark, and suspended him in the middle of the street. He had Harbor Smoke around him for hours."

"Harbor Smoke?"

"Yeah, a smoke that knits together around your alias, enclosing you in it—a free-floating jail cell, basically. You can't get out of it for a day and a half!" Camadro started cackling again. "The Holder does it. The only one who can do it. If you see someone in Harbor Smoke, you know they did something to piss him off."

Asillus shook his head.

"And everyone in Ruinnlark crosses that street." Camadro exhaled loudly. "Dude, have you told her about your next morphis mission?"

Asi seemed annoyed at the question. "Why would I do that?"

"Go on, tell her."

"It doesn't matter. Loxy, ready to go over some more training?"

"Why don't you want to tell me, Asi?"

Asi looked at me. "Can we move on?"

"He's gotta go—"

"Camadro! I said move on," Asi snapped.

"Fine, okay, okay. Was just sayin'—"

This is the moment, I told myself. *Take it.* "I'd like to apply to Sarkmarr."

Both looked at me with shocked faces. "What!"

"I'd like to join."

"You just heard what I went through, and Zulu." Camadro was baffled. "You're kidding."

"Why would you want to join, Loxy?"

I wanted to say: *Because, Elliott. You're not going through this alone.* But the words came out differently. "Well. Because. Same reason you guys want to. When you're in, everyone knows you're the best; that you endured hell, and still won out. I'd like to hope I'm that kind of caliber."

"No offense, Loxy, but the people applying have been in Edannair for years. You just got here. You're not even at Highmark yet."

"Camadro's right, Lox."

"You said so yourself—I'm way ahead, Asillus. I'm flying through my training."

"Yes, but this isn't just a few Ruinnlark missions. The Holder tests everything. Not just your in-game skills. He messes with your mind—with your outside life, too."

"You've been having fun in Edannair so far, right?" Camadro said. "I used to quest solo, without being a part of any groups. Just exploring the world. Stick to that. That's my advice. I'll see you noobs later, I gotta bounce."

Asillus leaned toward me. "It's insane. Loxy, seriously, you don't want to do this."

Yes I do. I have to, I thought. "Then why do you, Asillus? Why can't I want that same experience? To succeed at the impossible? I really want to."

"Edannair is more fun played casually. Most Sarkmarr members have no respect for anyone but themselves. I don't want you to have to deal with them. They're not worth it. Just forget about Sarkmarr."

"Elliott. I've been in a coma for a while now. Edannair has been the wake-up. And part of that is getting into Sarkmarr. It's me proving something to myself."

"What?"

"That—I can still play. Have fun at something. And show the Holder, or Rowley, or anyone else like them, they don't know what they're talking about. You can't judge a person from completing or not completing some random morphis mission."

Elliott nodded slowly, his eyes lost in thought.

"Can you imagine their reaction if I were to scorch a raid with the best of them?"

He didn't look up at me.

"Asillus?"

He stared at the mortar in the stone floor.

"Asi, I need your help."

"Loxy. These members, they won't hold your hand. They expect perfection. You can't miss a hit, a heal, an interrupt. You have to be on, one hundred percent of the time. I don't even think a girl's been accepted before."

"Good, I'll bring a refreshing change. Sounds like fun."

"Fun. Ha. We'll see what you say in a week."

"Thanks, Asillus." I hugged him. "What's the worst we could get into?"

"Uh, ruin any chances for unlimited fame, status, respect, the Stakes, the Holder's secrets, access passes to everything.... Nope. No risk at all."

I laughed. "We'll be fine. So, how do we do this?"

"Well, we need you to hit Highmark. And I don't know, a miracle? And you do realize Sarkmarr's applications cycle opens in a few weeks. And it only lasts a couple of days, twice a year. We need one hell of a long night with a *hell* of a lot of miracles thrown in the next few weeks."

"We can do it."

Asi sighed and then smiled. "I'll get a group together. You go talk to Pulm at the south tower in Ruinnlark. Fly to Kape-Fall and head west to Illinor Keep—the huge fortress surrounded by giant wooden catapults. Can't miss it. We're on the craziest deadline tonight."

CHAPTER ELEVEN

SIDESTEPPING OUT OF THE PATHS of flying carpets and small helicopters, I watched as giant Hoden bats were trained into submission. Emerald dragons with webbed feet and refractive blue-green skin bellowed to each other while eagles, almost as large as the dragons, ruffled golden-red feathers. South Bank's Landing was a flurry of flights that flecked the ground and sky.

"Excuse me?"

The flight master aimed his wooden walking stick at my navel. He was my height exactly, but looked down his nose at me with a smug smile. His exceptionally thin body, propped against his walking stick, made him look like a bicycle kickstand.

The Allika species, I remembered. Thinner than humanly possible, the Allika could move through mud or grass without leaving a single footprint and had the ability to communicate with all beings in Edannair.

"Yesss? Flight Master Pulmmm, at your servisss."

The flight master's lips were thin and, strangely, reached

almost entirely to each side of his face. His head was egg-shaped, and his small eyes—reptile eyes—flicked over me.

"I'd like a flight to Kape-Fall, please, Master Pulm."

The Allika rolled his shoulders, adjusting his tawny cape. He brought the walking stick down and placed both of his hands over the cane's head. "You're a new fly-yyer, aren't youuu?" He was still sizing me up.

Is it his wide mouth that makes him speak that way? I wondered. "Yes, I am. How'd you know?"

"I wouldn't beeee a master if I didn't know, now wooooould I?"

"May I have a flight please? I must get to Kape-Fall."

"Mayyy I havvve a flight, ppplease?" Master Pulm said, mimicking a female. "This isn't, 'Come onnnne, come allll,' is it? You're flying an Archimon eagle. Myyyy eagles. I must take a momennnt and innnspect—"

"Master Pulm!" A young Norseman boy with mud on his knees and face ran up the ramp to the circular landing where we stood. "I need a flight, sir! For Sarkmarr. I have news for Ilusas from the leader of Eludan himself!"

"Very wellll, young Ornwin." Master Pulm smiled affectionately at the boy. He grabbed the edge of his cloak with one hand, his walking stick with the other, and walked—no, more like floated—to the Archimons. The cane was clearly for show.

Pulm approached the eagles, which were pecking out of a communal urn filled with what looked like sunflower seeds. He lifted his hand to the face of one. The bird tilted its head into the touch. The master's fingers sunk in between rouge and yellow feathers, and he pulled it close. As he whispered to it, the eagle stretched its head, showing the length of the neck. The wind caught its feathers. The eagle knelt, and Ornwin jumped onto the bird's saddle and levered himself aright. His eyes were wide open, and his face glowed youthful and eager as Pulm spoke.

"I've told him to beee extra swifffft, for he is carrying a runnner of Sarkmarrr."

The boy beamed, his white teeth showing in a huge smile. The Archimon stretched its wings and lifted into the air, soaring high, until all I could see was the outline of wings.

The Holder's influence seemed to be everywhere. Even Pulm bowed to him.

The Allika straightened and finally remembered me. "Oh yesss, my new flyerrrr. Are you readyyy?" His eyes, beady and narrow, darted from me to the eagles, and his upside-down smile formed. "My Archimons know the path, Loxssivey. All I want youuu to dooo is keep yourrr feet in the stirrrups and hold on. Do not lean hithhher and tithhherr, do not sing or shout. In fact, it is better you tryyy and beee undetectable. Unless you'd like a fast exxxit to earth from a thousand mmmeters above?"

I shook my head.

"Lyrrriia!" An eagle slightly smaller than Ornwin's, probably female, raised her chocolate-colored head and approached the Allika. Pulm took her head gently and whispered. The eagle squawked, and Pulm gestured me toward the bird. She lowered her shoulder toward me. With a step I was astride, and seconds later we were in the air, rising higher and higher while Pulm and the other eagles shrank from view.

Up into the sky we soared. Edannair was even more magnificent from above: purple grasses, cliffsides, gullies, canyons, and neon flora and icetopias. This world was uniquely rebellious, possessing whatever season it wanted, wherever it wanted.

Lyrria glided easily with me as her passenger. We came across the Ridges of Belloy, an area enclosed by rocky slopes and craters. Red rivers laced through ashy soil and pools of lava. Fire elementals moved in figure-eight patterns, their funnels ceaselessly churning red magma.

All of the trees along the Ridges of Belloy had burned. The fire elementals consumed everything for miles. From the skies, the elementals looked serene and docile, but I'd heard they were terrifying in battle.

Lyrria left the blackened regions and took me into the ruins of Sul'Baron, the land of the ancient witch doctors. These masters had skulls for faces and wore long, tattered robes. The ground in their lands was covered in rubble and crumbling statues, with a few windswept areas that revealed ancient tile flooring. One witch doctor looked up to watch Lyrria and me. Slow and methodical was his stare. It sent a chill down my spine, and I gripped the eagle's saddle bar tighter.

We crossed into the borders of Ridges Point, above the Arrowhead Mountains. The ridges towered together, crowding and competing for the horizon, forbidding travelers safe passage. The imperial landscape made my stomach lurch. In Tacoma, Mount Rainier boasts its presence. To others, the mountain is a beautiful attraction, fit for visiting and pictures. For me, it's a gut-punch. Every time I stepped outside our home, I was looking at his graveyard, a colossal reminder of what had been stolen too soon from my life. My father…he was up there somewhere. He died alone, with no one there to hold him or remind him how much he was loved.

Living in Tacoma, with no way to escape that daily view, tormented me. I ran from it, but in moving away, I had put my brother and mother in greater jeopardy. I tried to push my past out of my mind. That is the curious thing about memories—they have a way of haunting us in the very moments in which we believe we have escaped.

"I can't find your brother!" I remembered Mum's voice after Hunter's first disappearance, her tone high and sharp like squealing tires. A tone I had only heard from her once before, that horrible winter.

Hunter started disappearing shortly after Dad died. The local quarries, the hidden estuaries, they became his oases. When Mum had called with her frantic news, I took the first plane back and we scouted the city for fourteen hours, finally finding him hiking a Forest Service road outside the city. Hunter wouldn't answer her questions.

He just sat with his forehead against the backseat window, the glass absorbing a halo of heat from his skin.

The disappearance before the last plagued my mind. *Almost a week?* I couldn't picture Hunter anymore without seeing the image of him, tattered and thin, stumbling through the front door.

Kape-Fall's greenery was a welcome interruption. Wildflowers grew in patches of grass, and the grass overtook the stony slopes, giving way to rolling foothills. I could see Illinor Keep in the distance. The land was fully green now, and chaparral grew in clumps around stone-fenced pastures.

Huge wooden catapults guarded the keep's moat, and large sandbag dummies lined the end of a shooting range. Three tiers of disc-shaped landings protruded from the stone tower. It was a training fortress—a way to reach Highmark status.

Asillus stood outside arched double doors on the second-tier landing; three others waited with him. Lyrria swooped down and pulled up just shy of Asillus. He scowled at the bird. Lyrria squawked frisky chirps at him. I bowed after dismounting, and Lyrria stabbed her beak in the air, took flight, and doubled back.

"Blasted eagles," Asillus bellowed. "We're all here. Loxy, this is Furtim, one of the quickest rogues I know, and Dagan, one of the finest bowmen."

The ranger Dagan lifted his bow toward me politely. His scalp gleamed around a single dreadlock, and his plum-colored tongue licked cracked violet lips. His face was so hollow that his cheeks were more bone than flesh. The undead, I remembered. The Murinkai. The other, a Zana, matched me—the hybrid of cat and human features seemed fitting for this stealthy rogue, Furtim.

"And finally, meet Modaga, a very old friend of mine. We've been fighting together since the Qoointies."

"Nice to meetcha, Loxeh." Modaga's alias was armed with more trinkets and tallies than what seemed possible to carry, even with the large satchel slung over his shoulder. His shield was lashed to his back, and canteens knocked together on his belt along with knives, extra rope, satchels, a compass, and what looked like a cluster of charms hooked to an oversized key ring.

"You too! And actually, I've heard of you."

"Not surprised by that. I'm pretty important."

"Can it, Modaga," Asi teased.

"I mean, I've heard your voice before," I said. "When Asillus was introducing me to all this. The accent is pretty memorable."

"Sexy, innit?"

Groans from Asi and the others filled the speakers.

"Here we go," Furtim said.

"No one agrees with you, Modaga." Asi chuckled. "Let's head in."

We stepped through the fortress doors. Thick, fog veiled the entrance. The smoke swirled around our feet in random eddies. As we entered, it cleared, and the blurred surroundings of the interior came into focus. A white stone hall funneled us to a quartermaster who announced, "Fight and defeat every enemy."

Asillus turned to us. "Get ready, everyone. We have a ton to do for Loxy tonight. We need a miracle."

"Nah, no miracle needed. Just me warrior's strength and a bit of luck." Modaga winked, and in one fluid stroke, he unhooked his charm ring and kissed it.

"Thank you all for coming," I said.

"Ya know, Loxy, Sarkmarr's pretty intense," Furtim said.

"Coming from such an experienced source?" Dagan teased.

"I know I'm new to it myself. But I've seen enough to say the Holder's intense."

"Has anyone ever told him that?" I said. No one answered. "It seems someone ought to."

"No no no, lass. Some things are better left untampered with."

"Why not, Modaga? If not you, or Furtim, then who?"

"I like your spirit," said Modaga, chuckling.

"Let's go, guys," Asi said.

Drums rumbled like thunder between the stone walls. My group conjured Valiance, Resilience, Stamina, and Intellect, increasing our strength, spell power, and agility. Modaga drew his sword and shield, Dagan nocked his bow, and the two of them took the lead.

At the end of the hall, we came to a dimly lit room. The ground seemed fluid, like shallow water shuddering in a breeze. Our eyes adjusted to the shadows, and we saw the motion was caused not by a fluid on the floor, but by a slithering. Hundreds of yellow serpents masked the floor like a thick rug.

"Psst. Loxy."

I turned to Dagan. "Yes?"

His violet lips thinned in a wry smile. "Wager? Bet I can double your damage."

I looked at the oval room. Its floor was sunken below a raised colonnade, and the snakes filled the whole depression. "Uhh … I've only just started, but I'll give you a run at that," I said.

"Hmmm. Want to bet I beat Furtim, then?"

I looked to see if Furtim had heard us. He was gone. "Where is he?"

"Here," Furtim said, appearing from behind us. "And I take that bet. The winner gets a week's worth of minerals."

Furtim was quick and quiet—true to his feline nature. He touched Dagan's bow with his dagger to seal the wager, and the two got into position. Three giant python-like creatures, big as dragons, came slithering from the north, east, and west tunnels into the room.

"Imoogi," whispered Modaga. "They be cursed creatures. Hornless and limbless, they reside here and in the sea."

The giant Imoogi slithered down the stairs almost as if choreographed. They rose up when they reached the middle of the room and wove hypnotically back and forth, their green-and-yellow bodies twisting around one another as they hissed at the smaller snakes.

"Steady, lads." Modaga's tone was low. "On me mark. Let's go."

He stepped forward with the rest of us close at his heels.

As we arrived at the stairs, the Imoogi sensed us and formed a line, their tongues tasting the air and their green eyes ardent. Then they charged. The smaller snakes fled. Furtim crouched and darted behind the Imoogi. Modaga surged forward, his sword and shield brandished. Dagan fired an arrow, and then another and another, so rapidly their paths blurred.

Furtim slashed an Imoogi with his dagger. The Imoogi swirled around, mouth open and fangs dripping with poison. As the Imoogi's mouth snapped at Furtim, Modaga clanged his sword and shield together and slammed the haft against the snake.

"A lil help, Dagan!" Modaga called out.

Dagan dipped his arrows in an urn at his feet. When the laced arrow pierced the Imoogi, the snake went into some sort of trance and turned slowly toward Modaga. Asillus was beginning to sweat as he chanted a healing barrier of protection around us, and another Imoogi turned to slash at Furtim.

"Loxy, get this one!" Furtim yelled.

Think think think. Go! With clenched fists, I conjured the Seed of Inoga. My hands glowed, and from them, green flames swirled and grew, spitting out ribbons of magic. *Now!* I hurled the emerald light at the center Imoogi. The spell seeped into the beast's scaly skin. The Imoogi's attack speed slowed as it struck at Furtim. It wavered, and suddenly a green aura burst through its skin. Green wisps of smoke curled out of the snake as it sank to the ground. The other two screeched and wavered for a moment, then glowered. The nearest one looked at me, as if it knew who was responsible, and charged. Modaga struck his shield against the charging Imoogi, but it did not flinch. The Norseman looked to Asillus with panic in his face.

"Protect Loxy!"

"I'm protecting everybody!" Asillus yelled back.

The Imoogi snapped and struck at me. I dodged.

What was the spell I needed? My mind raced.

The other serpent was now free to attack Furtim. It whipped around and its fangs came arcing down toward him. Furtim ducked just in time, almost dancing to stay out of reach. He thrust his dagger into the Imoogi's abdomen. The giant serpent lashed at Furtim again. This time the rogue's duck was too slow. A fang sliced a shard of flesh from the Zana's arm.

Furtim shrieked.

Modaga turned back to help Furtim. His blade and bludgeoning shield caught the Imoogi's attention, and he jumped beyond its reach.

Augur's Cry! That's it! Closing my eyes, I recited the

chant. A terrifying sound echoed in the cave. The two Imoogi hung their heads—disoriented and dizzy—before pitching their heads back and panicking. They hissed and raced around the room in an erratic pattern. The distraction was just long enough. Dagan nocked more arrows and let them fly. But when the snakes came out of their frenzy, they headed straight for Modaga.

Asillus, still conjuring healing barriers, shouted out, "Running low on energy guys! Hurry!"

"Kill 'em!" Modaga yelled.

"Blow everything!" Furtim said.

A spray of celestial light rained down on the beasts. Modaga put his shield and sword together and struck the ground; the earth quivered and shook beneath them. Dagan peppered the creatures with splintering arrows that multiplied upon release, while Furtim slashed his daggers across scaly flesh. Another Imoogi finally sunk to the ground. The third took a dozen more arrows, and then its attacks slowed—it wavered and finally fell.

We stood together, looking at the beasts at our feet.

"That's one way to do it," Asi said.

"That was insane," I said. "I don't think I was breathing that whole time."

"Pay up, Dagan." Furtim smirked at the Murinkai bowman. "I obviously won. Look at this war wound." The Zana was tying cloth around his biceps.

The bowman sighed. "With the Holder's cheat, I would have won."

"Hmm? What Holder's cheat?" I asked.

"The Holder can cast this empowering enchantment," Furtim said. "It gives you an edge—a strength and accuracy boost. It's like a focus drug."

"Pixie Dust," said Asillus.

"Ohhh man, what that could do for me," Dagan said, lifting his bow. "It'd be amazing. Loxy, you could duplicate your Seed of Inoga more often, and that trio we just had…you could have owned."

"Who is this guy?" I whispered.

"We all wish we knew." Modaga's eyes were wild with the idea of it. "To know how he does what he does would be…well, I 'spect it'd be like knowing a god—and not even those powerful Shades know a thing. And they've been trying to catch him fer years."

"Shades?" I asked.

"Let's keep moving," Asillus said.

"Walk with me, Loxeh," Modaga said. "Let me enlighten ye on Edannair's dirty secret. Shades be the police."

Asillus led us at a quick pace through strange hallways, where the ceilings shed a faint virga that did not reach the ground.

"What are Shades?"

"Godly aliases. Can do anything. Ya might as well give up if ye come across 'em. I seen 'em bend steel and halve glaciers with nothin' but a whisper. Shades can disappear and appear as they like. They have the power to ban ye, kill ye, suspend ye, strip ye clean."

100

I listened as we moved along the winding through-way into a room where silvery ash covered the floor.

"They been trying to catch the Holder fer years. Nay, not one can. He's a charlatan to them, but a hero to the masses. A touchy position to be in, if ye ask me. No one knows how he's done it."

"Careful in here," Asi called out.

We entered a dim antechamber where water trickled all around us. I turned my palm up, and ink-black mud splattered my hand.

"I'd be thinking a beast is lurking in here. Better ready ye'self, lass."

ALL THROUGH THE NIGHT and into the twilight hours of the morning, we worked as a cohesive unit, surviving encounter after encounter. Fortress after fortress, we plundered, each more easily than the last. We claimed nearly forty enemies. By all measures, we shone—even without *his* Pixie Dust.

When I said goodnight and signed off, dawn lit my windowpane. My head pulsed for sleep. My body was lethargic. But I couldn't stop smiling. I had joined up with three strangers and a close friend, and instantly, we all trusted each other. We made an alliance and worked to keep each other alive. And on top of that, we had met the objective. A new part of Edannair opened to me: I had reached Highmark.

CHAPTER TWELVE

I walked into the stark auditorium and inhaled the heavy musk of mold and chalk. Danny and Eve waved at me as I climbed the classroom stairs to the middle row.

"Welcome, Ms. Ames." Danny greeted me in his usual calm, collected style.

"Hi, Kay," Eve said.

"You've created a monster in Eve," Danny began. "She hasn't stopped reading about food and drug companies and how to stay organic since you've talked about it."

"Well, Kaylie's right. We should know where our food comes from. And our baby's food." Eve looked down and touched her stomach gently.

I gasped and grabbed Eve's hand. "You're ...?"

She nodded and started giggling. "I'm not showing at all yet, still in the first trimester."

"No wonder you're glowing."

As Danny answered his cell phone, I leaned into Eve and rested my head on her shoulder. "How have you been feeling?"

"Really not bad at all—just having a hard time finding food I actually want to eat."

"Congratulations. This is such an exciting time for you both. Have you told your parents?"

"No," Eve said laughing. "I keep imagining it, but actually following through with it—I have no idea. Not looking forward to their faces. Danny and I are planning so much that I want to tell my parents about it, but I've barely been able to speak to them." She paused. "They have their own view of the way things should be. It's hard to convince them to see anything else. I've been waiting till it feels like the right time."

"I know you guys will be great, and everything will work out."

The professor's microphone scratched to life. "Class. Remember to review the art we discussed from the Renaissance and Baroque periods." Professor Ledson's monotone hushed the room, and a dusty silence fell over the auditorium.

The lecture made me wish for a coffee. The sleep deprivation was catching up to me, and it was hard to concentrate. My eyes felt like lead doors. I forced myself to draw and color shapes in my notebook in between my other notes.

My phone buzzed in my back pocket. Eve reached for hers, too. Somebody was blowing them up with messages—Sabrina. Two more buzzed in on the heels of the first. We told Danny about the urgent texts and snuck out of class.

When we entered the flat, Saby was sitting on the living room floor with her legs crossed. She cradled her face in her palms.

"What is it, Saby?" I asked. "Are you okay?"

"She's coming. My mother called."

Eve and I looked at each other and sighed relief. A hundred scenarios had run through our heads as we rushed from class.

"You both are so lucky your mothers live out of state. My mother insists on visiting!"

"What did she say?" Eve asked sweetly.

"She said it was in the cards; that she had to stop by today—"

A woman's voice outside the door made us all pause. It was faint, but we could understand a few words. "—won't do…have the perfect remedy."

Sabrina opened the door. Her mother, a robust woman with bushy hair, was standing in our doorway and stringing up several long strands of yellow beads. She was dressed in a skirt and henna-print blouse. "Hellooo!" It sounded like she was singing the word. "I'm here, darlings!"

"Mother! What are you doing to our door?"

"It was drab, darling, drab." Her voice was dry and raspy. "I'd say every one of these apartment doors is in desperate need of charm beads. And these. I brought these especially for you girls." She leaned around Sabrina and waved to us. "Hi, girls. Now, these yellow beads are special for studying goddesses." Saby closed her eyes and shook her head, embarrassed. "Yellow brings intellectualism—never a bad thing for college girls. They bring imagination, improved memory, and bold creativity."

After our door had a full curtain of beads, Saby's mom prattled on about the good spirits and how much luck we were going to have in the coming weeks. Eve sat down next to her. "Eve, darling, let me look at you. Palms up." Eve gave the prophetess an uncertain stare. "Something's weighing on your conscience, isn't it, darling? We are all elevated women here. We don't hold anything back from one another, so you don't keep anything inside. That would shorten your life span."

Sabrina rolled her eyes. "Mom, stop."

"Wait! I'm feeling something." Saby's mum closed her eyes before looking at Eve again. "You're not pregnant, are you?"

Eve's eyes got wide and her mouth opened. "Actually, I am. I am pregnant!"

"You *are*?" Saby said, astonished.

"Ah! I knew it! I knew there was a life force pulsating around you. The universe has really blessed me with this clairvoyance."

Eve and I were mesmerized. Saby looked at Eve. "How could you not have told me?"

"I just found out."

"Saby's mom put her hand out toward her daughter.

"Sabrina. My left forearm is aching, and you know what that means."

"It doesn't mean anything, Mother."

"Sabrina."

"All right!" Saby lifted her palm to her mom, sulking.

"You're too stressed, darling," she said, scanning Saby's palm. Then she pushed Saby's cheeks together and said, "My precious daughter." She pulled Sabrina into a huge bear hug. "You have my gifts, too, you realize?"

"Stop it, Mom. You're so embarrassing." Sabrina rolled her eyes, but as she hugged her mother, she was smiling. The moment, their warm embrace—I paused in a bit of stupefaction. *When was the last time Mum and I had a moment*? I tried to peg memories as they flashed in my mind. I realized it felt like decades, eons of time, since Mum had been anything like her former self. And watching Sabrina and her own family amplified the differences between Saby's mom and my own.

My phone rang. It was Elliott. I excused myself and closed myself in my room.

"Kaylie? Do you have time to talk?" He sounded exhausted.

I listened as he unfolded the memory that was troubling him. It sounded like a story he had told himself many times.

"I remember my mother's arms flailing. She was hitting the man, first with her purse, and then scratching at him with her fingernails. I was five, but I can still remember that image of her like it was yesterday. New York City isn't exactly the safest place to grow up. In fact, now that I'm older, I can't help but think that day was the reason why my parents moved us to Washington State in the first place. It felt like we'd been in that grocery store all morning. I was following my mother down the candy aisle. Rows and rows of candy. It looked so amazing. I couldn't help stopping. I fell behind, ogling those baskets of color-wrapped candy. I heard the voice of the man behind me, and I wasn't scared or anything. He asked if I liked candy. He looked like a regular Joe. He dressed like my dad—light-colored pants, shirt, and tie. He said he had even bigger baskets of candy outside, and that I should follow him, and he would give me all the candy I could eat.

"I never liked shopping with my mom in Chinatown. Those streets were unforgettable—there were so many people, and foreign signs, and this awful moldy-food stench that permeated everything. I didn't pay attention to any of that. I was so focused on the loads of candy I was going to get from the man. It wasn't until I heard my mother's voice screaming out above the other street noise that I had any idea something was wrong. And then the world went sideways—everything slanted as the man scooped me up and held me under one arm. He was reaching for a car door. I saw my mother in the street. When I think about it now, the way her face was like a wild animal's...her eyes about to come out of their sockets, her fingers digging into her face as she screamed my name over and over again at the top of her lungs. I wanted to show her where I was. She saw me, and she tore after us like a wild bull. And just as the man was shoving me in a car, she was on him. Flailing her purse, then her arms, yelling words I had never heard before. He dropped me. I remember hitting the pavement and crying out, first in pain and then fear, because my mother had transformed into a screaming, clawing animal. She yelled for me to get away from the car. The man grabbed one of her wrists and shoved her down on the concrete, and charged off, abandoning his car, leaping like a deer over trash bags and weaving between pedestrians.

"I've hated grocery stores since. I can't stand them. Can't stand the people, or the smell, the lights—none of it. Needless to say, Gage does all the foraging for the house. And then the Holder gives me my next morphis. It's in a grocery store.

"One ... one step inside the place, and I was five years old again. When I found the candy aisle, I think I was already as white as a ghost. I could feel my heartbeat in my feet, like my blood was trying to escape through my shoes, and my forehead was cold with sweat. I sat down, crossed my legs, and it was then that everything began to blur. The labels on the candy were as unreadable as those signs in Chinatown, and the lights were dimming above my head. I was either passing out or having a panic attack, or probably both at this point. It didn't matter that I was in a clean, suburban area. All I could smell were the dirty streets of Chinatown again, and the crowds of faceless people. I felt the world shrinking, and I was shaking at the memory of my mother holding and hugging me so tight my chest hurt. She was yelling in my ear and shaking me almost senseless while she explained what could have happened to me, how much danger I was in, and how strangers could kill me, hurt me, and take me away from her forever.

"But then you were there, and that jolted me from my flashback. The morphis said I had to sit in the aisle and blabber a speech until I got escorted out or kicked out—but I couldn't do it—I couldn't do anything. I don't know what would have happened if you hadn't appeared and gotten me out of there. So, thank you."

Elliott paused for a long time. "I don't know why I'm telling you all this, Kaylie. I—well, I never talk about my childhood with anyone. And I don't like talking about my morphises with anyone either. It helps, though, talking to you. It does. You kinda take the edge off somehow. I still can't believe the Holder passed me. How did I pass?"

I was listening to him; I felt almost in the same room with Elliott, but also a thousand miles away. I wanted to comfort him, tell him how sorry I was about what happened. How terrible I felt that he had to go through something like that at such a young age. But I thought of my brother, too. How panicked Mum and I were the first time Hunter disappeared. Kidnapped, lost, or murdered—the possibilities plagued the back of our minds, but we wouldn't say the words. Listening to Elliott made me re-imagine someone trying to snatch Hunter away, and instantly I was filled with rage. All I wanted to do was protect him from harm.

The words were faint, but I managed to get them out. "I'm glad I can help, Elliott. Even if only a little."

"I hope you see why it makes me even that much more nervous about you joining Sarkmarr. I'm worried about it. I don't want anything bad to happen to you. You're important. And I don't know what the Holder is going to ask you to do."

I felt nothing at his warning. I was numb to the fear or anxiety I was supposed to be feeling toward the Holder. All I felt was certainty—a certainty that I was in the right place.

"Don't worry, Elliott. No one is untouchable. Not even the Holder."

CHAPTER THIRTEEN

IN THE WITCHTOP MOUNTAINS, the stones on the ground were garnet and sapphire. Trees were crystal with diamond leaves that sounded like wind chimes in the breeze. Witches appeared out of the waterfalls—waterfalls that flowed upward from the ground. Survival here meant disguising myself as a witch. Normally, such a unique place could only exist in a dream. But Edannair broke the rules. It was all here—an illusion for the mind that made dreams seem real.

"Good morning, Kaylie." Sabrina's voice rippled into my groggy waking thoughts. "It's noon, actually. So, good afternoon."

It had been over a month since my alias hit Highmark, and after my adventures in Edannair, I was actually sleeping better.

"Another great night," I whispered and buried my face in my pillow.

"Who did you meet, and what did you do with him?" Sabrina asked excitedly.

I rolled over. "No, nothing like that."

Disappointment scrunched up her face. "Ugh, I thought I saw you up and getting ready this morning. Was I sleepwalking again? I did take my mother's herbs last night...."

"I just hadn't gone to sleep yet."

"You hadn't slept at all? Why on earth—oh, good gracious, do not tell me you were in that game thingy all night." I started to reply, but she grabbed a pillow and hurled it at me. "Kay. Are you kidding?"

"Hey, I'm armed, too." I grabbed the nearest ally. A stuffed Tigger.

"Knock, knock," said Marco's voice at the door. Saby leapt onto my bed, hushing me.

"Marco, come in. We're in bed," she teased.

He opened the door and glanced to me. "Elliott and Gage are at the door, Kay."

A surge of motivation filled me, and I hopped out of bed.

"Oh, so that gets you out of bed?" Saby rolled her eyes. I gave her a playful shove on her way out.

I dressed quickly, combed my hair, splashed my face with cool water, and met my mentors in the living room. Gage was standing at the edge of the dining room, asking Marco about the blueprints sprawled on the table, while Elliott sat on the corner of the sofa, arms crossed and head down, eyes darting around the room.

"Kay," Elliott said, sounding relieved.

"Ah, the Highmark Queen." Gage high-fived me. "Great job. I knew you were starting to like Edannair, but enough to work as hard as you have?" Gage clapped his hands. "And today's the big day. Application day."

We excused ourselves from Saby and Marco and went to work. We were all business today.

"Now, Kay. Elliott helped you get to Highmark. I'm going to help with Sarkmarr's application." Gage's hands flew over my keyboard while he spoke. "After applying on the website, you'll get a generated interview time and meeting place. The application cycle ends tomorrow. Not a lot of wiggle room. Ah, here it is. Fill this out."

Gage and I switched places. *Sarkmarr.com* was laid out like most group websites. A logo, a colorful, artistic backdrop, and several tab options: Application, Progression, FAQ, and Member Forums. I clicked on the first and scanned the list: Aliases, Stats, Specs, and Unique Talents and Abilities. Gage and Elliott helped me answer each question, posting links and stats that showed my alias's progression.

"Picture?" I asked curiously.

"Yeah." Gage laughed. "Everyone's gotta do it."

I searched my picture folder, found one I liked, and linked it.

"Describe your goals in Edannair." I thought about how I would really like to answer that question, but I typed what Gage and Elliott coached me to say. "To participate in high-level content, to achieve and surpass the expectations and trials put before me, and to prove a worthy and beneficial member of Sarkmarr."

It went on: What is your current time zone? When are your available interview times? Available raid times if accepted? Why are you considering a move from your current group? What is your typical rotation and priority? How would you rank the following alias stats? It felt like a visa application.

"Finished."

"Good. Now let me see if we forgot anything else before we submit." Gage navigated expertly through the site. "Remember, the interviews are done by the highest-ranking officers in Sarkmarr. They will ask you questions and judge your answers. Listen carefully, and answer honestly. The Holder doesn't accept just anyone, so try to stand out, but also be prepared for anything.

"Interviews can be hours long, with questions about your upbringing, career, whatever, or they could be short and sweet. Findail was my officer. He asked me things like how I started in Edannair. What I liked most and what I hated. Compared to Elliott's, my interview was easy. He had Riscanth, who was way more of a jerk. He grilled Elliott about his parents, college, career, childhood, everything. So, the interviews are all random, making it hard to prepare you exactly. Just be you, and I'm sure you will do fine."

"Kaylie?" Elliott interrupted. "This is it. Are you sure? We can't predict what the Holder will do."

"I understand, Elliott. I'll be fine. If I have to sacrifice a few nights' sleep or deal with some embarrassment, so be it."

"Clearly, I underestimated just how competitive she is," Gage said. "But I love a good shocker-story. Here we go. Clicking submit."

CHAPTER FOURTEEN

THE ALAMO DRAFTHOUSE WAS A STUDENT FAVORITE in this city—a movie theater with classic Austin flair. The place always ran special showings, like a timeless trilogy as an all-day event, or a live comic-book reading before a Marvel movie debut. Besides that, there were long tables along each row of seats so the restaurant could serve food and drinks during the films. It was lucky my Sarkmarr interview was slated for here. Some people had to fly from out of state to apply.

I was directed to theater four. Reserving the entire auditorium for an application process was an impressive move. Then again, everything about Sarkmarr had been unexpected. I glanced at the paper in my hands. "Officer Perdonic, 2:00 p.m." I glanced at my phone—ten minutes till. My stomach still felt knotted up with nerves. Gage thought it was the competitive side that got me here, but I knew better. It was the investigation and the surprising escape Edannair offered that had me hooked.

Walking into the theater, I realized how very far the Holder's reputation reached. Dozens of people, all male, filled rows of seats. At the top of the auditorium were a few empty rows reserved with laptops and papers. I found an empty seat near the middle next to an unintimidating stranger.

"Hey, I'm Kyle." He reached out his hand; he had kind, boyish eyes. "Or Lyndona, whichever you prefer. I play a druid."

"Oh, hello. One of my friends also plays a druid. I'm Kaylie, or Loxy, I guess."

"Loxy is a...?"

"Shadowlock."

"How long you been playing?"

"Not that long. A few months."

"Wow. I'm going on three years. That's pretty cool you're app'ing here already. And I thought I had ambition."

"What made you wait to apply till now?"

"Eh, a lot of things I guess. I was just casual at this stuff at first. Messed around on the weekends—that kinda thing. I didn't believe any of the stories about the Holder back then."

"Which stories?"

"Them all, really. That he could change the world for you. Inside Edannair and out. All the elite stuff: the Stakes, access passes, secret skills, mechanic-manipulation, and then the outside stuff too that his people were getting. I just thought there was no way."

"What changed your mind?"

"A friend of mine. Good guy. But he had bad luck.

117

Struggling at his job. Until he passed Sarkmarr's tier four, then things started changing for him. A call here or there from the Holder, and he had a cushy office job in a few weeks. So I started checking into it. And turns out, the Holder's one of those guys who knows someone, somewhere, in everything. Ever since I started seriously getting ready for this day, I've been training and studying his events. If you can offer a skill he can use in the Stakes competition, you're golden. So, what about you?"

"A little different. Honestly, I feel pretty out of my element."

"Eh, I'm sure you'll do fine. We got here, didn't we? Getting past all the paperwork and up to an interview, and we've already beat out thousands of others."

"Kaylie Ames. Alias Loxy," a voice called out through a speaker. "Please come up."

"That's me. It was nice to meet you, Kyle."

"Likewise. Good luck."

The house lights gave a low glow over the top few rows. As I neared, I noticed a polygraph machine set up beside penholders, papers, and laptops.

"What have I got myself into?" I whispered.

"Hopefully, an endless adventure." A clean-cut, average-statured man with short, curly brown hair held out his hand to shake. He wore a polo and khakis and looked to be around college-age or a little older. "Welcome. Loxy. I've already heard a lot about you."

"I can only hope good things. And you must be Perdonic?"

He nodded. "Let's have a seat. I hope you'll understand we will keep to using our alias names. Something to do with preserving culture." He grinned. "So, how are you?"

"A little nervous. I have the paperwork detailing my experience, alias stats, and assignments completed so far." I handed him the papers.

"Sure, sure," he said putting them aside. "But getting down to brass tacks here, let me ask you the most obvious question. Why are you here?"

"I'm going to assume you want more than the obvious reason." I paused. "Um, well, honestly, I would like to explore what this is all about."

"What do you mean? What have you heard *this* is?"

"For one: that just sitting here with you is a privilege. Two: I know you don't have to be in Sarkmarr to enjoy Edannair, but you do have to be in Sarkmarr to enjoy the best. *This*, as I understand it, is the leading edge of progress, power, status, access, and the only way to experience the secret side of Edannair."

"Hmmm. Interesting. And I take it you want to challenge yourself. Prove something to yourself."

"Sure." It sounded right for now. I wasn't ready to say that the Holder needed to be knocked down a peg.

"I remember growing up feeling the same way. Competition was everything. I fought for the smell and taste of victory before the race had even begun. I wanted to be so far ahead in the race that my competition couldn't catch me if they tried. My father used to say, 'You can never go wrong, going on in things of war.' I didn't know what he meant for years. I mean years. Night after night, when I was a little boy and he was putting me to bed, I would unleash some tirade about Simon Hill and Tommy Rider, and how there was no way they should have beaten me. He would smile and repeat the phrase like a goodnight prayer."

"Did he ever tell you what he meant?"

"You'd think so, but no. To this day, I think about asking him, but I don't. Because I've decided I already know." The officer watched me carefully as I listened. "My advice, Loxy. Get outta here. Don't apply. Hang out in Edannair. Forget about Sarkmarr, the Holder, and all this. It sucks you in. To be a part of the Holder's lair is to give up a part of yourself. Do you understand what I mean?"

I started to answer, but he continued.

"You are going to have to sacrifice some part of your life that could be the most dear to you—family, pets, friends, coworkers, classmates. The things you are asked to do could turn some or all of them against you. Do you see?"

"I believe so, yes."

"Your family could be persuaded to believe you are giving up your favorite cheese—or moving to New Zealand. You could be the humiliation of the five o'clock news or the spotlight of a Friday night play. You lose control over part of your life. You seem like a sweet girl. You don't need this."

I sat there for a moment. As I began to speak, it felt like my vocal cords were being crushed. "My dad also had a saying. He told me life was like a tornado. And I think he meant more than just we'll absorb our surroundings. He meant it's a funnel that needs wide-open space. If you try to control the twister all the time, you'll just end up being beaten."

Perdonic smiled. "What does he say about Sarkmarr?"

It felt as though all of me drained from the room. What I wouldn't give to be able to talk to my father about Sarkmarr, about anything again.

"Loxy?"

"He—" I swallowed hard. "He would say…" I found the marble in my pocket and clutched it. "I don't know. I lost my dad two years ago. So I don't know what he would say."

Perdonic's gaze fell to the floor. "I'm sorry." He leaned toward me. "Take all the time you need. I respect your courage coming in today—"

"Wait. I know what you are going to say." He looked startled. "And you may be right. I don't need to apply. But I want to. It would mean a lot to me to be considered."

"Edannair has tons to offer in and of itself, without Sarkmarr and our elitists."

"I'm aware."

"Nothing, huh? None of this scares you?"

I shook my head.

He took a deep breath, and his eyes fell to the papers on his desk. He looked sincere. "Well. Quite simply, here's how it works. You're applying for the AVE side. There are four tier systems and five ranks per tier. Tier one, pretty straightforward—your app gets approved, this interview gets approved, and you join us as a rank one of tier one. You'll attend meetings and WAMs, but you'll be judged on how you complete solo and group work. That's how you'll move up in the ranks. You will have to survive encounters, whether that means mind-controlling enemies off the Cliffs of Kalleen or crowd-controlling enemies in Teroca or Ulion. You don't have to memorize all that; lists of the tier system are in this." He handed me a manila folder. "There are time limits, and the faster you get them done, the more impressive it is, and then the more opportunities you'll get. Missions set up outside Edannair are part of what we call your 'morphis.' These morphises can be assigned at your work, school, with neighbors, anything. And they start once you've hit tier two. We do not know the morphis missions beforehand, so don't ask. They are designed and given out by the Holder. He will pass them down to officers, and the officers will pass them on to you. If you have any questions, ask an officer."

I nodded.

"In tier three, you will be given harder Edannair assignments and harder morphis assignments. Once you hit tier four, you're home free. You've got access to the restricted, rare stuff, as well as the opportunity to compete in the Stakes. You'll be somewhat of a celebrity at that point. Be prepared for fans. They will approach you and ask you questions about Sarkmarr. So ..." He reached for an envelope and handed it to me. "Remember the privacy addendum you are signing today. Read it in detail, because any slip of the tongue will forfeit your role, your tier, everything. Even if you get in, work perfectly at everything, climb the ranks, and pay your dues, if you forget your place, boom! You go from top to bottom in seconds. There's always someone waiting to take your spot in Sarkmarr. We're very competitive.

"I kind of went through everything a little fast. Do you have any questions?"

"Is that it? I mean, aren't you going to put me through an interrogation of some sort or hook me to the polygraph?"

He chuckled. "Only if we feel it's necessary."

I raised an eyebrow.

"The orders for you don't include anything like that, so you're good. And come on, you're too pretty for that anyway. We don't want to scare you off. Any other questions?"

"There was one thing, if you have time. I was rather curious about the Stakes."

"Sure. Basically, it's Deluvian Games' huge industry conference. It is an incredibly competitive event where the best talent from all over the world goes head-to-head. There are exhibits for new games, sneak peeks, and sequel work. Developers give live talks about current and upcoming work. And of course, there's the Stakes competition itself, which was originally the Holder's brainchild—though Mr. Charles Luvi will never admit that."

"Who's he? The owner?"

"Yes, the *owner* of Edannair, and he'll make sure you know it, too."

"And the Stakes. There are two sides to the competition, correct?"

"Yes. AVA—alias versus alias—and AVE—alias versus environment—championships. You and me, we're the latter. Our goal: to get through a maze never before seen by anyone. So essentially, we're going in blind. No beta testing, no practice. All the teams are thrown in against brand-new masters, and we have to defeat them on the fly. It's an extreme challenge. There is a time limit of six hours. Many teams don't complete even half. The prize money is hefty, though—two hundred and fifty thousand dollars."

"Oh. Wow. How long have you been doing this?"

"I've been with the Holder for some time now."

"When did the Holder become *The Holder*?"

"Quite a while ago."

"You seem vague."

"You seem curious."

We both laughed.

"You must like Sarkmarr? I mean, you've been with the Holder a long time."

"It's the best an alias can get. I can't do the explanation justice, but you don't get this kind of gaming experience as a normal Edannairian. With the Holder, you go beyond end-content to the unseen, unspoken tricks and trades of the world." He glanced down, smiling at a memory. "What I am saying is, with the Holder you can be great; you can be greater than you ever thought possible. Get to the top, and you can literally get anything you want, become anything you want. Like I said, it changes your life."

"You make it sound all groovy, but what I've seen is the Holder and the morphises racking people for no good reason."

"Didn't Horace say, 'Adversity has the effect of eliciting talents'?"

"The Holder seems to thrive on adversity."

Perdonic caught the edge in my voice and smirked. "That would be a discussion for a whole other time. All right. Your application will be processed through our Archnigh officer, Ilusas. We'll be in touch after that. Thanks for coming in. Will you tell my assistant I'll see Beardrum next?"

CHAPTER FIFTEEN

MUM'S NUMBER FLASHED ON MY PHONE. My first thought was, *What happened with Hunter this time?* I stood there watching her number on the screen, listening to her ringtone. Half of me felt guilty for not answering, and the other said to ignore it.

I have finals this week. I need to study.

Sliding the volume button down, I silenced the call.

I STUDIED FOR JUST A FEW HOURS. Thankfully, the tests didn't seem that difficult. With spring semester finished, free time beckoned. I was growing fond of the lands in Edannair—the serene and unexplored ranges, colors, music, and multitudes of exotic and beautiful creatures inspired my imagination more than any film I had seen. I was content to be lost in this foreign world, welcomed into its secrets.

Dragon-plunging became one of my favorite activities. Diving over the Cliffs of Namaste on the back of a dawn dragon made me feel as if my own life had been locked out for a moment and my painful memories along with it. Dawn dragons were the best for dragon-plung-ing. Smaller than most dragons, with vibrant yellow eyes and gray bodies, they blended into the clouds and were quick and agile.

Friends of Gage and Elliott steered their dragons over and under mine, and abiding by dragon-plunging rules, we tagged each other only during a dive, making it all the more thrilling.

"Hey, Loxy," Perdonic said. His Quarlin alias stood apart from others. His seemed more humanoid than zebra, his stripes thinner like pencil traces across his skin. He appeared in the sky atop a breathtaking thing—some sort of undead dragon, skeletal but animate. "I have some news for you."

Switching out with a partner to take over my chase, I stopped beside Perdonic on the cliff's ledge, away from my teammates.

"You've had me in suspense." I braced for the worst.

"I have your application results. And, you made it in. Are you ready?"

My stomach lurched and my heart sang. Before I could reply, he added, "No harm in declining, remember."

Hearing his warning again made me hesitate. Was I doing this for the right reasons? "I can do it, Perdonic. I want to."

"You sure?"

"I'm sure. Thanks for looking out for me, but I really want to push for this. I want to be a part of the best."

"No other reasons?"

I froze for a moment. "Well, I—" *Don't say it, don't give anything away.* "I feel I have something to prove."

"All right, Lox. Good luck. Oh. There's one more thing. You'll need this." Perdonic held up a medallion with the lynx symbol. "I get to knight you." I bowed my head, and he placed the pendant around my neck. "It's official. You're a part of us now."

"Thank you." I had a sinking feeling and the urge to confess my true plan. Perdonic genuinely seemed to have people's best interests at heart, and yet he worked for the Holder—a strange duo.

An invitation appeared on my screen.

"Perdonic has invited you to join Sarkmarr. Accept or decline?"

Accept.

Immediately, a steady string of speaker icons popped up on my screen, showing the names of the aliases speaking on Sarkmarr's group chat.

[Thadys]: The healers couldn't push it to phase two. Plain and simple.

[Brambt]: With me healing we could have done it.

[Nyx]: Lol.

[Syntax]: You're a healer, Brambt? I thought you just stood around and looked pretty.

[Modaga]: I thought that's what Perciphony does?

[Syntax]: Eh. Him too.

[Svar]: Hi, Loxy.

[Furtim]: Loxy. Loxy. No way. What's up girl?

[Polixus]: Welcome, Loxy.

[Kronium]: Welcome.

[Lekar]: Hi. Hi. New person.

[Flogg]: Who's the newbie?

[Modaga]: Loxeh. You made it!

[Loxy]: Hi, everyone. Thank you so much. I'm excited to be here.

[Kulnuir]: The female that app'd, Flogg. Loxy, ignore Flogg, he never knows what's going on.

[Flogg]: Woot. A girrrrl! Hi Loxy. I'm Flogg.

[Modaga]: Down boy.

[Brambt]: We allowed a girl in here? What were we thinking?

[Syntax]: Same thing we were thinking when we let you heal?

[Brambt]: Hey, we stopped wiping when I started healing!

[Rynq]: Brambt's dyslexia is kicking in again.

[Thadys]: Loxy, you sound European or something. Where are you from?

[Loxy]: Tacoma, actually. But my mum's from England.

[Thadys]: Ah. Makes sense.

[Flogg]: Loxy, ever seen an Eagle Eye Shot?

[Loxy]: I haven't.

[Svar]: Loxy, he's gonna try and show you his bow.

[Polixus]: Run for your life, Loxy.

[Flogg]: Hey. It's cool. I'm pretty much top damage all the time.

[Furtim]: Lies.

[Rowley]: Well if it isn't the shadowlock I met at the caves. Who let you in?

[Loxy]: Hey, Rowley.

[Rowley]: Did the requirements drop for becoming a member? Are we just taking anybody now?

[Furtim]: Here we go.

[Braxas]: Rowley, what could possibly be wrong with some female presence in here, man?

[Rowley]: What do you think?

[Furtim]: Uh oh. Rowley's soapbox lecture's coming.

[Snome]: She's gotta be good. She got in.

[Rowley]: I'm just calling it as I see it.

[Kulnuir]: I saw her app' pic. Nice.

[Kronium]: I want to see.

[Grimm]: Guys. Shut up. Meeting tomorrow night. Seven o'clock.

[Arano]: Woot.

[Grimm]: Who's in for this week and who's out, we're gonna find out.

[Findail]: No rhyme intended.

[Brindle]: Grimm thinks he's an officer.

[Grimm]: Too bad, suckers, none of you topped my numbers last week.

[Rynq]: Yeah, okay Grimm, keep telling yourself that.

[Arano]: Give me one time where I don't have to protect, Grimm. Then you'd feel some real competition.

[Brambt]: I'll stick with healing.

[Syntax]: You would, Brambt.

[Logos]: Let's duel right now, Grimm.

[Grimm]: I'm going to bed. Wake me when the actual competition shows. Peace.

[Flogg]: Night, Grimm.

[Logos]: Bah.

[Kronium]: Night.

[Oster]: I wish I could go to the meeting.

[Flogg]: Me, too.

[Furtim]: Be better.

[Flogg]: I am better. The Holder just hasn't seen it yet.

[Oster]: I just want to see people get owned.

[Syntax]: Tomorrow should be interesting. The Holder's got me trudging through mud for two hours. He called it, Pig in Its Blanket.

[Oster]: Haha.

[Syntax]: It's cause I'm fat, I know it. He's making fun of me.

[Lekar]: He makes fun of us all.

[Kulnuir]: At least he didn't specify you having to be naked or anything, Syntax, be grateful for that.

[Syntax]: I'll prolly do it naked anyway.

[Arano]: Ewww, TMI.

[Polixus]: TMI!

[Ilusas]: Loxy.

[Loxy]: Yes?

[Ilusas]: Your evaluation is tomorrow. Five o'clock.

[Flogg]: Yesss! Haunted Temple tomorrow! Maybe?

[Loxy]: Okay.

[Brindle]: Already, Loxy? Jeez.

[Furtim]: I remember my first.

[Snome]: I never thought I'd get my first. Took like a month.

[Furtim]: It's all about the foreplay, Snome.

[Xuvy]: Ohhh!

[Snome]: Good one ... I'm laughing so hard ... ah-hah, ah-hah.

[Brindle]: The first morphis is always the worst.

[Svar]: True.

[Brindle]: My first was Aquatica. I've never been so cold in my life.

[Thrill]: The gates of hell have opened for you, Loxy. Hope you're ready.

[Brambt]: Yeah. You seem like a nice girl. Why are you here with us locos?

[Loxy]: Same reason as you, right?

[Brambt]: I forgot why I came here a long time ago.

[Loxy]: Challenge and rewards?

[Brambt]: Yeah, something like that.

[Nyx]: Lol.

[Thrill]: Nyx, you would say that.

[Syntax]: Nyx. Never says a damn thing but, lol.

[Nyx]: Lol.

[Brambt]: Well. Good luck, Loxy. Ask us if you need anything. We're in this together.

[Syntax]: No one's in this with you, Brambt.

[Rowley]: Brambt and your *diplomacy*. You're as cutthroat as the rest of us.

[Brambt]: Rowley, not all of us have quite your… what's the word, thirst for blood?

[Rowley]: There isn't a word.

[Kulnuir]: Some advice for tomorrow, Lox. If you find yourself in Kirin's Pen, summon your Nillekma. That was my biggest mistake ever made.

[Furtim]: Kulnuir's Failure. I'll never forget that day.

[Oster]: Who could? His Nillekma—right there the whole time. Tragic!

[Loxy]: I'm not sure what you mean.

[Kulnuir]: You know. When your alias reached Highmark. You got a Nillekma from the dark-elves.

There was a long, uncomfortable pause.

[Kulnuir]: You haven't gone yet, have you?

[Loxy]: No, not yet.

[Svar]: Ah, Loxy. He's right. We forgot to take you.

[Kulnuir]: If you end up going there, you could survive the whole thing but without your Nillekma at the end, well...

[Furtim]: Blehhh.

[Kulnuir]: Like Furtim is so discreetly pointing out, you die.

[Loxy]: I...

[Kulnuir]: I'm not doing anything, I'll take you. Can you

meet me at Inlet Wood? It's the passage between the Fjord Islands. Take the flight path north to Cerulean Harbor. The blue grass under white trees will give it away. Actually, just wait for me on the dock. We'll go together.

THE ARCHIMON EAGLE LET ME DISMOUNT and jetted into the sky. I stood on the landing pier, staring up at a colossal landscape. Monstrous black mountains gouged the sky, and a purple-gray fog concealed their exact height. Thickets of trees—leafless, white skeletons—speared the ground. I stepped off the dock onto hard mud. It cracked; the tidal wash of seawater had left a margin of ice along the shore. The silt feathered into short, ice-blue grass. A gust of wind ruffled my hair, and a white light the size of a quarter started to flicker ahead of me. The orb grew, swirling and whining like a hurricane wind. A small, mousy-faced humanoid appeared beside me wearing midnight purple witches robes. "Hey!" There was maturity behind its childlike features. Despite their appearance, Elowfons were master sorcerers.

"Kulnuir. How'd you … you just zapped here beside me!"

"Mage-gates. Gotta love 'em. Come on. Let's save a Nillekma."

We walked down through the blue-bladed meadow toward the fjords. The cliffs stretched up and around into the sky above us. Inlet Wood lay at their feet.

"These trees have seen their share of magic," Kulnuir began. "They belong to the dark-elves."

"I see. Um ... Kulnuir. What exactly is a Nillekma?"

"Oh. You don't even know what were looking for. That would help, wouldn't it? Nillekmas are in the family of unicorns. They have a lion's tail and two curved horns instead of one straight horn."

"Why are they in need of saving?"

"During the Elder Wars there were many battles between the sea-elves and the dark-elves. When the last dark tower fell, the sea-elves banished them to the under-growth, also known as anywhere there's no sunlight. Like here."

We entered the forest, and as I looked around, I realized that the sun did not penetrate to the ground any-where—despite the leafless canopy.

"Caves, trenches, tunnels, or forests had to become the dark-elves' home. Hey, watch yourself!"

I stopped a few inches short of where the footing eroded down into a gully. "I didn't even see that. Thank you."

"It gets freakin' dark in here. No wonder the dark-elves are so angry."

"What happened?"

"Over time, they became bitter, so full of hate that they started ravaging the upper lands. In the dead of night—well, no one knows, because the dark-elves are never seen—but after they emerge, a part of a land's natural beauty vanishes. Sacred ponds, vital lagoons get destroyed, and the water nymphs and mermaids along with them. And now Nillekmas, too. You been to Elavion Forest or Hennowa Valley? Herds used to graze all around those parts. See, Nillekma are sensitive, dependent on each other. They rely on their herd for everything; they find food and water as a unit. They are not survivalists. The dark-elves broke up the herds and blinded them so they could never find each other again. Many of them have already died from shock and loneliness. When we find them and take them in, the bond we form is enough to calm them. They will always come when summoned; you become their herd."

"And you were saying we need them for what?"

"Well, their horns have the only antidote to masters who use Crux poison."

As we walked, the shape of the trees changed. Their bone-white branches stooped like weeping willows. It made walking through them difficult. Every few minutes, Kulnuir would stop and listen to the forest or look to the ground for hoofprints. But all we could see were the skeletal trunks and tree limbs disappearing into darkness.

Then Kulnuir touched my arm and motioned ahead. A Nillekma, between the branches of two trees, stood angled away from us. The dirt in its coat hid a sheen of bronze fur. It breathed in short, guarded breaths. Then its ears swiveled in our direction, and when it turned its head,

I saw that its eyes were covered. A sickly olive-colored enchantment wrapped its head, holding a hood in place.

The faintest sound, a nicker, escaped on its breath.

"You have to break the spell," said Kulnuir.

"Right. Okay. How do I do that?"

"Touch the cloth and say, 'Liberate.' Go ahead, Loxy, before you miss your chance."

I moved slowly, speaking quietly to the animal. The Nillekma's shoulders started to shiver, and it threw its head in the air as it struggled to back away from the sound. From what I could tell, it was a mare. I tried again, speaking softly and slowly. I reached out to pat the animal's shoulder, and her hooves danced. As I moved my hand to her forelock, the Nillekma reared, hooves punching the air. In one quick motion, I touched the cloth and said the word. With a loud crack, the enchantment broke and the hood slipped from her eyes. The animal bolted, and I stumbled backward to avoid getting trampled. She galloped in a crooked circle before stopping a few yards away from me. She lowered her head, and I thought she might accept a caress. I stepped toward her, but this time her hoof pawed the ground.

"Watch it!" Kulnuir shrieked.

The Nillekma aimed her horns right for me and charged. Kulnuir touched my hand, and we vanished. We reappeared several feet from where the animal had thrust its horns through the air where I had just stood.

"That was close!" Kulnuir said. "That must have been my fastest teleport yet. Whew. Now. Go try again."

"You want me to go up to that crazy thing again? After an attack?"

"If you survive the attack, you must approach her again before she attacks again."

"But—"

"Try again. Quickly! Go on!"

I did as he said, inching up to her. The Nillekma watched me, exhaling sharply through flared nostrils—which I interpreted as *Come and get it*. But instead of rearing or charging, the Nillekma nickered and nudged her nose into my abdomen. I looked at Kulnuir. He was smiling.

"See?"

I smiled. "Easy, girl. No more darkness, okay? It's all right."

CHAPTER SIXTEEN

"EVERYONE'S GOING TO BE THERE! You have to come with me."

I couldn't look at Sabrina. I was staring at my cell phone. It was ringing, displaying Mum's number again, and I knew I ought to answer.

"It's the kickoff party, Kay, to a great and wonderful, sacred summer. So, you'll come?"

"Sure, Sabrina," I said.

"I'll see you at Wes's then!" she said, skipping out the door.

"Wait, what?"

My mind felt muted under a weary morning fog. Going to a damn party was just as good of an excuse as any to get out of the house. Even if it happened to be at Weston's.

"WESTON'S SUMMER BASH!" Signs had been taped up all throughout the dorm hallway. Wes could have lived anywhere, but he wanted a down-and-dirty setting—at least, that's how I remember him describing it. He picked the foulest dorm hall because it was the one with the most character. Huey, Wes's roommate and best friend, waved as I walked up. He was a giant of a man—not fat, simply an inheritor of a large frame.

"Lil Kay," he said, giving me a bear hug.

"Hi, Huey."

"Get in there. The party is already heavy-deep in slurring and bad karaoke."

"On guard duty, huh? I'll be sure to bring you a drink, then."

"No rush. I'm still finishing one."

As soon as I entered, my stomach flip-flopped. I was torn between being excited to see Weston and horrified at the idea. Yet another person I hadn't been there for. I spotted a familiar group: Elliott, Gage, Danny, and Eve had claimed a corner of the party. As I approached, Danny had the group mesmerized with a story. There was a hint of elation in his voice.

"I couldn't believe the man was asking me to hold his child. People don't ask strangers for the time anymore, let alone to hold their baby. But, with me being a daddy soon, I said yes. So there I was next to shopping carts and sliding doors, with the tiniest infant in my hands. Mind you, at this point I'm freaking out inside. It was the craziest day!"

Gage crossed his arms and said, "I think I would have blanked if someone had asked me to hold their baby. I would have just stood there staring."

"Was it a boy or a girl, honey?" Eve asked.

"Tiny three-month-old baby girl. Her name was

142

Savannah. She was wearing a little tiny visor. The father was so cool; it was weird. The sleeve tattoos usually make me a leper to suburbanites. They have this wariness, like I'm hazardous to their health. But this dad wasn't like that at all. Holding his little baby... I can't believe we're going to have one of those, Evey."

"In Edannair, the more tattoos the better," Gage said.

Danny's eyebrows rose. "I know Edannair. Well, a long time ago I did."

"Really?" I asked. "What class?"

"A Murinkai samurai. I got pretty into it. In fact, I was one of the leaders for Eludan."

Gage almost jumped in the air. "Ha, no way! You're only looking at your archrivals in Sarkmarr!"

"No kidding?"

"Hey, guys." A familiar voice, Weston's voice, spoke up from behind our group. "Am I interrupting the geekfest?"

"No, man, go ahead," Danny said. "I just finished."

Weston nodded to Danny. "Thanks. I saw Kaylie over here and thought I would say hello. I don't think we've met." Wes turned to Elliott and extended his hand. "Wes Caine."

Elliott looked put-off. "I'm Elliott."

"Nice to meet you." Wes shook his hand and introduced himself to the rest of the group. "How do you all know Kaylie?"

"Since forever ago," Gage said, smirking. "We went to school with Kaylie way back in the day."

"Wes! We need more ice!" We all looked across the room to where someone had yelled.

"Well, I'd better get back to hosting. Enjoy yourselves tonight." Wes turned to me. "Kaylie. Glad you could make it." He held out his hand to me. As I took it, Wes pulled me into a soft hug. The rich, clean scent of his cologne instantly brought me back to being in his arms, and suddenly, I wanted to be even closer to him. He put his mouth to my ear. "I heard about your dad. No worries, okay? I'm sorry, and I understand. Have fun at the party, and stay as long as you want."

I watched him walk away. When Wes caught me staring, he smiled with a soft and open expression. He knew there was more to my past than I could explain.

CHAPTER SEVENTEEN

THE SARKMARR PLAYERS' NERVES WERE TIGHT as violin strings. Officers barked orders back and forth. Ilusas would be picking the people for the challenge tonight. Perdonic said everyone wanted a chance to showcase for Ilusas. He was the Archnigh, the right hand of the Holder. Riscanth called out items from checklists while Perdonic distributed potions and elixirs. Even though I was fairly new to Sarkmarr, I felt that I was now a part of something large, a family with a common goal. It created an unspoken bond and immediate trust. With that kind of group expectation, the pressure to be good enough was daunting.

[Ilusas]: Sarkmarrs.

Everyone's chatting stopped.

[Ilusas]: I will need: Thadys, Lekar—

[Lekar]: Woot.

[Ilusas]: —Polixus, and Loxy. Gather what you need.

[Rowley]: I guess I can take a nap now.

[Brambt]: The pressure's off; they're picked. Anyone want to do anything?

[Snome]: I'm up for some faction hunting.

[Xuvy]: Oh yeah, I'm down. Let's go.

PREPARING FOR A RAID was like preparing for a war—or what I imagined preparing for battle would be. Gage and Elliott told me which dungeons not to choose if the decision was left to the group. They told me the Holder had taught Ilusas how to teleport himself and others to anywhere in Edannair. And that no one was supposed to be able to do that. No one except Shades.

While I double-checked my supplies, Lekar pulled me aside. "A visit to the blacksmith for armor repair would be good. You can buy reagents from him. You'll need a good stock. Devout candles for Endrilliance and sirtha powder for Power Aura Transfusion. It'll increase your perception and sharpness."

I thanked him and did as he said. Edannair cities were busy. The sea-elves, Zanas, earth-trolls, the witch-child Elowfons, even the carnivorous orcs—all were a part of my family now. Most were friendly, and even the most shy or cynical still lent their skill or aid.

"Loxy, I'm going to summon you," Ilusas said.

I disappeared. White light flashed all around me, and when I reappeared, Ilusas stood beside me. His alias was

146

one of the cunning and powerful Murinkai, with dread-lock hair and a violet mouth.

Ilusas looked at me. "Let's see what you can do. Your focus above all else: Stay alive. If your performance has to suffer, so be it. You're no use to me dead. Thadys, you will be healing. Lekar, hybrid fighter, and Polix, protector."

Polixus nodded, and Lekar yelled out, "Yes, sir!"

"I assume you are ready, Loxy."

"Any questions?" Polixus said.

Ilusas laughed. "Polix, when have I answered questions? Follow me." Ilusas disappeared through a charmed archway. Its teal vapor swirled around his alias, concealing him. Polixus and Thadys followed.

Noticing my hesitation, Lekar approached and said, "Don't be nervous. Think of this like practice." The Elowfon smiled confidently.

"Practice graded by the Holder's highest-ranking officer."

"Well, yes. But don't think about that. We'd better get in there."

Lekar disappeared behind the vapor, and I followed him. At first I couldn't see anything but the color teal. When the world finally came into focus, a huge circular cave opened up like a grand ballroom above me. Markings on the cavern's wall read *Red Cave*. The ground was hard-packed red dirt. It looked like we had been transferred underground. The music that created an ambiance in the cities of Edannair was gone. It was dead silent. It was then that I realized there was no "we." I was standing alone, feeling minute in the belly of the cave. Above me, tiny galleries were cut into the cave's walls. Three of the largest of these cells were only about ten feet above me, and mist poured through them. I heard something rummaging in the dark. My heart climbed into my throat.

I heard a low hum, then a raspy whisper, "Who dares enter here, in my cave depths, shambling near?"

I had never heard a master speak before. I could see a form emerging from the gallery's shadow. It looked half-man and half-beast. He walked upright but had a toothy, canine face and dark brown fur. His eyes narrowed to slits. A crown gleamed in between four ears.

His head cocked curiously. "Here now stands one where there used to be none. Wait, five were by your side, oh my—you shall surely die." He murmured another low hum—half-song, half-growl. "Move quickly to free your friends, small one. When their lair doth lose its air, their fates grow dire, and their lives expire." He flourished his clawed hand in the air.

As I looked up, I saw Lekar, Ilusas, Polixus, and Thadys trapped in cells high above the ground, caged behind some magic barrier. Lekar moved his palms like a mime's against it, while Polixus and Thadys conjured spells that sparked and sputtered out against the barrier. Ilusas stood at the center of his cove, perfectly still, looking right at me.

"Loxy. Listen to me." His voice startled me. I didn't expect to be able to hear Ilusas from behind the cove's barrier. "The Red Cave divides the group. It separates one from the rest to be the Guardian. The Guardian's job is to defeat each spawn that Master Greckmon will summon. They'll come through the tunnels in front of you."

"Greckmon being the rhyming beast-man, I take it?" My voice croaked like a frog's.

"Yes. There's more. Each of our cells is on a timer. Before each of our timers expires you must free us. Look above our cells. Each one should have a symbol. Do you see them?"

"Yes."

"What are they?"

"Lekar's has a White Demon."

"He will be freed first, then. Those are Valdry demons, and they always lead Greckmon's battles. Defeat a Valdry, and Lekar will be released."

I was listening, but my rapid heartbeat was making it hard to concentrate.

Fighting alone? My first Sarkmarr test! I'm panicking.

From behind Greckmon, a white cloud twisted and turned in the air. The cloud began to take shape. A womanly body emerged, ghost white. Instead of legs she had a funnel of pale smoke. A green headband held thick, luscious ebony locks back from her face, and strips of brown leather were tied around her chest to make a sort of bra— the hyper-feminization of this character design was clear. She moved toward me, hovering above the ground, wings fluttering noiselessly. She moved with a deadly purpose in her eyes.

"Think it through," Ilusas said. "She is a white demon. She will be susceptible to black magic."

"Um. Corruption?"

"Good. Now cast!"

The dark spell began forming in my hands. Corruption's purple flare grew until I punched the air and the flame hurled toward the ghost-woman. When it hit, the Valdry screeched, her voice high and piercing, and she sped along her path toward me.

A rumbling sound echoed from the cell behind Greckmon, and pebbles and stones began to clatter at my feet.

"Loxy." Thadys's voice was riddled with concern. "What are mine and Polix's symbols?"

I looked frantically in between casting and backing away from the Valdry. "Wolves. Digging, I think."

"Loxy. Those are Greckmon's earth-core hounds. They come in pairs."

"What? *Pairs*?"

The Valdry was gliding closer.

"Don't panic. What's next?" Ilusas asked.

"I—I don't know. Wait. Boding Fire can stun!"

"Use it now!"

A shot of adrenaline jolted me. The smoke from Boding Fire whipped around my palms and formed into a sphere. As I released the orange-and-red orb, the sphere grew tentacles that wrapped themselves around the Valdry's neck. She screeched and struggled against the magic.

Now, Black Poison! Immediately, the ghost-woman's life started to drain away.

The rumbling from the cave was louder now. An enormous animal lunged from the darkness, snarling and tossing its head. A mutant wolf. A second one emerged beside it.

Greckmon spoke again. "You take too long, little magic caster. Less than half the time is left—go faster." In one fluid gesture, Greckmon drew a pearlescent wand from his sleeve and flourished it above his head. The walls began to shake and crack. Chunks of dirt crumbled away from the ceiling, and Thadys and Lekar spun away from the rain of falling earth just in time.

The Boding Fire was wearing off of the Valdry. I renewed the spell to keep the Valdry in place, because the mutant wolves were already advancing, snarling and slobbering. *Augur's Cry*, I thought and threw my hands in the air. A shrill screech sounded from everywhere at once, and the wolves howled and fled the noise. Thadys's cave symbol started to glow. More earth-core hounds coming. Within seconds, two more wolves came charging out. The other two rallied, and all four hounds stalked toward me.

Time! I needed more time!

Honeydew Floor, I remembered. I shoved my mace into the ground, and a thick honey-colored mucus flooded the floor, coursing over the hounds' paws and binding them to the ground. The hounds whined and struggled, but struggling only worsened their predicament.

151

What's next? What's next! Impudence! The blue shards hailed down, slicing into the pack of mutant wolves. The white Valdry came loose from the orb-tentacles, and I turned with barely enough time to duck her bolt of electric-white current. Amidst sibilant whispers, the Seed of Inoga emerged; its green aura swept inside and around the ghost-woman and then burst. The Valdry's wings froze. She dropped to the ground. Lekar's barrier vanished.

"Now I can kick some ass!" Lightning bolts cackled and shot from Lekar's staff. He thrust it toward the hounds, and its force threw them against the cave wall. One of the wolves recovered fast and leaped toward me. Lekar stepped in between us, knocking the animal down again with his staff.

The last symbol started to glow above Ilusas's cove.

I renewed the Honeydew spell over the floor to slow the wolves. "Lekar. Ilusas's symbol—more are coming!"

A giant reptile appeared, larger than the hellhounds we were already fighting. It surged toward me, lashing out with an impossibly long tongue. It struck my armor and knocked me back. I tried to conjure something to slow its follow-up attack, but the lizard knocked me down again. I scrambled to my feet and conjured Boding Fire. As the orb left my hands, the thing's tongue whipped out again and extinguished the spell. "A little help when you can, Lekar!"

"Almost got these two ... there!" Lekar killed the second of the four advancing hellhounds, and Polixus's barrier vanished. "Help her, Polixus. I'll get the dogs."

Polixus threw his axe in the air—it turned a few somersaults and then split into multiple axes that flew into the reptile.

"Shock it, Loxy!"

Harnessing the orgone energy, I conjured Siege-Flay and Dark Shock, but the reptile dodged and lashed both the first and second attempts with a lightning-fast tongue.

"Watch out, Lekar!" Polix yelled. "Beside you!"

Lekar shrieked and ducked from the wolves. "Damn it!" He conjured rippling currents of Depravity that finally finished the hellhounds. Thadys was free. He joined us against the iguana. In a susurrant music made of combined spell energy, our power engulfed the cave and rained deliverance: shocks, slashes, and shattering blows. The ground and air seemed to join in a whirling force that threw the green reptile against the wall. It slid to the floor, and Ilusas was free.

The five of us looked at Greckmon. The Beast Master sighed and turned. We watched him as he retreated into his lair. Just before disappearing, he turned his head and said, "A victory I see your ally brought, but we'll meet again before you rot."

The black shadows of the tunnel enveloped him. Our aliases started to glow, and in a swift moment we were teleported back to the city of Ruinnlark.

The city looked grander somehow, more colorful and exuberant. My first battle with Sarkmarrs, and I didn't fail. The union in there, the tension, the quick decision and reaction time—it was amazing. Chatter flooded my feed.

[Brambt]: There they are. How'd it go?

[Ilusas]: It was Red Cave, with Loxy as the Guardian.

[Flogg]: Loxy!

[Thrill]: Wow. How'd you do?

[Rowley]: How did she do?

[Ilusas]: She did fine.

[Findail]: How was her execution?

[Ilusas]: Quick assessment and good execution of spells.

[Rowley]: Beginner's luck.

[Brambt]: Grats on the victory, little lady.

[Furtim]: Being the Guardian is crazy. I remember the first time. That iguana freaked the hell out of me.

[Windvar]: Finally found something that can dodge as quickly as you can, Furtim?

[Furtim]: Just about.

[Snome]: Hate that tongue.

[Loxy]: It was intense. The rush was insane.

[Furtim]: WAMs soon. Let's go!

[Oster]: World Arena Matches!

[Syntax]: WAMs for the win!

[Loxy]: I've heard a lot about those; I'd really like to see one.

[Kronium]: WAM virgin alert! Brambt. You buying the drinks?

CHAPTER EIGHTEEN

I SAT IN THE MIDDLE ROW of the stadium, ensconced in the roar of a thousand cheering fans. Lekar sat on one side, and a Norseman and a female sea-elf on the other. We watched as aliases battled each other like gladiators in the arena below.

"Your first time at War-Nook?" The sea-elf woman looked almost disgusted.

"Not just War-Nook, Sorkah," Lekar said. "This is Loxy's first WAM ever."

"What a baby."

"She's gone through some growing pains," the Norseman said. "She's in Sarkmarr, after all."

Sorkah agreed with a reluctant nod. "Today's the day, Aerum. I can feel it. My warrior is going to take the house down and bring home the money."

"Who's your warrior?" I asked.

"See there—" she pointed to an orc below— "That's my man, Krow."

Robes, armor, colors, and shapes blurred. More than

fifty aliases bobbed and weaved to miss blows and channel spells.

"How much you bet this time, Sork?" Lekar asked.

"Only my Ferosha."

"What? It took you three days to find the silk for that."

"Well, they don't want more gold, do they? Don't worry, I'll make it back when we win."

"You are so confident betting against Sarkmarr's AVA team. I'm not so sure Eludan can take them," Lekar said, chuckling. "They're good and all but—"

"I'd worry about that little one about to be smothered by one of our Murinkai."

"Oh that's little Nozey. He may be an Elowfon, but he is lethal."

"Lethal? Against who? How did he even make the Holder's team? If it were AVE that'd be one thing. Then he'd at least have the protector and other members. But alias versus alias? He's gonna get creamed."

Across a ravine in the valley, I watched the littlest alias move across the field. He did seem out of place. Yet little Nozey was holding his own. He threw his hands in the sky and whipped his wrists; sharp golden spellcasts hurled across the dirt, and long ribbons of fuchsia light collided with opponents.

The crowds wore red and black tabards for Sarkmarr and blue and orange for Eludan, cheering alternately as one team's fighters smashed against the other, and those fighters returned the attacks with five-edged swords, battle-axes with blades on both ends of the haft, and spells. The arena below the stadium resembled military training grounds the size of a football field. Lekar said that if we had been watching a duel between two aliases it'd be in a smaller ring, usually a one-room stage, similar to theatre in the round.

"Krow, behind you! Behind you!" Sorkah yelled from the edge of her seat as Krow dodged between spellcasts from a Quarlin and Nozey.

A Sarkmarr turned from the row below us and glowered at Sorkah. It was Rowley.

"What? What are you looking at?" Sorkah taunted.

Rowley sneered at her and turned back to the battle.

"Yeah, you better turn around." Sorkah gestured rudely at him.

Rowley was seated in a clump of red Sarkmarr tunics, and all of them began turning in our direction.

Lekar leaned in and whispered, "Do you have to cheer against his brother, Sorkah?"

She shrugged. "I'll cheer against Xuvy and any other Sarkmarrs."

"Cheering against Xuvy makes sitting with you rightly uncomfortable. Rowley's gonna kill us."

"Xuvy's time is done. It's Krow's time," Sorkah said proudly. "There, look at him now!"

A quarrel between battling aliases unraveled in casts and blows on the road between two depressions in the land.

I was starting to understand. In each depression was a flag-pole. Flags anchored a base, either Bloodrun or Vows, and two teams attempted to claim the base by stealing the flag. If the flag remained in a player's possession long enough, the base was won. When this happened, the flag morphed from neutral colors to the flag holder's team colors.

Rowley stood up, throwing his hands in the air. "What are you doing? Razen! Come on! Fighting on the road? Cover Xuvy!"

Razen's body was so large it was hard to glimpse his katana as it slashed and whipped before him. He paused, pointing his sword toward Krow. Both orcs blasted for each other, their strides long and heavy, but agile. Out of the corner of my eye, I glimpsed a shadowlock's aura—and then the smoky black shape of the shadowlock dodged behind the cover of a stone barrier. He crouched, sneaking behind the orcs to claim Bloodrun Base.

"Come on! Xuvy, Bloodrun!"

"Rowley, calm down."

Rowley turned with a scowl. "Why don't *you* take a seat, Aerum? You're blocking everyone behind you."

Rowley turned back to the ring. Aerum did not sit down. His Norseman alias had a blond beard longer than the mane of hair that covered his shoulders, and the bones of his victims had been rigged throughout his chainmail armor. Gathering the full weight of his presence, Aerum raised his chin. "Razen will fight anywhere, and it's a danger, too. He leaves the base open like that for anyone on Eludan to take. Uh-oh, look there, look there!"

Arrows flew from Xuvy's bow toward the creeping shadowlock. One arrow grazed close enough to cut through the player's hood.

Lekar winced. "Oooo, good thing that shadowlock didn't have a Demon-wisp. Xuvy would have been down before another arrow left his bow."

Xuvy staggered suddenly. He turned, exposing a rogue dagger embedded beneath his shoulder blade. Rowley stood from his seat, yelling. Magenta flashes from the shadowlock's hands rained down even more damage on Xuvy.

Aerum winced.

"Wooohoo!" Sorkah screamed.

The crowd started to murmur and roar as Nozey bounded through the fray, hurling lightning bolts at the shadowlock.

"What!" Sorkah said. "No, no!"

The Elowfon was dodging and whizzing about the ring. As the shadowlock turned his attention to the child-sized wizard, Xuvy regained his footing. Together, the two Sarkmarrs brought the shadowlock down.

Nozey reached the flag and began unwinding it from the flagpole. A moment later, a horn signaled that the flag had been taken. Razen and Krow froze midstrike and looked toward Bloodrun. They took off toward the basin, one to defend, one to avenge.

"Oh, now you go!" Rowley shouted at Razen.

Krow tore after Nozey and stripped the flag from him.

"Yes!" Sorkah screamed.

Krow sidestepped Xuvy's attacks. He moved wildly as his opponent forced him closer and closer to the edge of the ring.

"No. Careful. Watch out!" Sorkah gasped.

It was too late. Krow stepped out of the arena and into the void zone. Gasps and oohs flew about the crowd. The flagpole shook; the flag disappeared out of Krow's grasp and reappeared again at the base. A bell rang—time had run out. The crowd jumped to their feet.

Sarkmarr held the majority of flags and had claimed more bases. Red-clad fans cheered and celebrated another Sarkmarr win.

"I'm sorry, Sork," Lekar said, patting her back. "Your team will get us next time."

Sorkah grumbled an inaudible reply.

"On the bright side, Sorkah, you won't bet against your dear friend's team anymore!" Aerum said.

"I'm an Eludian. I'll always bet against Sarkmarr. And they win too much! But 'grats, good game."

"You think the Shades have a showcase planned today?"

"That would make today better," Sorkah said.

"What showcase?" I asked.

"Shades sometimes give a little show at the end of WAMs."

"What kind of show?"

"Pfft, so many. It's kind of like a grand-reveal type thing. It promotes new events coming up, newly invented creatures, new spell abilities....Shades have even shown themselves a couple times."

"You've seen one?"

"Not me. I wish. But I heard it was freaking amazing."

We watched in silence, scanning the footprinted pitch. Wherever the spells had struck the ground during battle, colored smoke vented into the air.

"That was one exciting match. Such a better day already."

"Long day, Aerum?" Lekar said.

"I'll tell you what. I'm a judge outside Edannair, and I have to listen all day, every day, to so many unhappy stories."

"I didn't know you were a judge, man. That's cool."

"Or depressing," Sorkah said.

"A little bit of both, actually. No day is exactly the same. And my wife learned a lot of phrases I brought home from divorce cases. That's how she told me she was leaving, actually. 'We need a bifurcated divorce,' she said." The Norseman exhaled. "Didn't see that coming."

"I'm sorry, man."

"It's all right. It was a while ago, and not the kind of talk for a fine, fun event like this."

The crowd had thinned.

The Norseman stood. "I guess no Shades are coming this time. How was your first arena match, Loxy? We'll see you next week?" He clanged with every movement as bones and tallies hit his chestplate. "The best AVA fighters of the second and third divisions are next week."

"Definitely. If I can get a ticket."

He laughed. "You're in Sarkmarr. We can get pretty much anything we want. Didn't you know that?"

CHAPTER NINETEEN

SABY INSISTED ON COOKING a Fourth of July feast because none of us was going on holiday. She hung a "do not enter" sign on the kitchen door and banished us to the living room while the smells of spice and simmering marinades teased our appetites.

"Danny, you were at the Stakes two years ago?" Gage asked.

"Yes, he was," Eve said.

"Yep. Me and some of my best gents were there. Sarkmarr barely beat us." Danny grinned. "We were peeved."

"We heard about that year," Gage said. "The Holder even tried to recruit some Eludans afterward I think."

"That he did—"

"You met him?"

Danny looked at me quizzically.

"The Holder, I mean."

"Only briefly," Danny continued. "He asked if I was interested in moving over to Sarkmarr. But I wasn't too keen on switching sides after the amount of team-building we had done preparing for the Stakes."

"The Stakes is no joke," Gage said.

"Not to mention, my entire group pretty much hated the Holder."

"Hated him?" I asked.

"Well, you know, the Eludans were pretty much a group of Sarkmarrs that didn't make the Holder's cut. We were good, but we either didn't make it through the Holder's web or *refused* to make it. And a lot of us didn't agree with the fact that he cheated. So we separated."

"Cheated?" *This could be the key*, I thought. Danny could offer more clues to understanding the Holder and this whole stinking business. *I must play it cool, though.* The last thing I wanted was Danny or Eve thinking I'd taken this game too seriously.

"Well, technically, there's no proof that he's cheating, but come on. The Holder knows how the game is coded, and how is that fair? Not only can he manipulate the game engine, but you guys, he shares secrets about hidden places that even the most veteran Edannairians have never heard of. When the Holder competes at the Stakes, his performance blows any records that exist. How does he explain that?"

"So, he competes then?"

"Not anymore, Kay," Elliott said.

"Yeah, he just scouts for talent now," Gage said.

"Why doesn't he compete anymore?"

"The added attention and investigation that's happening. Shades are in overdrive to find him."

"What will they do if they catch him?"

"Track his IP, ban him—"

"No," Elliott snorted. "They'll destroy him. And in that one stroke, everything the Holder could have done for us will be gone."

"If they haven't been able to do it by now, what's gonna change? They have no chance of catching him."

"He's good—no doubt about it," Danny said. "But, Jesus.... Some of the things he asked my buddies and me to do scared or pissed us all off."

"What kind of things?"

"Loads of questions tonight, huh Kay?"

I blushed.

"Nah, it's fine. Hmmm." He shifted in his chair. "It's been a while. Ah. Okay. There was this one gent, a kid who had a real, truly real, fear of blood. Good kid. Enthusiasm and heart up the wazoo. Really wanted to do well and move up the tiers. He had a really bad problem with blood though." Danny sucked his teeth. "The sight of blood—his, a friend's, or even on TV—would make him pass out. Even in movies. If red food coloring was dripping from the actors, he got lightheaded. You can bet he lost sleep over the Holder's next assignment."

"Oh, no," Eve said.

"The Holder, in all his greatness, tells the kid he has to take a knife and cut his kneecap without passing out."

"What?" My tone got sharp.

"Yeah, and the kid did it, despite everything. He took a knife and sliced his knee. No one thought he'd do it."

"Did he get in?" Eve asked.

"Not until his fourth try. He passed out the first three times."

"Hey, Danny," Gage said. "Did you ever know a guy named Brambt?"

Danny shook his head.

"He has the biggest fear of heights, right? He had a morphis that demanded he walk the perimeter of the Empire State Building for something like two hours."

"How does the Holder make sure the morphises get done?" I said.

"Depends. Sometimes you use your phone to document it with video or pictures, or sometimes he designates witnesses for it."

"He has no regard for people. It's awful." I could feel myself getting angrier. The thought of the Holder exposing his members—preying on their vulnerabilities....What about me and my weaknesses? Since my father's death, everything had gone wrong. My mother and brother fell apart, and me as well. I haven't been myself in months. I'm my own shadow, stitched to a series of scholastic habits. What if the Holder exposes me? "Why would he do this?"

"Who knows?" Gage shrugged.

"I want someone to confront him—to tell him to go to hell."

"You'd be hard pressed to find anyone able to talk to the Holder, let alone willing to scold him. It's like getting to the president. It has to be arranged and every rule followed," Elliott said.

"I've seen him before. How hard can it be?"

"Stop, Kaylie, please." Elliott said softly. "You could jeopardize everything we've done to get here."

Danny's eyebrows rose. "You're in Sarkmarr, Kaylie? Right on, right on." He paused. "Ya know, Kay, if you want to get a message to the Holder, trying to speak with him as just another member is not the way to do it. He speaks to the talent."

"Loxy's got talent. She beat Red Cave as the Guardian in her first challenge."

"I had help, Gage."

"You can't be modest about Red Cave, Kay. Everyone knows whoever ends up being the Guardian determines whether everyone lives or dies. Ilusas and the other members are impressed. And you're not even done with tier one."

"I'm almost done."

"No, no, that's great," Danny said quickly. "I'm not trying to take any credit away from that. That is impressive. But not enough."

"Well, what then?"

"He needs to be caught off-guard, surprised—slapped in the face, so to speak."

Gage and Elliott looked at each other. "So, what are you saying?" I asked.

"There is a way you can get not only his attention, but you can get him coming to *you* for answers." Danny had us all sitting stone-still. "You need to go beyond member status in Sarkmarr. It's true there aren't many members in Sarkmarr compared to most groups, but there's still enough to make your progression through the tiers ignorable. You need to attack what the Holder worries about most each year. You'd be the first girl to go, that's for sure."

"You mean…?" Elliott looked mortified.

"You need to get to the Stakes."

"What?" Gage screeched. "Danny. Come on. That's ridiculous. The top players from all over the world compete in the Stakes. She'd be one in millions, literally, trying to get a spot."

"That's why it's going to work. If you get to the Stakes, you'll not only see the Holder for prep and the competition, but you'll be at the Holder's afterparty, and depending on how you do, you'll most likely be invited into the private meetings just like I was."

"But you were not in Sarkmarr," I said. "He was trying to recruit you."

Danny shook his head. "Hear me out. You make the team, you go, you prep, you win, and you're skyrocketed to fame. We're talking interviews, articles, magazines, e-sports coverage.…You'll be on TV, Kaylie. And then there's the afterparty—where the catch will be. You have an announcement to make."

The living room went silent; even with Sabrina clattering about in the kitchen, all our focus was on Danny.

"Picture it. Everyone's celebrating, having a great time, you're there, you're part of the festivities, and right as the Holder moves to give his famous victory speech, you interrupt it all and announce to everyone that you quit."

"Why would she do that?" Gage hollered.

"First of all, no one's ever quit before—that's a huge blow to his reputation—which will kill his ego. Not to mention, you'll be able to articulate any message you want to all of Edannair. Anyone who's anyone is going to be there. If you have something you want to say to the Holder, you can bet he'll listen."

"I could speak for all the people he's humiliated."

"Kay, you could tell him what it means to lead, and why he is not a leader. Hell, you can tell him you're going to defect to Eludan, a team with better leadership." Danny slapped his hand at his heart. "That would burn him alive."

"I've heard enough." Elliott stood from his seat. "Gage, stop this. We're not doing this."

Gage looked at Elliott. "No. I think it's a good plan."

"Have you lost your mind? Remember, she's tied to us. It's not only going to come back to us when this goes down, but it's going to stir up all the wrong kind of attention."

"God forbid any attention."

Elliott glared at Gage. "This is a terrible idea! If the Holder finds out what she's trying to do, we're done. That's it. No second chances. How hard we worked to get in, to rank, will all be for nothing."

"He won't find out. And if he does, so be it, we'll be famous!" Gage said. "And don't forget how many times we've wanted to kick the Holder's ass ourselves with the things he's asked us to do, or had our friends do. It will be nice to give him a taste of his own medicine—humiliation."

"That's what I'm talking about," Danny said. "You know how much publicity the Stakes teams go through? One of them resigning? That will reflect too poorly for him to ignore. So, Kay, what do you think? Ready to go after this guy the real way?"

I hesitated. *A competition as grand as the Stakes? The lights, cameras, pressure to perform, no room for a single error....* "I don't know, Danny. I don't think I can."

"Kay. Come on. This will work. I have a good feeling. You can do it."

You can do it. My father would have said the same thing. He would have said it with the same grin. Was this my moment? Hunter didn't achieve that day at the Tour without first making the decision to get there.

"All right. Let's do it," I finally said.

"Kaylie, please. None of us know what the Holder is capable of doing," Elliott said. "Don't do this."

"Elliott. It will be fine. We need to do this. And we need to do it together."

"Yes!" Danny pumped his fist. "Wow. I don't know why I'm so excited about this."

The front door opened. Marco gave everyone a hello and stood there, unsure of where to go even in his own flat.

"Saby's making dinner in the kitchen, Marco. She's cooking up a storm."

"Mmm, I'm starving. I better check on that." Marco walked through the dining room and disappeared into the kitchen.

"Now," Danny continued, "the Holder has a knack for getting to people and breaking them, which will make this harder, but so much sweeter in the end. Even a Shade once told me that the Holder knew too much about him."

"You met a Shade?" Gage's eyes were saucers. "Are you kidding me? How? Shades don't show themselves for anything but a WAM."

"One of them made an exception—Sillek. He told me he'd been tracking the Holder for months and asked me to tell him everything I knew. He said the owner was firing Shades every month that they failed to take the Holder down. See, anytime players submit a complaint about the Holder, or a sighting, or even rumors about the Holder, a Shade is sent out. They track the complaint, reverse any traps or immobility the Holder had forced on the alias, and so on. Unlike us, Shades have all the power. They can move like no other alias—they have no delays, no restrictions, and they have secret zones that no other alias can access."

"Like Shade Islands."

"That place isn't real, Gage," Elliott snapped.

Pans clattered and clanged against each other, reverberating as they hit the ground. "Guys?" Saby sounded rattled as a cooking timer buzzed. "Dinner's going to take—just a—little longer."

"Can I help?" I hollered.

"Just give me a few more minutes."

"Take your time," Danny said.

Elliott leaned in over the coffee table. "That place is just a rumor. Right?"

"No, it is very real. I've seen it. When the Holder tried to recruit me after the Stakes, he took me all over Ylora."

"Off the continent?"

"Yes! That's what I'm saying. No one can move continents. I don't think even Shades can. And he did! And you know how in battles we can't physically grab someone else or pick them up? It's not so for the Holder. One second we were in…what's the name? Oh, Caves of Anach, and next thing I know, we're flying up with no griffin, nothing. He had me by my shoulder armor, and as we're getting higher and higher, the sky is changing color. He wasn't restricted at all—"

"How is that possible?"

"—So we're flying up, and the sky just….It's just going nuts with color. It's like the sun takes over. We cross into an atmosphere of white and yellow. I swear, if the sun had its own world, this alien stratosphere would have been it. It was so freaking bright. I'm giggling like a little girl. We're getting higher, I see we're getting closer to these circulating streaks and masses of cloud—not cloud, exactly, but the constellations we can see from the cities. It seemed to have a gravitational field of its own, like a black hole except bright. We head right for the mass's center and get sucked in. I'm out of my mind at this point—in total disbelief. We drop into a foggy land, some sort of island. I couldn't see it from the outside; it was camouflaged by the galactic mass. But there it was, this hidden gorgeous zone, with a three-hundred-and-sixty-degree view of Ylora. I could see Edannair, the oceans, the Outer Reach, even the Elder Cities' continent. I could see everything.

"I remember a thin layer of fog covering the ground beneath our feet. But in between the fog and the ground there was a blood-red, swirling mass. When I realized it was some kind of lava, I panicked, but then I realized it wasn't hurting us. We were hovering above the lava with no enchantments or anything.

"Just then I saw a Shade fly above our heads and dive down into the lava right in front of us. When he came up, the Shade had transformed into a phoenix, fully on fire and everything. He started spinning and whirlwinding. I saw him knock down two other Shades as if they were light as feathers. I'm not sure, but I'm guessing this place is a training ground or social hall for the Shades."

Gage and Elliott's mouths dropped open.

"I kept looking around, and there were more and

more weird phenomena happening everywhere. I thought I was in Zeus's lair or something. It was incredible. All the rules changed. Their aliases were doing the craziest things. Moving so fast, defying gravity, walking upside down, even levitating."

"And how did you see all this without them seeing you?" Elliott said.

"No kidding! My thoughts exactly. When I realized we were surrounded by Shades, I knew we were screwed. Anyone disobeying the rules is gonna get banned. But, who knows how, none of them could see us. Maybe the Holder manipulated the stealth codes that Shades use, because there we were, invisible to every single one of them. The Holder has tapped into their godlike powers. It's no wonder he's driving them nuts."

"You must have been psyched," Gage said.

"I was. This sky-island had everything—all the elements, all the seasons. Huge snow-covered cliffs on the north side where Shades manipulated snowdrifts and swung sheets of ice around like baseball bats. There were grasses on the south end that a Shade transformed to a bed of snakes, and another Shade turned a bit of cloud into hawks, and at a wave of his arm they swarmed downward and devoured the snakes. Others manipulated the air, turning white particles dark and drawing lightning from them. This place was unreal."

Gage shook his head. "Holy God. That's insanely cool! In the very lair, standing next to the Holder, right with the police that would pay in limbs to take him out! Ohh man. So cool. No wonder the Shades bribe us for information."

"Why don't they just ban Sarkmarr, Danny?"

Danny looked at Eve and smiled. "Well, they would if they could. But remember that it draws a lot of people to Edannair. There would be a lot of angry aliases out there if it suddenly disappeared. Hundreds of teams practice for the Stakes and try for a chance to beat or compete with Sarkmarr. Eludan came so close. Take out the number-one group in all of Ylora, and they've just lost their moneymaker. Shades would rather take the Holder out quietly, leaving Sarkmarr intact and in the officers' hands. The Holder is the only one who holds the Shades' secrets. He's their only threat."

"I think he's passed some of his information down to Ilusas," Gage said.

Danny folded his arms. "The Shades probably don't know that."

"The Holder's a genius."

"Not enough of a genius to see Kaylie coming. Loxy's going to be the Sarkmarr he never expected. Once the Shades realize what you're doing, I bet they'll even help you."

"Thanks, Danny." I felt my cheeks flush. "Let's hope we can do it."

Saby walked in from the kitchen, looking more than distressed. "Well, the rolls are overdone from me trying to cook the duck a nontraditional way, but dinner is in fact ready now. That one mistake better not take away any of this meal's glory."

"Nah, this will be the best Fourth of July feast ever," Gage said, smiling at Saby.

As we gathered around the table, the computer in my room beeped with a new message alert. I excused myself from the table and slipped into my bedroom. When I saw it, I stiffened. The subject read: Morphis Assignment.

CHAPTER TWENTY

BUT I SHOULDN'T HAVE A MORPHIS YET. I'm not tier two. What is going on? I opened it and began reading.

Greetings:

Your morphis is to be completed by noon, July 5, and is as follows:

Using the uniform provided, you will impersonate a physician. Arrive at the NorthPoint Hospital at 8:45 a.m. Go directly to the fourth-floor neuro ICU waiting area. There will be a wife and child waiting to hear about the father, Luke Mason. Luke was suffering from blunt trauma to the frontal lobe and has been in a coma for two days. You are going to deliver the bad news. You will tell the family he has died. He coded during the night, every aggressive action was taken to save his life but was without success; you give your condolences.

Remember. None of the reasons why you are completing this morphis may be revealed to anyone. Should you have any questions, your assigned officer is Perdonic and he can assist you. Good luck.

Sarkmarr

What…? I bit my lip and stared at the screen. I must have misread—it had to be a twisted joke. My pulse fluttered as I read it a second time. A burst of anger clawed my stomach. No, this was real. This was the Holder's command. This was how he'd decide my worth, my effort, and how far I would go for him. *This is what he does*: he'll push, prod, haunt you until he sees what he wants— who's willing.

DRIVE, Kaylie. Instructing myself to do one thing at a time made my movements mechanical and driving while wearing a white medical coat ignorable. *Windows down. Stereo turned up.* Anything to just get there without thinking.

Park. Walk—across the parking lot, past an idling ambulance and a man hobbling on crutches. My footsteps were footsteps through an older memory. It soon felt as though I was dragging lead.

Don't look around. Just walk through the entrance. When the hospital doors opened, the smell of anesthetic and disinfectant was immediate and strong. The busyness of the staff, the sounds of machines, it all drowned out the undercurrents of human sadness and hope.

Find the elevator. Move, Kaylie. I felt like an insane person, having to instruct myself to perform each movement. The elevator accelerated upward; I watched each numeral light up until the fourth-floor button illuminated. My heart raced—a drumroll in my ears. The more I thought about what I had to do, the more I blamed the Holder. Anger seared my flesh like a hot iron. *How could he ask this?* And he had given no time to prepare last night.

Last night. There was no backing out, not after last night. This was only my first morphis. The Holder would not beat me, not this easily. He would regret trying to humiliate me and everyone else.

Move, Kaylie. I crossed through the waiting room's clover-green archway. I tugged the white coat around my small frame, attempting to look professional. The mother and son were easy to spot; they were the only pair sitting together. A coloring book lay open on the boy's lap, and he pushed a crayon up and down the paper. The mother studied the tile. All at once, I saw my own mother and brother outside our house as the uniformed man walked up. I saw the hesitation in the man's stride, his constant need to swallow, and the shadow of grief already darkening his face. Only one thing can consume a human that way: the fear of delivering the worst possible news.

The hospital air tasted like floor cleaner, heavy on the chemicals. As I walked up to them, the mother and son's expressions perked up, and the speech I had attempted to memorize vanished. I was my own worst enemy, here

180

to deliver the most horrible news. And they would hate me for it.

There was a timid inflection in the mother's voice. "Is there news about Luke?"

"Yes. I'm ... I'm Doctor Ames."

"Yes?"

"I've been—well I've been recently added to your husband's care team." My throat went dry; it felt impossible to make any sound. "You see ... it's with the deepest regret that—"

"Wait!" Her eyes, terrified, darted toward her son. "Bobby, run and get us some more water."

"But Mom ..."

"Go on."

As he walked away, the woman was upright in an instant, standing too close to me.

"Your husband—" A shadow began reaping the life from her face. "You see, last night there was a complication—" My lungs began to constrict, and I felt a pricking in my eyes.

I can't do this.

"Actually, I have to step away. I'm so sorry." The words escaped like soft mouse sounds. "Another doctor will be along shortly." I turned around and kept walking even as she called out after me.

"Wait, what about my husband? Luke? Doctor!"

I didn't wait for the elevator but shoved myself through the stairwell door instead. The tight solitude of concrete walls and endless steps was a haven. Several people stared when I shoved the front doors open and tore my way through the parking lot. I slammed the car door closed, yanked off the white coat, and threw it behind me.

My own family's grief mauled me. The way the uniformed man looked at us...the way he searched for words....All of it stared me in the face again. "We don't know how it happened, Emma. One minute he was with us, and the next, the blizzard was everywhere. None of us could see an inch in front of our face, in any direction." Mum teetered, and the uniformed man had steadied her. "I'm afraid we've lost him." *I'm afraid we've lost him.* Lost him. Lost him. Lost him. We couldn't comprehend those words in that moment. And then we lost ourselves, too. Now, Mum, Hunter, and me....We're castaways in a sea of no answers. We don't even have each other anymore.

I wanted to puncture the air with screams or crack the bones in my body; I wanted to feel some other pain to diminish the aching holes caving in under my skin. What happened to my family? When will it be okay to grieve with my brother or cry with my mum? I want to honor the life my father lived, not bury his existence. The anxiety inside me felt as though it would explode, like it would blast out of my chest and leave nothing of me behind. My hand found its way into a fist, and I slammed the steering wheel. It was the Holder's fault! He asked me to do this. He brought on more pain and relished doing so.

I hate him. I hate him for this.

Feeling more drained than if I had run a marathon, I arrived home and locked myself in my bedroom. It was then when I realized what else had happened. I didn't pass the morphis. And what this inevitably meant.

Who cares? I'll be damned if I care. I don't care.

I dragged myself to my computer and typed out the morphis report detailing what I had done and what I didn't do. With that one tiny click of the submit button, I knew, any moment, the Holder would be reviewing the morphis and would have more than enough to say.

Fuck him! How dare he make these bullshit missions for his own gain!

I closed my blinds and buried myself under the bed covers. The idea of sleep was comical; my mind was stuck in hyperdrive. I dwelled on what was to come. I imagined what I would say to him and what he might say to me. I knew at least what he'd say about me being in Sarkmarr. People have been thrown out for less. If staying in Sarkmarr was what mattered most, I sure as hell didn't perform well enough, as per usual.

Just before dawn, just as my eyes were heavy and my mind slipping into unconsciousness, I heard the phone.

Ring… Ring.

"Hello?"

"The Holder wants to see you." It was Ilusas. I could easily tell by his military way of speaking. "In Edannair tonight. At Bounty Bridge. Confirm?"

"Yes." I hung up the phone and sat in silence, staring

off into the distance of my dimly lit room. This wasn't routine. He could have sent a form letter. Why schedule a meeting with me? How curious. *Instead of kicking me out privately, he wants to say it to my face.* This wasn't going according to plan, but now I had my chance. *I can confront him. This is it.* It would be personal, without fanfare, but at least I could get it all off my chest. *I'm sorry Elliott, Gage, Danny ... and Hunter for failing you all. If this is going to be my last opportunity before getting kicked out, I have to make it count.* Yes ... confirmed. Bounty Bridge, tonight.

CHAPTER TWENTY-ONE

IT WAS MY JUDGMENT TIME, so my job was now to wait. For a long time, I waited. The thought of him was revolting. The Holder reveling in my failure—it was disgusting.

A new, achy feeling spread across my stomach. More than the Holder's outrageous rules and missions, I hated that he had the power to make me say farewell to all of this, to the experience of Edannair. Granted, I never expected this game to do anything for me, but it had. I somehow felt like I needed it. Deep within, somewhere inside me, I knew this place was pulling me from a dark coma. It was the only thing that gave me moments of freedom. Now, when I had learned so much and worked so hard to get here, I would be banned. I thought of the moment in Ruinnlark when I had first heard the Holder reaming Elliott for his failures. How confused I felt when Elliott was so hard on himself, and how funny, now that I realized and understood.

A crackling of leaves sent a chill through my blood. The Holder had arrived. It was time.

I couldn't see him well. He wore the same high-collared coat and dark bandana tied low around his forehead—just below the eyebrows. I shivered, but not from the temperature. His eyes seared through me, and immediately I forgot my intentions, where I was, and what I was going to do. What was I doing here? I had failed my mission, that's all I could remember. Overwhelmed, I couldn't focus on anything but the failed morphis.

"Good evening." The Holder always spoke as if he knew something—something privy to only him.

I nodded. "Hello."

"You were given an assignment today. Your first morphis, am I correct?" His voice was a low musical pitch. His presence exuded mastery and ease. No wonder everyone was uneasy around him. "Mind telling me exactly what happened?"

"I didn't … I didn't complete it—"

"Don't," he hissed. "Don't dare to waste my time. Tell me *what* happened."

Why was he making me nervous? Why was I hesitating? I didn't owe him anything. Tell him what happened! There was nothing to hide. But nothing came. Here, in front of the Holder, and I couldn't find a damn word to say.

"Speak, Loxy." Everything blanked. I sat quiet. "Have we lost our words?"

Isn't this what I wanted? The Holder was right here in front of me. Why couldn't I say anything? The edge in his voice, his charisma—he had me paralyzed.

"Interesting," he mused. "Every poor thing I've heard about you must be true."

What? What things had he heard? Possible answers went awry, firing-off.

"It matters not—"

Without knowing what to say, I just started speaking. "It—It's hard to explain...."

"It?" he snapped. "Are we talking It-with-a-capital-I, the word of grand generalization? Or a specific 'it,' upon which you might be so kind as to elaborate?"

Responding felt like choking on mud.

"When I read it—when I read the morphis—I thought I could complete it. I had every intention to. Even though just driving to the hospital took effort. By the time I had taken the elevator, I was still pressing on—holding on to some belief that I could. But standing there...standing in front of the family in the waiting room...I couldn't. I started to. I tried to. I was giving them the news when..."

"When what?"

"When everything changed in the room. It was me I saw in her eyes. She was my own mum. My brother. How we sat there, too, while some stranger told us my father was never coming home again...that'd I'd never hear his voice again...I'll never get to tell him anything ever again."

The Holder watched me. He stood there in his all-encompassing way, letting the silence linger. His jaw tightened. "You know what your failure means."

I nodded.

"The consequences of failing a morphis…"

I looked away, staring off while listening to him.

"Go and tell Ilusas then. You have been ranked to tier two."

My gaze flew to his. "But I thought—"

"Discernment and strength are difficult to come by, I know. I'm bored of searching for these qualities in people anymore. But you came close enough for now. Go. Before your future in Sarkmarr changes yet again."

And then the Holder disappeared.

GAGE LOOKED AT ME, perplexed. "Wait. So, you got the morphis *before* tier two, you went to the hospital, didn't complete it, and he still said that?"

"Yes."

"This doesn't make any sense. I'm baffled. I'm truly baffled."

"All we can really tell is the Holder has a purpose in mind," Danny said. "Otherwise he would have kicked her out that second. Or at least given her some sort of hell to make up for it."

"Right." Gage nodded.

"But what could that mean?" I asked.

"It means we are in over our heads." Elliott looked sick to his stomach. "Just like I said we would be. He knows all about our plan already, I'm sure of it."

"We don't know that. Everything can still get underway," Danny said. "Maybe he just wanted to make sure she'd put in the effort. Or maybe he's just curious about her—that's good."

"I don't know what to believe," I said pausing. "And honestly, I'm relieved. I wasn't ready to give this up. Sarkmarr has been a…I don't even know how to describe it, but it's been a haven from daily reminders I don't want to remember. Even though this brought me face-to-face with the worst kind of morphis, I'm glad I don't have to leave Sarkmarr so soon."

"How did he seem, Kaylie?" Danny said.

"It was strange. For a moment he almost seemed human. As if he let his guard down."

CHAPTER TWENTY-TWO

IT WAS 7:30 IN THE MORNING, and already it felt impossibly warm for a jog. But fresh ideas often come alive when I'm running. Edannair was taking me deeper into the Holder's world. He was still an enigma, though, and there was more to Sarkmarr than what I'd assumed. And Perdonic was right about the fans. They were beginning to coagulate around me already—in every city there was always someone else desperate to know about the Holder, about what it was like to be the only girl in his group. Other female aliases stopped and thanked me for representing them in an admirable, competitive light.

I tried to keep my breath steady as I jogged. My father's advice swirled through me like oxygen in my lungs. *Push yourself to lead and make decisions. Competition is healthy. It is not something to be feared.*

Heaving, I slowed at the corner that rounded back to my flat.

How is it that I'm even still playing this game? The normal social scene didn't apply in Edannair. The other aliases challenged me, but somehow not in an alienating way. I could earn their respect by doing well in the game, and in the process, I could take pride in my work. It was more satisfying than school—almost more satisfying than my real-life friends.

I spent the rest of the day researching the Stakes, stopping only for laundry and a lunch break. Elliott and Gage said I was becoming a kind of journalist with my note-scribbling, interviewing, and forum-reading. I found old players who had known the Holder before he called himself by that name. His name used to be Lorgen, and he had once been the same as any other sea-elf. Those friends described Lorgen as very good at what he did—not too talkative, but when he did speak it was relevant. So, he wasn't a Shade, nor a renegade. But what happened to him? Why couldn't I place his race when I saw him?

I worked for hours before recognizing that twilight had fallen and the whole apartment was dark. Oh no, 8:43! The concert. I had to be in the heart of downtown at 9:00! A little extra eyeliner and lip gloss would suffice. I swooped purse and keys off the floor and jetted for my car.

Luii's was one of my favorite Austin venues. It was a small establishment but huge in its unique appeal and popularity with students. An eatery during the day, it transformed at night to host intimate band concerts. Tonight Luii's was in full swing. White Christmas lights made the outside sparkle year-round. As I opened the door, an adorable golden retriever panted a tongue-lolling smile at me from under his owner's table. The crowd inside made it hard to walk without bumping shoulders. Every barstool, table, and couch was full. I made my way to the bar for a better view of the stage and seating. The bartender, an energetic and handsome guy my age, handed me a colorful cocktail on the house.

Studying hairstyles and body compositions the way I did in Edannair, I spotted a girl with a ponytail of bouncing brown ringlets—bright red tank top—hand on hip. *Sabrina!* I slipped in and out through holes between waists and shoulders, careful to dodge people's drinks.

An announcer breached the cacophony. "And now, for our opening performance of the evening, put your hands together for Overwhelming!"

The crowd clapped and hollered. Ashaad counted off, cracking his drumsticks together; the reverberation of double bass drums, distorted guitars, and bass unleashed a kraken of heavy metal.

I mouthed hellos at Danny and Eve and hugged Sabrina, and then praised the band with thumbs up and smiles. Eve said something to me, but the music was too loud to understand. She was five months along, and her belly was growing ever bigger. Gage stood center-stage, his fingers clutching the neck of his guitar, his voice meeting the instruments in a battle of chords and vocal power. The band played a dozen songs before taking a

192

break. Gage finished the last verse with one arm raised, his hand forming the rock symbol.

"Thank you very much! We're going to take a little break before bringing you more tunes! We're Overwhelming, and we want to thank the house and the crowd. You guys are great!"

Gage set his guitar down before waving and hopping off the stage. "What's up, guys? What do you think of the band?"

"You guys are great!" I said.

"Not bad at all," Danny said.

"Sabrina?" Gage asked. "What did you think?"

"Loud but good."

Disappointment fanned Gage's face.

"Where's Elliott?" I asked.

"He had to finish a morphis."

"Oh, I didn't know he had another."

"Yeah, You-Know-Who is piling them on pretty thick."

Three teenage-looking boys shimmied out of a crescent booth next to us. Danny motioned behind Saby and mouthed, "Grab that booth."

After Gage said good-bye and disappeared behind the stage curtain, Sabrina threw her hands on the table. "Well, my gypsy mother is trying desperately to organize another visit. She uses every ounce of guilt mixed with clairvoyance, doused with prophecies, and salted with karma to get her way."

"Sabrina, how are you and Marco doing? Has he, ya know." Eve giggled. "Are you official yet?"

"Not yet official. I coax him into trying restaurants with me. That's about it."

After twenty minutes, the band's music filled the bar again with a harmony of bass and guitar. As I listened to the band, I couldn't help thinking of Elliott. He was going through so much for the Holder. We all were.

AFTER THE GIG AT LUII'S, Overwhelming received some recognition from a music promoter. Gage was ecstatic. The promoter asked the band to play in the Summer's End Festival Bash in Dallas. Gage, Elliott, Ashaad, and Ben packed out the following week, leaving me with clear instructions: keep my eye on the prize, and give the Holder what's coming to him.

Gathering information and completing assignments without their support was going to be difficult. Half my team was gone, and Danny was swamped with Eve and the pregnancy. I had no choice but to face my future with Sarkmarr on my own—at least for the time being.

CHAPTER TWENTY-THREE

I CALLED HUNTER'S CELL. He didn't answer. What was he up to? How was Mum? I wanted to know the answers, but most of all I felt a lingering hangover of guilt since my morphis mission. It was as if I'd broken bad news to my own family, and their silence was a judgment on me. I wanted to hear their voices and be positive for once——but Mum's cell went to voicemail, too.

I'll call again tomorrow, I promised myself.

THE MORE I INTERACTED WITH OTHER PLAYERS, the more bizarre the Holder seemed. On Ylora's other continents maybe it was different, but in Edannair his thoughtless self-centeredness didn't make sense. Most everyone, excluding protégés like Rowley, worked together to progress. It was one of the coolest aspects about this place. Complete strangers investigated and worked together like best friends. In the day-to-day world, it was hard to even ask a person for directions anymore. In restaurants, elevators, airplanes—even on campus—if we have a choice to talk or not, the majority of us don't say a word. We're all inde-pendent people working and intermingling, but we act like we belong to separate species. The fact that it was the opposite in Edannair was so incredibly refreshing.

Why the Holder and his enterprise then? Why was he determined to bring real-life dares and missions here? I thought about Rowley, too, with his certainty that I couldn't compete. Stubbornness drove me to work faster and more efficiently. I studied this world as if it were a new language. I practiced the offensive and defen-sive strategies; I watched and listened closely. When the Holder—and even Rowley, for that matter—saw me again, I would be more than they could ever expect.

"Tickets! Get your tickets for exclusive access to the most popular event—World Arena Matches!"

A dozen Sarkmarrs and I sat in front rows at Glock-World Stage. A proportion of attendees bled Sarkmarr colors and lynx insignia. Merksril and Arano sat with me. Rowley and a few of his groupies sat a row behind, and in front were the officers, Ilusas, Riscanth, and Perdonic. WAMs were the nightclubs of Edannair. If I wanted to inquire about the Holder and snub anyone like Rowley, I could use this avenue. Just how would I go about it?

Eight single and pair divisions were competing today in the World Arena Matches. Half were teams of three, the other half one-on-one duels. We watched a shaman named Jagg competing for Bararm against our Xuvy. They somersaulted and dodged about the ring, Xuvy shooting a crossbow and Jagg summoning totems. The seating was so much more up close and personal here. *A bit too close*, I thought as sweat and blood splattered the first row.

"Arano. Can I ask you about the DarkSwells in Eve Keep?"

"Sure, Loxy, what about them?"

"You can ask me." The hefty dwarf pointed at himself. "I, Merksril, know more than little brother here."

Arano shook his huge Quarlin head at Merk, waving away his best friend. "Shut up, Merk, she didn't ask you. Go ahead, Loxy."

"How many times do we need to let Swells disperse before we can dispel? For the achievement, I mean." I fumbled with my words, feeling jittery over asking about Sarkmarr strategies.

"You don't have to worry about that, Lox. That's a Stakes strategy."

"I know, but I—I'm curious."

"Well. We have to do a couple things before we can dispel."

"A couple?" Merk scrunched his forehead at Arano. "Or five, but what do I know? She asked you."

Arano threatened to backhand his know-it-all friend.

"Going to peck me with those dainty fingers? You can barely lift that shield. You know my cousin wanted that shield—and could have used it better than you, I might add."

I giggled. Those two were always together, and they bickered like an old married couple.

"A-ny-way." Arano looked back to me. "Like I was saying, a couple things we do: we let the DarkSwells disperse three times before a dispel. Dispelling before then causes the Swell to burst, and then the raid damage would be unrecoverable."

"Ahem, ahem."

Arano stared at his best friend. "What now?"

"Hmmm? What? I didn't hear anything?"

Arano shook his head and turned back to me. "But we also need to make sure to dispel at the third dispersion or they will cloak."

Merksril forced another cough noise. "It's not slowly floating to the ground or anything."

"Oh. Yeah. Well, I was getting to that. You won't see it falling right away but…Whoa!" We heard a thud against the arena wall below our seats. Xuvy's body had slammed into the side of the arena, blasted back by an air totem's windblast. The crowd grimaced. "That was insane! Haha. Whoa. What a hit." Arano wiped his brow.

Xuvy dove to avoid another burst of current from the shaman. They darted around each other.

"Um, anyway, what was I saying?" Arano looked at me and back to the ring in rapid succession. "You don't want a DarkSwell to touch the ground. They will start to lower to the ground after their first dispersion. Satisfied, Merk?"

Merksril seemed proud.

"And you were talking earlier…" I searched for the correct vernacular. "Something about the best position for attacking a Parudien?"

"Parudiens have no peripheral vision, but they can see behind and in front. So, attack from the sides and you're golden."

"If you have a pack of them, though—"

"A pack? Oh, damn. You'd need a shadowlock with a Demon-wisp. You'd be wiped out otherwise."

"How do you even conquer a Demon-wisp? It's incredibly rare, so I imagine incredibly hard."

"Ask Ilusas. He went through that hell."

Those of us sitting in his proximity looked at Ilusas.

"Curious cat we have here." Ilusas's curt tone unnerved me instantly. His eyes never left the ring.

Rowley snorted. "Loxy's asking irrelevant questions again."

I ignored Rowley. It was Ilusas's tone that worried me.

Ilusas continued. "Why can't you answer these questions yourself, Loxy? What is the best position? What are all the best positions we use for the Stakes, or for Sarkmarr in general for that matter?"

"I—I'm not sure."

"I wonder why that information is not more readily available to everyone, don't you, Arano?"

"Yes, sir. I mean no. Sir?"

"What tier are you now, Loxy?"

My voice caught in my throat. "Just t-tier two."

"Halfway ranked to tier three now. Don't be modest."

"All right, that's enough." Perdonic spoke with an edge to his voice. "I think Xuvy's about to lose this one. Ilusas? We should go square our bets, don't you think?"

Ilusas looked at Perdonic. Something unspoken passed between them. "Yes. Why don't we?"

They took their time filtering down the aisles. Ilusas whispered something, and Perdonic furrowed his brow. I heard bits and pieces of curt words.

In the ring, Xuvy was taking a beating. He couldn't get his paralyzing darts or dizzying arrows off as long as the shaman did mind-control chants.

"Did you hear that? Loxy a tier three?" Rowley scoffed. "That will never happen. Rumor has it you choked at your first morphis."

Before I could answer, Lekar interjected. "Never say never, Rowley."

Rowley hyenaed a laugh. "Loxy. I swear, you rank tier three, and I'll take you for a Demon-wisp myself."

Shocked looks wrangled around Rowley.

"What?" He looked around. "Not like she'll do it."

But Rowley had ignited an acrid competitiveness foreign to me. I bit my tongue and did my best to watch Xuvy and Jagg in the ring.

AFTER JAGG HAD DISPATCHED XUVY, Sarkmarr members swaggered out of the theatre despite the loss. Anyone could recognize the elitism on display in their walk, and their decorated, rare armor. With the best of everything in the game, it was no wonder that the adoring wannabe Sarkmarr fans always begged for our time. We were Edannair's aloof and untouchable gods. I was starting to understand the appeal, but I remained suspicious of it.

After the match, I left the ring and stopped by the Lake of Elouise. The teardrop-shaped lake was best known for being haunted. Legend said that a kidnapped woman, forced to blackmail her family into fighting in the Elder Wars, had been killed in the water while trying to escape. It's believed that her spirit became one with the elements and was trapped at the lakeside. The breeze hooked the gray water in all directions, creating an uninviting, choppy surface. On the smaller point of the lake, I found a spot on some half-submerged stones. Perdonic must have seen me, because he stopped and took a stone for himself.

"Hey there, Loxy." His large, muscular alias looked massive next to mine.

"Hey."

"Pretty intense out there sometimes, huh?"

I hummed an agreement. "He really knows how to get to you."

"Ilusas? He can get like that this time of year. During Stakes season, he always gets jumpy. But don't hold it against him. He does it to keep Sarkmarr safe."

"From me?"

"Not just you, no, no Loxy," he chuckled. "New members, nonmembers. There is a lot of attention on Sarkmarr these days. Ilusas has been with the Holder for—huh, I don't even know how long. So morphises, drills, Shades, fans, not-so-nice fans… it gets to be a lot."

"Yeah, I bet."

"And then mentioning the Demon-wisp. That will rub him the wrong way."

"I've never seen his Demon-wisp with him. I didn't even know he had one."

"I'm not sure you ever will. It is his greatest regret. Anything that reminds him of what happened… well, it's going to get uncomfortable."

"What happened?"

"It's not really my story to tell. After all, officers are pretty closed off. We don't want to go bruising their egos."

"You're an officer too."

"I guess you're right. Better lump me in there."

"The way he referred to me, like I was overstepping my bounds or overstaying my welcome—Ilusas seemed like he hated me right then. It was like Rowley all over again."

Perdonic laughed. "Rowley? Come on now, no one can be that overzealous. Don't sweat it. Ilusas—well, I guess Rowley, too—they're the type that scrutinize and criticize as a defense mechanism. They micromanage aliases, all the way down to the questions you ask and your reactions." He paused. "If any of those things alarms them, they don't have the best way of communicating their concern."

"It felt like I was the enemy. My whole existence was all of a sudden a threat." The thought of Danny, Gage, Elliott, and our Stakes plan hit me with a surge of panic.

Well, you want to be a threat, Kay. Don't you?

"Not at all," Perdonic continued, not noticing my unease. "They just don't care to see the good along with their suspicions. The pros and cons of what a member can and will bring to Sarkmarr. If they don't see themselves in others, they forget to look for anything else. Other resources or approaches are suspicious to them. And for that, I'm sorry. We want you to feel at home in Edannair and Sarkmarr. New members sacrifice their time, give a huge effort, and demonstrate loyalty every day to Sarkmarr. You're a good example of that."

"I am?"

"You may have asked how DarkSwell works, but I know you're not an undercover Shade looking to find some chink in Sarkmarr. But give Ilusas some grace. He would give anything to protect us, and that says a lot about his character. Not that he should come down on you for asking questions. That's the elitist showing. Between you, me, and the trees, you're kicking major butt in Edannair. No girl has done that. And that's worth some praise."

"Wow. I really appreciate you saying that."

"No problem. You're performing really well. Even better than some of our most tenured."

I smiled, and in the privacy of my room, warmth filled my cheeks. I was glad Perdonic couldn't see me.

"Keep it up, Loxy. No other girl has ever come as far as you have. It's going to drive them crazy." He laughed.

"Oh great."

"No, no, it's a good thing! I have a feeling you are going to move some mountains around here."

"Thank you."

"Our AVA teams, though, I don't have the same confidence with. This loss against Bararm was not good. Not good at all. I have to head to an officer meeting about just that, in fact. See you tomorrow, Loxy?"

CHAPTER TWENTY-FOUR

HUNTER WAS TALKING ON THE LINE; I was sitting at my window, staring at the landscape. "She doesn't listen, Kay. She's more like a zombie than a mother. I don't know if I can take it anymore. She leaves nothing alone, yet she does nothing. I feel like I'm drowning in stagnant water..."

The plants that were once green, vibrant, and excited about spring were now strangled and limp. This year's drought season was already crushing the city. I wondered if any of it had any chance of coming back to life. I listened to Hunter's diatribe in cool, conditioned air, where I should have felt separated from the summer's devastation. But I felt the dryness as if I too were a dying plant.

"...nothing means anything to me anymore, Kaylie. I've gone through whole weeks as a drone. Everything I do is out of habit."

"Me too," I said softly. "It's like a ritual to get through the day. I don't remember conversations or care to, and if I sleep my dreams are about Dad."

"Yeah," Hunter sighed.

We hovered on the line together. When he finally

spoke again, his tone was solemn, dark. "How am I going to cope?" There was a throbbing in my chest. It felt like being crushed. "Everywhere I turn she's there, changing something, or pecking at me. I'm walking on eggshells all the time, because if anything Dad comes up, she turns crazy. I need an escape. That's why I run away. I have to get a break from here."

"You have to stop doing that, Hunt. Do you realize what you're putting us through every time you disappear?"

"Do *you* realize what it's like here? What I'm going through? No. You have your new life, in your new part of the world. But what do I have? I have nothing. Nothing that can help get this, this shit out of my head!"

"There is one thing that's helped me," I said timidly. He stayed quiet. I hesitated. "This game. Edannair."

"I've heard of that," he said quickly.

"You wouldn't think it'd be my thing. But honestly, it impressed me. The role-playing, the cities and scenery, with extra twists that turn them mystical…it's a fusion of a film and novel. Your alias has a life, a history, lore, secrets, and ancient spells that have haunted their families for decades. It's this phenomenal story revealed as you go. And something huge has happened."

"What are you saying?" he asked coldly.

"Imagine being part of a legend, Hunter. Imagine being an essential part of a group striving for achievement—the training you put in beforehand, the learning, the anticipation, the intensity as you're all threatened, your performance being crucial for survival. The killing blow as your enemy drops and the universal glory of the victory afterward."

Hunter's demeanor changed minutely. "It sounds like you're telling me some big secret."

"I feel like I am."

"How many people in this thing?"

"I don't know, somewhere in the millions."

"No. In your group."

"Oh, should be forty-nine, I think, now."

"Why so few?" he said.

"The things you have to go through for this group, a lot of people don't make it."

"Why even bother with it then?"

I smiled to myself. "Because it's supposedly worth it."

He exhaled and said, "So, you can play games again, huh?"

"Well. I mean. Not at first. But it has actually helped. I think to cope—"

"So you've replaced the loss."

"No. What? No."

"Uh-huh."

"Screw you, Hunt. You don't know what the hell you're saying. You sound like you're comparing me to her now."

"Well?"

"Well nothing, Hunter! Why don't you listen to me instead of jumping to conclusions and assuming you know everything about what I'm going through or how I'm dealing."

"Like I don't know?"

"I was hoping you would. I was going to tell you that something pretty rare is happening. I'm getting the opportunity to be in a world-renowned group. It's like when you and Dad trained—"

"Don't do that. Don't bring him into this, pretending it's all okay."

"But it's a really great thing."

"Since when? What are you going to tell me? That you can compete? You can't. You choke. Why do you think Dad had to hold your hand through everything? Because you can't handle the pressure—any of it."

It felt like the wind had been knocked out of me. I wanted to hang up on him.

"Humor me; this is funny. What are you going to do, Kay?"

"This isn't a joke, Hunter. Why—how can you—why don't you tell me again about your least favorite human flaws, because I see no differences between you right now and what you say you hate in people most."

The phone went silent.

"Are you still there?" I finally asked.

"I'm here."

Silence.

"Go on," he murmured.

"Go on, what?" I asked.

"I want to hear about it, okay? Go on, what is it you're doing?"

CHAPTER TWENTY-FIVE

TIME WAS RUNNING OUT. The Stakes competition was only two and a half months away, and my A-Team's plan was still far from blossoming. Gage and Elliott e-mailed and called whenever they could. They were doing really well and enjoying the gig a little too much, they said, slurring one night in the middle of a drinking bout. When I told them I only had one rank to go before making tier three, Gage was overly congratulatory, but Elliott didn't say anything. Gage begged for details on the morphises, and I reluctantly told him about how bizarrely outgoing I had to be, hitting on five men, *so embarrassing*. I was starting to feel callous to my own discomfort. And I didn't know whether that was good or bad.

I told Gage how Ilusas had been selecting me for quite a few raids and I was getting the handle on strategies, the dos and don'ts, and crucial times to aid group members. It seemed I was getting noticed—I was certainly moving up the ranks, so all was on track for our plan to work. I didn't mention the rising pressure. The closer we edged to the Stakes, the more I grew dependent upon and obsessed with winning. Success started to feel more than pivotal; it gave me the edge to get through another day. The Stakes wouldn't just bring the Holder a fancy surprise. It would bring me the proof that I still had some fire left in me.

"To rank tier three: only one in-Edannair assignment and one morphis assignment left, Loxy." Perdonic forced a smile. He seemed disconcerted. "The Holder's assignment for Edannair is vague. It says, 'Speak with Riscanth in Gallop Haven. And beyond the journey, in the peak's high elevation, find the source of the water and bring back the prize.' That's it. So, let me know if you need anything. Otherwise, I'll leave you to it. I need to get back."

"About that, Perdonic. Are you okay?"

"Yeah. I'm fine."

"You don't seem as cheery, is all."

He sighed, stretching his neck as if he'd been holding tension there for days. "A decision's been made, and I don't agree with it."

"What decision?"

"Officer business, Lox. Really nothing I should question. And nothing you should worry about."

"I will worry, regardless. I can tell something's wrong."

"I guess everyone will know soon enough anyway. But for now, keep this between us."

"Of course."

"As you know, our AVA team has lost a few more

matches. The one against Bararm, another to Voodoo, and two more against Eludan. And ... well ... the Holder decided to pull all the AVA teams from the Stakes."

"What?"

"Shhh. Keep your voice down."

"He can't. Why? Why would he do that?"

"The Holder says our AVA teams have lost too many matches."

"But they've still qualified. With only a couple of losses, they must have still qualified for the Stakes, right?"

"Yep, they still qualified; they're sitting fifth, and the top six AVA teams make the Stakes. But that doesn't matter, apparently. They're not performing to the Holder's standards and he pulled them."

"Duels, threes, and thirty versus thirty?"

"All of them." The fighting spirit of Xuvy, Nozey, and all the AVA duelers who worked so hard in alias-to-alias combat flashed through my mind. "Now our only representation at the Stakes will be on the AVE raiding side."

"And who's our team for that going to be?"

"That hasn't been completely decided on yet. The top nine raiding groups from every continent qualify for the Stakes AVE raid, and Sarkmarr's more than fine there. We're still ranked number one. I gotta get back to the meetings, and you, you do well on this assignment."

I nodded slowly.

"Hey, chin up. It will be fine, I promise."

LEAVING PERDONIC ON AN ARCHIMON EAGLE, I flew past Quillinthos to Aldium. As far from Ruinnlark I had ever been, I sat quietly on an Ulu train. The futuristic train cars were without walls, hovering along the tracks like a flat conveyor belt. *How could he?* I smoldered. The Holder's decision to cut the AVA teams seethed in my subconscious, threatening to boil over. I could not believe it. It was a complete overreaction to a couple of match losses. All of Sarkmarr's AVA competitors … what will they do? All of us watched and cheered them on in so many arenas and battlegrounds. They've worked hard all year long. The news would crush them. All those matches. All that effort. For nothing. I thought of how I would feel if it were the AVE side that had been pulled. Pulling the raid side would have sunk any plans for me making it to the Stakes, but it seemed my chances were still open for now.

The train jerked through sharp, irregular turns, and my thoughts followed a similar path. From Aldium to the east, and on to Gallop Haven, bolts of electricity made sparks below the train cars and lit up the path as we raced along. It looked as if I was zapping through time.

The Ulu train rumbled to a halt and dropped me at Gallop Haven. The Holder's officer, Riscanth, was waiting.

"Greetings, Loxy. Here you go." Risc handed me the reins of something comical—a giant chicken, flightless and bright yellow. "Ride for forty-five minutes. Don't bother looking for the peak—you won't see it." He sounded rehearsed and bored. "Follow that trail." He pointed to a path not wide enough for a person, let alone a rider and her mount. "Keep going even when you think you've gone too far. Are you good?"

"Sounds like I should have kept my eagle."

"You can't fly where you're going."

Into a strange forest, the hybrid chicken and I went— barely fitting under tree roots that had grown out above the ground. Like coiling fingers, they grabbed hold above boulders and other trees. Gallop Haven? Or hell? A play on words, considering that my mount was galloping across the most unforgiving, uneven fields and stone-pocked lands I'd seen. The chicken darted through rocky passes and bubbling mud. The animal seemed to know the route, or maybe just loved to run, for nothing seemed to slow it.

Crossing into a garden, we found the first patch of level ground within miles. Lilies dotted the earth, shining among the ferns like pale lanterns. A snarling sound from behind the shrubs made my mount jump and squawk. A giant green-yellow bee creature appeared out from under the brushwood. Scrinbees! A predator with tiny legs and wings, the Scrinbee's body was plump like a bumblebee's. It had a face like a grasshopper and a deadly stinger.

I spurred the bird on, and we galloped forward. The mutant bee hovered for a moment and then tore after us, darting along the ground. I held on for dear life as the bird darted and ducked from the bee-creature biting at our heels.

Finally, we lost our attacker. I kept the bird moving, though, reminding myself what Risc had instructed: *Keep going even when you think you've gone too far.*

After we squeezed between clumps of heavy boulders, a riverbed appeared.

In the peak's high elevation, find its source.

The path was getting harder to see as a fog descended, spinning its arms of gray along the ground. My mount stopped abruptly and refused to go any further. Dismounting, I moved forward on my own, and within a few yards I found an earthen wall: the peak. I followed a stream upslope, using vines and rocks to scale the steepest slopes. The fog was so thick I could barely see a foot in front of me. After a long climb, the incline finally leveled and the sound of plunging water echoed around me. Mist funneled from everywhere and mixed with the fog. My eyes finally adjusted, and beyond the fog I saw plunging water. A waterfall fed into a half-moon cove into a pond. It seemed sacred. Pacing along the pond, I strained to make out anything. It was when I stood still that I saw them. Aquatic fairies, or pixies—I couldn't be sure, but they looked familiar. There were so many—sitting, standing, lying out, and hovering in and around the cove's water. They had petite bodies, long hair, four translucent wings, and webbed feet and hands. *Asrai.* That's why they were familiar. Pearls laced their hair and wrapped around the curves of their waists and arms. One with long red hair hovered within inches of the waterfall, flittering her wings and splashing the water. Another was dipping in and out of the pond like a water bird after a fish. Two others were screening the water—foraging for something.

I stepped closer. My foot touched the water, and instantly one fairy became aware of me. She flew straight up. Her body tensed, and her back arched as she drove toward me. Her serene face transformed: her brown eyes turned an electric green, and her petite mouth opened, revealing a mouth of razor teeth. I stepped back out of the water, and the fairy instantly retreated and regained her soft expression.

A golden-haired fairy drew a screen from the water. Fog lifted and fell, hiding and revealing her as she moved. Lying on one of the flat rocks, she pulled a pearl from the screen and laced it into the hair of a fairy next to her.

It was the pearls. They were the prize!

The water. They were protecting it, maybe in awe of it. My hands went to work. I conjured a water spell and hurled it into the cove. The spell–water hit the back of the cove's wall and dissipated. A fairy or two looked toward the commotion for a moment and then turned back to their toil. I tried again, but nothing.

Wait. The demonstration spells. I had forgotten about those. Arano had explained that these training spells could hold their shape if another spell was cast around it. *Tangle the spells together.*

Water orbs formed, and I gently released the hovering spell. They moved slowly over the water, swirling in and around each other. *Now. Shackle.* The swirling orbs expanded, but before they could climax and disappear, I caged them together. It was working. The fairies watched the orbs in awe. One after another, maidens flew to it, hovered around it, circled it, and pointed at it, sniffing.

Tiptoeing back to the water's edge and sinking my hands in, I grabbed a handful of mud. Dirt and rocks fell away as I sifted through it, and under the last little bit of sludge, three white pearls glistened. The demo-orbs were beginning to dissipate, I stepped back, holding the pearls, and my foot splashed the water.

As one, the fairies' gazes snapped up. Their faces went livid and fixed me with terror-smiles full of glimmering razor teeth. And all at once they flew at me. I staggered back and fled down the mountain's steep slope. The thunder of beating wings surged after me as I leaped off the edge and somersaulted through the air. Landing hard, I struggled to get to my feet and continued running; the wings and gnashing teeth grew louder and closer. The red-haired fairy's razor fangs snapped within an inch of my ear. Before I could duck, a hand grabbed my arm, and suddenly the mountain, the soil, the sound of the beating wings, and the fog disappeared.

What was happening? The world evaporated in an instant.

As the haze and smoke dissipated I glanced left and right, desperate to get my bearings. I recognized the clumps of heavy boulders. I was standing back at the bottom of the peak.

"Quite a trick up there," a voice called out. I spun around. A foreign figure stood a few yards away. He wasn't a normal alias. "I was wondering how you were going to proceed," he said. "Nice diversion, I must say. Quick thinking."

Not an earth-troll, not a Norseman. Not a Zana or orc. He didn't look completely alien, but what was he? He had smooth skin, long messy hair, a man's muscled body, human except for the hands and feet. They were longer, thinner—clawlike. And the eyes. They were alien and depthless, with no distinction between iris and pupil. A hint of a smoke swirled around him—an aura falling gently from his naked shoulders like a mantle. He had no armor or weapons on his body and wore a single cloth tunic.

I looked for an exit.

"Before you think about doing that, let me introduce myself. I just want to talk to you." The authority in his voice made me believe I wouldn't get very far. "Have you ever met a Shade before, Miz Loxy?"

I shook my head.

"You can say you have now. I'm Vsin. And I'd like to ask you, what were you doing up there?"

"I—"

"That's a restricted part of Edannair."

"I didn't know that. Honestly."

"Who sent you here?"

"I must have wandered too far; I was exploring."

"Ah. Exploring." The Shade took a few steps away. With his back to me, I could only tell he was looking down. His elbows and shoulders were moving, cradling something perhaps. He turned around, careful to hold his arms in position. He held—no, more like hosted—an illusion. It was the mist-shrouded pool under the water-fall. "They are called the Asrai," he said. I looked up from the image when he spoke; he was watching my reaction. "Water imps. They are obsessed with the water-pearls, and protective of them, obviously."

I considered the Shade's ability to hold an illusion and felt a little afraid of the illusion itself. The fairies were swarming in the watery reflection, fighting with each other, tumbling in and out of the cove water, snarling and biting at each other in frantic, searching dives.

"Dangerous to aliases as well, the Asrai. Did you know their touch stunts an alias, making it unable to cast or even wield a weapon? And as you just observed, they have no qualms about killing." The Shade clasped his hands together, and the watery mirage of the fairies melted away. "We've thought about extinction. Wiping them out before they become more of a nuisance. It would be terrible to think your exploring there was on purpose, wouldn't it? Who knows what could have happened to you?"

It was hard to look at him without wanting to avert my

eyes, even though I was safe behind my computer screen probably a thousand miles away from this Shade, Vsin.

"We're just looking for some information, Miz Loxy."

"I don't have any. I've been here barely a few months."

"Indeed. And already a part of the great Sarkmarr. You must be very proud of yourself."

"Thanks. I think."

"Miz Loxy. We try to keep a balance in Edannair. Protect each alias. And ensure a good experience for everyone. If that balance is interrupted, tipped to one alias's advantage, we rely on good people, like you, to help us flush out the disturbance." We looked at each other a few seconds. "If you think of anything, don't hesitate to contact us. And be careful where you stray. You were very lucky I happened to be there to grab you in time."

"Thanks for that."

He bowed his head. He clenched his fist, as much as the long animal claws would allow, and turned it back and forth over the grass. The ground around him started to turn colors. Blades of grass bleached white. I staggered away, but he stood still—accustomed to the effect. The aura around him thickened, and in seconds he was gone. A mirage—a ghost of him—was all that remained.

Chapter Twenty-Six

Sarkmarrs had crowded into Taby's Tavern and were already deep in heated debate when I entered. Ilusas nodded to me after reviewing the pair of pearls I handed him. One of Sarkmarr's favorite hangouts, Taby's Tavern was a pub with unique appeal. The mahogany spiral staircases rose like columns throughout the room, each with balcony seating built outward at the middle and top levels, allowing three stories of conversations. But you didn't need to shout across rooms or over too-long tables—this was Edannair, and people seated at midlevel could easily talk with those below or above them, no matter how far away.

[Merksril]: He can't go through that again, Ilusas. There has to be a different morphis Arano can do.

[Syntax]: No one made an exception for me.

[Brambt]: He'll be fine. The Holder knows what he's doing.

[Merksril]: This is ridiculous. Don't do it, Arano. I'll quit with you right now.

[Windvar]: Calm down, Merk. You'll give yourself a heart attack.

Arano shook his head and gestured at Merksril to settle.

[Findail]: Arano will still need a witness.

[Merksril]: I'll do it. If you're going to do this to him, I'm going to be there.

[Findail]: No, Merk. Not you. Has to be someone else.

[Merksril]: Not me? Fin, you're kidding!

[Findail]: Leave the tavern, Merk, before you get thrown out.

Merksril looked to his best friend, who nodded, and the dwarf hissed at Fin as he stormed out the door.

[Findail]: Well? Sarkmarrs?

[Modaga]: Me. I'll be the witness.

[Findail]: No, Modaga. You're not in the same state.

[Modaga]: Oh, right.

Seconds of silence circulated within the group.

[Findail]: No one else?

[Rowley]: Have Loxy do it.

I looked at Rowley.

[Rowley]: You're in the same state, aren't you?

I looked to Ilusas, but he was watching me like everyone else. I was quiet, an actor on stage who'd forgotten the next line.

[Findail]: How about you, Row? You're eager enough.

[Rowley]: Sure. I've done plenty before. What's one more?

Arano's head sank. Clearly he didn't want Rowley.

[Loxy]: Okay, guys. Just fill me in. I've never been a witness before, but I'll help if I can. What do I need to do?

Rowley sat back, looking smugly at me and then at Fin. I tried to give a discreet, reassuring nod in Arano's direction.

[Findail]: Good. It's settled. Now. Loxy. Do you have any rope?

ARANO DROVE THE THREE BLAND HOURS from Houston to Austin. I was early, and I waited for him downtown in an unused parking lot behind a bank and a law firm. I thought about Merk, the way he hesitated to talk about Arano, and the advice he had finally given me outside the tavern. "When Arano puts on a brave face, don't take him for a hero." Merk had crossed his arms and glowered at his shoes. "His claustrophobia was his worst nightmare in high school. A prank gone wrong, he almost drowned trapped inside a barrel. And now the Holder's bringing it all back."

Arano pulled up in a blue pickup truck. He was taller than me, though not by more than a few inches, and 5' 5" is not much of a record to beat. He was small-boned and seemed lethargic.

"Hey, what's up?"

"Hi."

We made small talk about Austin, the sights, and what he did the last time he had been here. When I asked him if he was ready to get it over with, his face turned pale. The mint green poly rope I pulled from my car was coiled and knotted neatly. It was the climbing cord I had only used once before for a rock-climbing weekend with Wes. The rope didn't come within an inch of him before Arano's breathing became irregular.

"Hey, hey, we can take our time," I said, letting the rope lay limply against my thigh. Arano had not taken his eyes from it. It felt like I was acclimating a wild animal to a leash.

Arano set up the camera and started the recording. He looked at the ground a long time, regulating his breathing and mumbling, "I can do this."

I started at his feet as I tied the rope around his ankles. Working my way up, I wrapped the rope around his calves, knees, and thighs, around his waist and wrists at his sides, around his chest and shoulders. By the time I finished, he was fully cocooned.

I knotted the end and started the timer.

His forehead was sweaty, and he heaved like he was going to retch. When I thought he might be hyperventilating, I went to untie him, but he shook his head and coughed out, "No, don't." The confinement was torture. It was ravaging his face. I begged him to stop halfway through, when it looked like he might retch again. His curses kept me away.

It was the longest half hour.

My phone's alarm went off. Something in him snapped, and he begged to be untied. I undid the rope as fast I could. Small tears trickled down the side of his nose. With the rope dead at his feet, I put my hand on his back.

"Hey, we're right around the corner from Austin Java." He was bending over and taking deep breaths. "It's one of my favorite places. Best pineapple smoothie you'll ever have."

"I WASN'T ALWAYS CLAUSTROPHOBIC." Arano was tipping his glass left and right, waiting until just before the smoothie spilled out before he balanced it upright again. We sat at an outdoor table where it was less crowded. "It's ironic really. I was a wrestler, if you can believe that." Arano looked down at his body and sighed.

It was true—to look at him, you wouldn't think he could have wrestled. He seemed frail. "Since I could crawl I was trained in wrestling. Being pinned down was nothing new to me, and I had no problem with it. But high school came, and well, the rest is history."

"What happened?"

"Nothing really to tell. I was a freshman kid who got cocky and paid for it."

Hunter and that Johnny Winters kid flashed in my mind. "That sounds like something to tell."

"Ah, well, as a freshman wrestler, I figured I was invincible. And I acted that way. Blake, a senior on the varsity wrestling team, told me and a few other freshmen the rules: we were the new kids, and we were to know it and respect it. I ducked behind him and threw my hands under his into a full nelson, right there in the locker room." Arano laughed softly. "Like I said, I was cocky.

"He and three other guys cornered me after school. We took a drive to some old factory. I remember pulling up and seeing rows and rows of barrels. Tons of barrels. They dragged me over to one. I was outnumbered; the coward wouldn't take me on alone, but I gave two of those boys a good welt or two before they were lifting me over a barrel. Blake slapped my face, saying, 'What now, little shit? Where's the big moves now?' His boys held me in the air. Blake's face was upside down, but I could tell he was grinning. What a coward." Arano looked at the ground. "Of course, it wasn't until I was being submerged into that black water that all the cockiness in the world, boom," — he snapped his fingers— "left me as quick as that. It went dark. They closed the lid over the barrel. I wriggled around so that my head was close to the top. My added weight pushed the water up so close to the lid I could barely get any air. I pretty much thought I was going to die. I couldn't breathe. I couldn't see. The pain of that panic," he shivered, "was infinite." He paused. "My head's messed up now, I can't wrestle or come close to anything confining. Well, today I did, but that wasn't very pretty, was it?"

I GAVE ARANO A HUG before we parted. I waved good-bye and stood in the parking lot for several minutes. I felt heaviness weighing on my being. He had driven away with a drained but grateful expression, but he shouldn't have had to go through that. It wasn't right; the Holder can't tread that personally.

I thought of Vsin.

Sarkmarr *was* better off with the Holder turned over to the Shades.

As soon as I was home, I made a copy of Arano's video and started an e-mail to Vsin. Together, maybe this Shade and I could help each other. When I attached the file and went to press send, something in me hesitated. *How do I know I can trust Vsin?* Would he punish all of Sarkmarr for our link to the Holder? We knowingly benefit and reap rewards from the Holder's power....What would Vsin do?

I fell asleep to these questions, with Vsin's letter saved and unsent, for now.

CHAPTER TWENTY-SEVEN

"I DON'T THINK YOU'D WANT TO DO THAT. It's three o'clock in the morning, and we just drove an hour to find this place. And trust me. It's hard enough the first time you drag yourself to do a morphis, let alone leave and try again." Perdonic was looking at me. He had a gleaming white smile, and his curly hair had grown out since last I'd seen him.

I glanced at the gravel under my shoes, then to the mansion behind the gated entrance in the Hills. Turning the pebbles with my shoe, I procrastinated. A morphis assignment was the last thing I wanted to be doing—images of Arano were flashing through my mind. I felt the urge to bolt; can't imagine what my body language was saying to Perdonic. But he'd flown in from California, and I knew I couldn't refuse. I tried stalling instead.

"Being there with Arano...do you ever think these morphises get to be a bit much? One day, the Holder's going to end up really hurting someone."

Perdonic stared straight ahead as if formulating what to say to me. "This isn't nervous talk, is it?"

"No, but I mean, harmless escapades are one thing, but treading too personally is another. He asks people to do these outrageous things and we do them, we comply. Why?"

"A lot of reasons. People are seekers. We want thrills, don't we? Power and challenge—the Holder gives us the opportunity to have those things. Come on. Let's get this assignment out of your hair and off your mind. You can climb the wall to break in there."

I looked beyond, where Perdonic pointed, and my stomach sank with fear.

AND I WAS RUNNING. I had the small marble lion head clutched in my hand, and the fountain behind me had one less decorative piece of art. One of the many mansion doors slammed again, and a gruff voice was yelling and cursing. Then came the sound of shots. Sheer panic hit me. *Run!* Racing to the wall, I pulled myself up and over, sliding down as another shot shattered part of the cinderblock near me. I jumped in the passenger seat and screamed, "Go! Oh my god, go!"

CHAPTER TWENTY-EIGHT

THEIR WHISPERS WERE STEADFAST AND SHARP. I was about to enter the tavern when I heard my name. I flattened myself against the wall next to the door. I turned up my speakers to hear better.

"I can't believe Loxy made tier three." I recognized Brambt's voice.

"Loxy got off easy." The voice was flat, almost a drone—Riscanth.

"She had the lion head, didn't she?" Grimm was speaking now, or maybe Aerum. "She earned her tier three, fair and square."

"What the hell was the Holder thinking?" Rowley hissed.

"What the hell were you thinking?" The voice sounded irate. It was Ilusas.

I slid under a window and peeked through its slats. The place was empty, save for a few tavern workers and the Sarkmarrs. Ilusas and Rowley stood. Aerum, Riscanth, and Brambt sat around a small table against the wall, the barmaids opposite them.

Ilusas stared at Rowley. "None of this would matter except that my dimwitted protégé swore to escort her if she made it, for Demon Paths Converge, no less!" Ilusas gripped his fist in his opposite hand. "Why not take her to Shade Islands next! Dumbass rogue."

"How about I just don't do it, Ilusas? I'll pretend to, but I won't take her the right direction."

Ilusas shoved his forearm into Rowley's throat, pinning him against the wall.

My jaw dropped. No one in Edannair could physically jar an alias like that without a weapon and without being in an arena or battleground. That is, no one except Shades or the Holder. And now Ilusas?

Brambt and Riscanth stood like soldiers coming to attention. Ilusas was choking Rowley so hard that Rowley's health bar started dropping. The tavern staff ignored what they'd rather not see and kept pouring ale and cleaning platters.

"You will take her. You will not spoil Sarkmarr's name or taint our reputation another ounce. Have you not gotten it into your pea-sized brain that everything you do, everything you say, reflects on us! To think I saw potential in you, and took you to Vile Xors in the first place. I should break you now."

Brambt moved in. "Ilusas. He will go. You can finish him afterward if he doesn't."

Ilusas released, and Rowley grabbed at his throat and gasped, wide-eyed, at his mentor.

Ilusas adjusted his shirt collar and straightened his sleeves. "I've summoned her here tonight, Rowley. Loxy's on her way. Get this embarrassment over with."

"Tonight?"

Ilusas glared at Rowley.

"Tonight's fine. I'm going, I'm going. I was just asking."

I slipped away from the door, spacing myself from the tavern. Ilusas had only alluded to why he summoned me. Now it was confirmed. Voices grew loud and died out again from inside the tavern. The entrance door swung open. Riscanth and Ilusas appeared. Our eyes met.

"Ah. Loxy. You're right on time." Ilusas swung the door back open for me. "Your escort eagerly awaits. Congratulations on tier three." Ilusas spoke with a sarcasm so thick that it almost sounded sincere.

Riscanth and Ilusas walked away toward Nimbus Square, speaking on some subject I didn't understand. I stepped into the tavern. Aerum, Rowley, and Brambt edged nearer to the door.

"Hey, Loxy." Brambt nodded to me. "We'll see you later, Rowley."

"Uh-huh. Later."

Brambt and Aerum let themselves out.

"Ready?" Rowley's disdain hung thick in his tone. "Let's go. I don't have all night. And this is going to take many nights."

FROM RUINNLARK, we traveled east, past Quil's Quandary and the Alabaster Hills. He didn't speak and neither did I. We moved carefully through Para's Thornwick and followed the white streams of Milkwood. As we entered the Sunlit Canyons, our pathway narrowed. At one point we could barely fit walking shoulder-to-shoulder. The sinuous walls were a deep red, and wherever the sunlight reached, the walls shimmered golden white. There was a special quality in all these lands. Edannair resembled our familiar Earth, but it was the epitome of what it could have been like: wild, unpolluted, highly evolved. Ylora gave us the best of our own world—the most exotic earth, rocks, and trees; the richest colors; and the most interesting animals.

"This place. It's incredible isn't it?"

Rowley said nothing.

The silence seemed to revel in itself. And for another long span, I let it.

Ignoring his demeanor, I finally tried again. "You've done this walk before, right?"

"Don't talk."

I grit my teeth. *Not going to give up.* "What is your problem, Rowley? We're going to travel all this way together. Humor me. I won't tell a soul. Promise."

"I don't care what you do."

"Isn't it difficult being that angry all the time? I mean, I would think it would be. The scowling, the tension, sore shoulders. You get a lot of headaches?"

"Stop. Please."

"I'm kidding. I'm kidding, Rowley. Where are we going, anyway?"

"That's it. Right there. What you just said. You girls come here, no research, no effort, and look, you're being guided to *the* hardest accomplishment in all of Ylora. Something wrong with this picture? Useless...."

"I have done research. A lot of it. There's hardly any information out there about Demon Paths Converge or the island of Vile Xors. Trying to find a specific answer to a mission as rare as this one is next to impossible, and you darn well know it. Besides, you were the one who gambled on the tier three thing, Rowley, not me."

"You had it too easy. You should be treated just the same as us. Come on, the lion head? Really? For your tier three?"

"Take it up with Lorgen, then."

"Don't speak his name. You don't hold that rank. Have you lost all respect, too?"

"The Holder. Excuse me."

Rowley glared at me before turning and resuming his quick pace.

"You know, I've never asked you for anything, Rowley. I've taken this place as it has come to me. And if I've taken anyone's help, it was offered freely. If you want to be mad at girls, pinpoint the ones constantly trying to get attention, like Minikit. Everyone says she's beyond annoying, so go give her hell."

"Maybe I already have. What do you know?"

"I don't, that's why I'm asking."

"I don't care what any of you do, as long as you keep out of our way."

"Done. I'd like nothing else, either."

The journey started to feel impossibly long. I followed Rowley out of the canyons onto a gray beach. The sky matched its dull color, and a hot, dense steam rose from the ground. I bit my tongue as Rowley needlessly stabbed beetles and whacked turtles napping on the hot rocks.

"Bathin's Beaches," Rowley whispered.

The steam faded away, and Rowley stopped where the land unfolded into the tongue-shaped gully called Yogoro's Crater.

"What is it?" I asked.

"We're done for tonight."

"Why?"

"It's four o'clock in the morning, that's why. I'll see you tomorrow."

"Okay. Hey, Rowley, thank you. For tonight. I know it's the last thing you wanted to be doing. It may not sound like much but I do appreciate it. I have to admit I'm getting excited thinki—"

"I'll see you tomorrow."

"Right. Night, Rowley. Oh, what time?"

"What time do you think? Same time. Can't do anything else this side of BFE."

THE FOLLOWING EVENING, I arrived a few minutes early and waited for Rowley. When my silent partner appeared, he started on ahead of me, absent of a hello. And we traveled some more—out of the cratered ground and into a weedy wasteland that gave way to miles of sand dunes. Farther we went, and then even farther.

We had to postpone after another seven hours of traveling. Both exhausted, we nodded a mutual goodnight.

Into our fourth hour on the third night, I was certain this place was infinite. No mounts—flying or otherwise—were allowed this far out, and the slow increments of distance we covered were unfathomable.

Following Rowley's tall sea-elf figure for a thousand miles should have felt like an honor, but was feeling more like punishment. I thought about Demon Paths Converge and what Rowley had said about it being the hardest achievement. I pieced together the bits of legend I'd heard in the cities, but details were missing.

"Rowley?"

"What?"

"Why do Demon-wisps have to serve a shadowlock? What makes them surrender?"

He shook his head.

"I know I know, I should know this already. But seeing that I can't do more research right now, would you tell me a little?"

He exhaled slowly. I could almost hear his internal debate.

"Ever heard of Beleth?" He turned around to look at me. "He's a high king of the underworld. And he was Ash-shaytan's Archnigh."

"Hey, that's what they call Ilusas."

Rowley nodded slowly. "Stemmed from a joke a long time ago, and it stuck. Anyway, Beleth led over eighty-five legions of Demon-sheiks, also known as Demon-wisps. He rode a horse so pale the animal was often mistaken for a ghost. He had two sons, Limo and Reden. He taught his sons how to hear and answer summons invoked by conjurers. When Beleth answered the summoners of the highworld, he would act very fierce, try to frighten the conjurer, and see how courageous he was. If the conjurer was brave and could draw the demon's sign with some special wand, then Beleth would give the conjurer a Demon-wisp to command.

"It's said that Beleth admires men but loves women most of all, and will do just about anything to fulfill his lust. He prides himself on giving power back to conjurers of the highworld and has helped his favorite summoners build armies and win wars.

"His sons, though, became obsessed with the power growing in them. The eldest more so. Limo would condemn any spirit or being who did not bow, show enough respect, or raise a silver ring to their head in homage to him or his brother. He taught his brother to demand this respect and to use demon legions against not only the highworld but the underworld as well. They plagued any people, spirits, or demons that didn't comply and tormented them until they worshiped the brothers. When Beleth found out, he was outraged and cursed his sons to silence, and he released every legion from under their command. For seventy years, they could not wield demon powers."

Rowley turned back to me; I had fallen behind a little ways.

"Don't lag."

"I'm sorry," I said, catching up. "Then what happened to Beleth's sons?"

Rowley sighed. "Well. The younger one, Reden, learned from the lesson and apologized to his father. Limo, though—the humiliation was too much, and he vowed revenge. He planned and poisoned his brother's mind until together they tricked their father into entering a forbidden level of the underworld, the Lomna level, by disguising it as a lust chamber. And Beleth, being the lust-lover that he was, suspected nothing."

Rowley crouched and touched the granules of sand at his feet, which were changing color from beige to gray. The gentle breeze carried wisps of hot steam from the ground ahead. He stood up, and we stepped over ash-colored rocks and into the clouds of steam swimming through the air. The sky was gray—so were the rocks, the sand, and the steam.

"Rowley, didn't we pass here already? Bathin's Beaches, right?"

"You would think so, wouldn't you? They're very similar."

"It isn't?"

"Nope. That was South Bathin's. We're in North now. It's meant to look this way. It's confusing and way too familiar. Gets people lost all the time because they think they are going in circles. They turn back and retrace the map over and over. It makes even the best groups give up after days of circling."

"How can you tell?"

"I'm a rogue. It's my job to know our footing. Besides, why do you think I've been smacking turtles around? It's one of the tricks to keep track of where we're going—or, rather, where we've been."

The same bleak surroundings, the same rocks, the same turtles, and sky…I could have sworn we had gone in a circle.

Rowley stepped carefully, glancing at rocks and touching parts of sand and looking from east to west. He was delicate with each movement, and his face was set in deep concentration. In this task, he was brilliant. *No wonder Ilusas brought him to Vile Xors.* Following him through the terrain was difficult, even the second time around. We stepped over steaming rocks and followed sand and water paths hidden in the thick steam.

"Rowley. What happened to Beleth?"

Rowley heaved another sigh. "He lost everything. His power. His control over his legions. He's cursed and remains cut off in a lower dungeon of the underworld.

Limo was elected the next Archnigh in Beleth's place. Which meant no more Demon-shieks to the highworld. No more help."

"That's awful."

"Yep. Sucks to be him." Rowley took a long pause. He searched the sky while shaking his head before speaking again. "Reden, though, in his guilt, still answers conjurers just as his father did, and had taught him and his brother to do. Unknown to Limo, of course, Reden will still appear at Vile Xors and help the highworld. Catch is, he'll only appear for shadowlocks now. And sometimes he'll give them a Demon-wisp, if they prove something or other—the hell I know." The sound of shooting water exploding startled me. "It's just geysers, Loxy. A good sign. We're headed right."

The gray, waterworn pebbles were small at first, but as we walked they grew into boulders, and then we were walking in a maze of rock canyons. We came to an opening where the ground was riddled with manholes large enough to swallow trees. The mesa wall was too high to climb and stretched on until disappearing in the steam.

"How will we get up there?"

A geyser sang out somewhere in the distance ahead, hidden by steam, then another to the left.

"Like this!" Rowley took off, heading straight for one of the black manholes. He jumped over the opening. Just as his body started to descend, the geyser shot off, propelling his body into the sky and throwing his tall form beyond the wall. The geyser sprayed its water over the wall, then backward, and straight again. I heard more shooting water behind me, then another to my right and left, and another farther ahead. I could hear Rowley's muffled catcalls from above. It wasn't for many moments that the chorus of shooting water paused.

Rowley had jumped perfectly. How did he know when it would spew? Was it after the first geyser or second? Did the warning come from behind me or ahead? The geysers had all gone silent. I was scrambling to remember my cue.

A geyser exploded up ahead.

Running, I let my feet move on instinct. A second geyser blew, farther to the side. I half halted, doubting my timing, but I already had momentum—I leapt with no other choice. The dark hole below me was massive. Enough to swallow four of me. I descended into the gaping mouth. I had leapt too early. Panic flew down my body like a current. Then a rumbling sounded below; a pillar of water rose and propelled me upward. I landed next to Rowley.

"Look." Rowley's expression was tense. "Here we are. The Outer Reaches."

We had traversed into a realm surpassing anything I had yet seen. The sky was cloaked with a rust-colored haze. Churning, behemoth tornados swept the cracked, scorched land, each one ten miles wide at least. After scanning the span of what seemed a never-ending horizon, I spotted a tiny seam in the heavy red atmosphere. Light beamed through, illuminating a dark shape against the tan and red of the earth and sky. Small shadows moved around the jetting shape.

"Fasten your seatbelts." Rowley said pointing. "There's the island of Vile Xors. The summoning circle."

Chapter Twenty-Nine

We moved carefully, almost holding our breath as we made our way between the mammoth tornados. Rowley calculated each of our steps to avoid them. If we were to be sucked into a funnel, the giant cloud would kite us from the Outer Reaches all the way back, kicking and screaming, to Ruinnlark.

We followed the cracked plain to its edge. A cliff separated us from seawater below. I peered over the ledge. A black ocean stretched from cliffside to horizon. We could see the island more clearly now, isolated by a long span of dark water. Experience told me it was too far away to swim to. The shape I thought I had seen from the mesa was actually multiple shapes—monoliths dotting the island of Vile Xors.

Shrieks sounded in the distance. It was the shadow of movement—something flew toward the sky, into the light, above the monoliths. I couldn't tell what was out there.

"Orexia's Sea," Rowley whispered. "Black water. Death's water. Those gray streaks—that's from all the decomposing bodies. Anyone who enters her sea dies, whether they swim or go by boat. She always gets them. Good luck finding your way across this. Even took Ilusas a while." Rowley crossed his arms and smirked at me.

I took the challenge. I looked over the edge again as Rowley made a seat for himself on the ground. I paced the cliff's edge before finally committing to a direction. I walked the edge for a long while, listening to the water's steady whisper. The waves of Orexia's Sea lapped the ground like warning lashes, threatening me to stay away. Rowley soon fell out of view. After a long straightaway, I saw a cape arching out into the sea. As I neared, I saw there was something at the cape's end. A rope hung from thin air, and from it dangled something. Hesitating, I moved toward it.

The thin creature was tied at the ankles, swaying slightly. Its skin was pale yellow and leathery, and its face was withered and masculine. Its—his?—large eyelids were closed. The rope was most definitely charmed. Its frayed edges swirled up into thin air. I imagined the creature to be the grandfather of an unfamiliar species; he was short like a dwarf, but scrawny. He wore threadbare clothes, and an injury just above his eyebrow dripped blood. He made no sound.

Is he dead?

His feet were three-toed, like a dinosaur's, and his long, pointed ears hung like antennae, making his uneven horns almost unnoticeable. I wasn't sure I wanted to touch him, but I did.

As my finger tapped his leg, his voice shrieked, "Terrible!" His wide eyes shot open, and bright turquoise irises darted around in panic. "Most terrible! They're going to leave me here," he sobbed. "Leave me here until I die off."

"Who are you, strange creature?"

"Strange creature. I am no strange creature. I am Matsees, a goblin of the Goblin-Quis!" He squinted at me. "Wait. Wait a second. You. You are no Aveolight, no demon, and no minion. You're a highworld creature. A Zanayin, if I'm not mistaken. What are you doing in the Outer Reaches?"

"I was going to ask you the same. Why are you hanging from the air, bleeding? What happened to you?"

"The Priestess. She's punishing me! Punishing all us Goblin-Quis!"

"Who is? Why?"

"Help me down and I'll tell you, kind Zana."

"I need more information before I let you down. You could be dangerous."

He laughed, a high cacophony of sound, before choking on his own breath. "I understand." He coughed again. "You're a careful Zana indeed. Well, I'll tell you. She's punishing me. That's why. Because I did not believe the stories."

I hesitated.

"Come now. Come now. The stories! The Demonsheik's 'good givings?' The Archnigh's son—helping the highworld. I told her it couldn't be true! All the prince-sons do is torture us, use us like puppets, demand we perform for them, and strip us of our Boudine. You've heard of that haven't you? Only the most powerful element found in all of Ylora! So she strung me up. Leaving me here to die!"

"I'm sorry to hear that. Having anything stolen from you is terrible." An idea came to me: *this Goblin-Quis could be more than meets the eye.* "Matsees? I need a way across the water. And you need help down from there. Maybe we could help each other."

"What good will that do? She'll do it again."

"You can come with me. I can protect you."

"No, no no, she'll want a gift. I'll need a gift. If you need safe passage, I can get you that. The Goblin-Quis knows all the Aveolight's secrets. I can get you across. I know the secret."

"So what will be our deal?"

"I need a gift for the High Priestess—weren't you listening?"

"I'm on my way to the Summoning Circle, Matsees. Just tell me what you want."

"A conjurer? You? On your way to Vile Xors? You! A Zana out of her mind! Look at you. This is not the attire of a great summoner. You can't know the deep magic that summons the underworld. Recite it to me, then."

Embarrassment flooded my cheeks and I grew impatient. *Improvise. Do something.* I pushed the rope away from me, dangling the goblin over the cliff's edge. "Onik'Ull,

245

arise!" I called, Twilight Smoke fuming in my palm. As the spirit–eel's shape took form in my hand, I shoved it closer to Matsees, and it lunged at the goblin. "I could throw you to the depths now, Matsees of the Goblin-Quis, wrapped in Onik'Ull to feed on you all the way to the bottom."

"On second thought, I see a sorcerer of great strength and dexterity. How about that deal?"

"Go on."

"You get me the gift, a rare necklace made from the glowing petals of the flower gods, found around the cliff's edges. That will please her. And I will get you across Orexia's Sea."

"Not enough, Goblin."

"What else can I do? I've gotten you a way across the water. What more could you want?"

"Recite the summoning ritual to me. Ten times. You seemed so keen to hear it, let's hear it from you. That should be apology enough for your disrespect."

The Goblin winced. "Very well. Take that thing away. Please! Take it away!"

"I will return with your petal necklace, then," I said, dismissing the snake.

The gift led me along the cliffs to the flower-god's gardens. Gardenias and tufts of moss grew thickly in crevices around the cliff's rock. The petals sparkled and glowed, and the plants were rooted so far into the ground that I had to use almost my full strength to pluck them. After an hour, I returned to Matsees with hundreds of petals strung into a beautiful necklace. I untied him and helped him down. "Here is the gift, Matsees."

His turquoise eyes widened. "Yes. This will do." He touched the petals as if they were gold. "This is perfect. This will win her over."

"You still have more for me," I said.

"Oh. The ritual. Seems nonsense at this point, but as you wish." He cleared his throat. "With this wand, drawing the demon's sign. First striking to the south, then east, and upward. I summon, I call forth a high demon to appear before me. I'll give my soul if he be harmed. I have no tricks waiting for him, I purely seek his help and power and will always admire and respect life of the underworld."

Silently, I repeated the words as he recited them. When he finished, Matsees bowed and began to walk away.

"Matsees. You are forgetting the last thing."

"What are you talking about?"

I grew impatient. Twilight Smoke rose from my palm and I threatened him with Onik'Ull again. "You still have to tell me the secret to the water."

"Ah. Yes, of course. The Asrai clams."

"Go on," I said, dismissing the eel.

"They are the only things the queen won't destroy. The Asrai made them using the pearls from Orexia's very

247

own sea. Before, nothing would survive. No ship, no species, no fish could move an inch in this water. Orexia destroys everything."

"Why doesn't she attack these as well?"

"She can't sense them. There is no difference between her own sea-pearls and the pearl clams."

"How do you know of them?"

"The wretched Aveolights, how else? Ruthless war they had with the Asrai over them. Many died trying to steal the pearls for the prince-sons. They tried hauling the stolen goods by ship or sea horse to the Summoning Circle. The Goblin-Quis celebrated every time another huntress died to Orexia. One fewer to pillage our Boudine. Until the Asrai clams."

"So now—"

"Now the Asrai clams have made the Aveolights' ravages even worse! The more they give to the prince-sons, the more greedily they take. It never stops!"

"How do I find these pearl-clams?"

"You don't find them. You call them."

"How?"

The goblin shrugged.

"Matsees…" I glared at him.

"Fine, fine." The goblin reached in his pocket and brought out a small opal flute. "Use this at the shore. They will surface."

"Thank you, Matsees."

He gave a good-bye nod and immediately went back to ogling the sparkling chain.

Rowley wanted to hear everything. I ignored him while inspecting the cliff for a place to scale. Rowley followed, and we both climbed down to the shore. When we made it, Rowley started again with the questions. "What happened? What did this goblin say?" There were no apparent threats on the shore, so I started playing the opal flute. "What are you doing?"

"Quiet, Rowley."

"Quiet? Don't give me orders!"

I blew again. And again. After some moments, bubbles started gurgling to the surface. Sure enough, giant pearlescent clams surfaced like submarines. They opened, revealing dark, brass-colored interiors.

Rowley's tone changed. There was a hush to his words. "He's not going to believe this."

"Who?"

"Demon Paths Converge changes every time someone completes it. No two people complete the same quest to get to Vile Xors. That way no one can carry someone else through the process. You found your passage across the sea. That's ... that's impressive."

"Thanks, Rowley. I think that's the nicest thing you've ever said to me."

"Don't get all happy. It's not like you'll get further. You're too inexperienced for a Demon-wisp."

"Why are you here then? Leave. You're not exactly pleasant company."

"The feeling's mutual, *Loxy*. I have to be here."

"No you don't. Leave. I'll make sure Ilusas knows you held up your end of the deal."

"You won't tell him anything for me!"

"Right. 'Cause you did that on your own in the tavern."

"What are you talking about?"

I realized what I'd said too late. I wasn't in the tavern with them. "He—just looked pretty uptight to me. You did something to piss him off."

"You don't know anything."

"Okay, I don't know anything. Get in your clam."

As we docked, the Aveolight huntresses appeared on the ramp, statuesque and emaciated. They veiled their faces behind painted skull masks, and their dreadlocks were blood-crusted. They were clad only in ropes, leaving their breasts exposed—their whips and weapons were their only protection. They were seductive, undead, savage. Ruthless cousins of the ghoul race, the Aveolights lined up in rows to guard the summoning circle, standing like the obelisks themselves.

We could see weapons ahead—spears thrust into the

ground, pulsing a red light around the circle. As we moved in between the huntresses, their heads turned, watching us pass. A half dozen Aveolights had gathered in the center of the circle. And when they moved away, she was revealed: the priestess, wearing a headdress of feathers and jewels. *The goblin's captor*, I thought. She looked at me over her shoulder, and as she turned, the glare in her eyes told me we had trespassed.

With the stride of a runway model, she stalked toward us.

"Stay still," Rowley said.

She stopped in front of me. I froze. She ducked and turned, inspecting me. She shoved me from behind, and Rowley moved after me. She drew a dagger and sliced at him, slitting a piece of his leather chestguard.

"Easy, easy," Rowley glowered. She struck at him again, forcing him backward. "I'm going!"

He faded into the distance. I stepped onward, and as I neared the circle, the huntresses entered with me and began some sort of ritual. They flicked powder at me, and the granules burst in the air like fireworks. Something halfway between bat and angel formed in the magic and whisked through the air, writing circles and figure-eight patterns in the sky. The Aveolights began a slow, humming dance around the edge. If I paused, the priestess forced me forward. I kept moving until I stood in the middle of the Summoning Circle. Covering the ground in the red dust was a pattern of slashes, circles, and triangles. The Aveolights hummed louder, and I felt almost drunk in the rhythm of it. As I raised my shadowlock wand, a silence hushed around the circle and all movement ceased. I didn't feel myself breathing. Where were the words? Did I remember them? I had to. It was time.

"With this wand…" My throat tightened. Being tongue-tied felt like asphyxiation. "With this wand, drawing the demon's sign. Striking south, and east, and upward. I summon—"

What was it? How did it go?

"I call forth—I call forth a high demon to appear before me. I…I pledge my soul that he will not be harmed, and…that I have no tricks waiting for him, that I purely seek his help and power, and will always admire and respect the lives of the underworld."

The ground cracked and groaned as something awakened beneath it. Rising like chimney smoke, a lavender aura escaped the breaking ground. From the portal emerged a spectral, ethereal demon. It was huge and powerful, and I felt as small as a bird. He stopped at his midsection, half hidden beneath the earth, yet still towering. Pale smoke radiated from him, and the priestess-obelisks glowed in his presence. He aimed his trident at me and held it there, an inch from my throat.

"Are you the demon-prince?" My voice sounded strange with fear. "Reden?"

Light illuminated behind his eyes and cheeks, and he had an austere expression. "You summoned me," the demon growled. "I ask you instead. Who are you?" His skin was ribbed with armor that flared into winged points at the elbows, head, and shoulders.

"I'm a shadowlock seeking your help."

"You've come a long way for one so young."

"I've done a decent amount, I think."

"NO! YOU HAVEN'T!" He smoldered. The smoke at his midsection swirled and spun around him as he grew even larger. "You come before me weak! Young! Inexperienced. I can taste the fear in you. I can smell the freshness of your weapon, the untainted boots and robe you wear. Next you will tell me you are seeking one of my own, little shadowlock."

"Ye-yes. That's true. I am."

A roar thundered from him. For a second, I didn't know it was his laughter. "How would you know what to do with the power of a Demon-sheik? Did you think that this would be it? You come and 'seek' one of my minions, and it would be given to you?" He broke his gaze and looked away. His tone quieted in words no longer intended for me. "This one does nothing to awe you, Father."

"I did not say I would do nothing."

"No? Your scent tells me otherwise."

"Challenge me." Unsure of what exactly I was proposing, I spoke the words from instinct. "I will complete any task you give. Lay down a duel or a quest. Give me a chance to show you what I can do."

"You will not find a Demon-sheik here. You are not

253

ready, little shadowlock. If you gain the power of a Demon-sheik unprepared, it can consume you—ruin you."

"Reden, I've seen that kind of power. Not in myself. Not in anyone I know very well. But a leader. A leader who's taken his power too far."

"In the highworld? No one has that power! I am a demon-lord!"

"He does. Trust me. I feel powerless by it at times. I need the Demon-wisp, Reden."

"Why?"

As I apprehended the full scope of power that Reden possessed, it dawned on me. With a Demon-wisp, I might have some way to challenge the Holder. "To do what you are doing, great demon-lord. To stop an obsession of power that has gone too far."

His scowl deepened. "Impossible. Nothing in the highworld has the power of demon-lords. And you, what makes you think you could challenge that power? You've never been close to Ultimates." His chest expanded, and he waved the trident toward me again. Just then something dropped from the sky, landing at Reden's feet. It was a winged spirit, translucent like his lord, but a quarter the size. The servant's wings folded behind his shoulders, and he kneeled before Reden. Without seeing him fly, I would have guessed that the points on his back were armor—these were not feathered wings. His breathing was labored as he spoke quietly to Reden, almost hissing.

The only words I made out were "rumor" and "Asrai."

Reden recoiled at the latter word. His entire being shuddered in anger. He looked at me with dissmissiveness in his eyes. "You come here in vain, little shadowlock. Be on your way. There is nothing for you here." The earth underneath him cracked and siphoned, and he started to submerge.

"Wait. Reden! If you would permit me. The Asrai, you know of them?"

He paused, the lightning behind his eyes fulminating. "They tried to destroy the Aveolights during the sea-war. Of course I know them."

"I've seen them."

"They are extinct. The Aveolights finished them off, and we control their pearls."

"But look." Fumbling in my rucksack, I found the small treasure and held it out in my palm. It was the third pearl, the one I'd held back from Ilusas after that day on the peak.

"What's this? Where did you get this?"

I stumbled backward from the force in Reden's voice. "At the top of a peak, quite a ways from here. Nor-north of Gallop Haven."

"Hiding! Hoarding what's left of the sea pearls!" He snapped his head toward the skies in uproar. "They will not hide long!" Before he vanished into the ground Reden looked at me, and his stern expression disappeared. He fixed a reverent gaze on the monoliths and reached his trident toward the pillars. As he swung around, the aura began funneling around his waist. Lightning leaped from the trident and each monolith. A sudden wind blew furiously around the island, and the sky darkened above the circle.

Reden chuckled—a horrifying sound, like dissonant chords in the ear. "So be it, little shadowlock. I'll give you Lixur, one of my Demon-sheiks. But heed this: If you use the Demon-sheik before being bound for two and a half moon cycles, he will kill you and anyone close to you. Then he will abandon you. *Do not* take this power lightly. Do not underestimate him." Reden began descending. "Destroy the one you say is too powerful. Lixur will help you."

I bowed to the demon-lord.

"Visit me again, little shadowlock. And I may bestow another gift upon you."

Tides of sand whipped in from the shores, dirtying the air and assaulting me from all sides. The wind erased the patterns in the summoning circle. The ground shook, and the wind lifted me. Reden funneled back down into the earth. The ground continued to churn, circling and spinning. When it began to cave in, falling into itself behind the rim of Reden's vortex, a growling sound echoed from the darkness below, familiar like a rumbling thunder. The spinning netherworld opened, and out of it flew a black vapor. It rose, and something twisted inside it, fighting to unwrap itself. The enamel-black essence formed into a hulking spirit, vaguely humanoid, that unfurled and stretched as if just waking, then screamed in terror as red rods of light shot from the monoliths. The red beams burned shackles around the spirit's wrists. They clasped closed simultaneously, and the spirit arched in pain. It turned. Its glowing eyes locked with mine.

I fought to stand still and tried hard not to shudder. And suddenly, I heard Rowley. His voice sounded small and very far away—he was cursing Ilusas's name. A shadow-air essence—deafening in power—a Demon-wisp, levitated in front of me. It made the familiar sound, that cursed exhalation, and moved. Graceful and submissive, it stopped at my side.

The binding had begun.

[Brambt]: Hey! Loxy and Rowley are back.

Sarkmarrs turned and looked. Mouths dropped open. Expressions changed. They were staring not at me, but at the towering black essence that followed me.

[Lekar]: Loxy. My god, a Demon-wisp!

[Grimm]: No way.

[Brambt]: That's incredible.

[Snome]: Congratulations.

[Furtim]: Serious congratulations. Wow.

[Logos]: Perdonic. You've got to see this.

Perdonic moved through the crowd. He looked at my follower, at me, and then at Rowley. He seemed more worried than congratulatory and whispered to us on a private channel, "Don't mention this to Ilusas. Not yet, anyway. And Rowley. Have you talked to your brother?"

Rowley looked at Perdonic quizzically. "No. Why?"

"The Holder's made an announcement. It happened while you were in the Reaches. He's—well, he's pulled the AVA team from the Stakes."

"What?"

CHAPTER THIRTY

EVERY SKI TRIP LEFT ITS OWN IMPRESSION, like a finger-print. The long drive wound across the mountain's face, determined to make us motion-sick, and the parking lot was a gateway to a magical adventure.

When my family and I went skiing, we stepped into a special realm of icicles and snowdrifts. Leading up to the lodge were stairs made from railroad ties, or railway sleepers, as Mum would call them. Mum and Dad always squabbled about the correct word. Either way, those stairs represented the hundred-yard dash to finally getting on the mountain. The four of us always found time to ski. No matter how much Mum grumbled about the cold, Dad knew how to get her on the mountain—the promise of teatime and cabin fires did the trick. Skiing came naturally to all of us but Mum. She'd fiddle with her poles for half an hour while the rest of us decided between the harder slopes. We always did a half-day of lessons, then freetime. One day after lessons, my instructor pulled my parents aside. After a long while, Dad called for me to join them.

"Your instructor told us you've been doing really well. Actually, that you've been doing really well all season, and you're good enough to join the ski team. Is that something you want to do, Kay?"

With smiles and raised eyebrows they waited for my answer. They looked like they had just handed me the world. It didn't seem that way to me. The idea of being a competitor... it was flattering, but terrifying.

"There's nothing to think about, sweetheart. It's a grand idea. Do you understand what your father is saying? You're good enough to ski competitively." Mum's smile slowly turned to a frown as I stayed silent.

"Why don't we get some skiing in, and you can think about it, Kaylie." Dad put his hand on my shoulder, thanked my instructor, and didn't bring it up the rest of the day.

I TURNED THE FRAME OVER, looking at the photograph of me on the ski slope. Saby and Eve had asked about the photo and were sitting cross-legged on my bed, hands in laps, listening. I handed Eve the frame.

"So, you never joined the team? That's so sad," Eve said.

"To think, Kaylie could have been the next super-snow-star." Sabrina smiled.

"Oh, Saby," Eve said.

The three of us left to go costume shopping. With

Halloween only a month away, Sabrina was anxious to get going. We arrived at Costume Castle, and the place was packed. There were aisles and aisles of every kind of outfit and accessory. Silk and leather, makeup and prosthetics—there were whole rooms dedicated to wigs and facial hair and entire walls for weapons, equipment, and masks. Anything we needed to transform ourselves into someone else was right here at our fingertips.

"I'm huge." Eve put back a pirate dress she had held up to her body. "I'll never fit in any of these outfits."

"You will do beautifully, Eve," I said.

"Try this, Kaylie." Saby handed me a tiny belly-dancer two-piece.

"Have you asked Marco about Halloween?" Eve asked.

"Yes, but he had vague answers, as per usual. I'm tempted to ask my mother for a tarot reading." Sabrina stopped suddenly and grabbed another costume. "Oh, here we go, here we go! I know what we should be for Halloween."

"No way, Saby. I'm not wearing that outdated thing. Let me try to find something."

I pulled a handful of costumes off the racks and hauled them to the dressing room. When I tried the first one on, I wanted to hurl. Drab colors with no sense of fashion whatsoever—I looked like a squirrel. I wanted something avant-garde, something that would make a classy but edgy statement. The next had a tag that said, "Harlequin Girl." *Hmmm*, I mused. *This looks promising.*

It fit perfectly. As I gazed in the mirror, something about the fabric or the fit snatched my attention. The midnight blue bodice hugged my curves; lace crept toward my neck and down my arms before turning into white-and-black-striped fabric. The draping along the floor reminded me of Demon-wisps. Gage and Elliott had said that Demon-wisps were the most powerful ally in the game. They could anticipate players' actions and act to counter them—protecting their masters from anything. *Too bad I can't do that myself*, I thought, smirking. But couldn't I use Lixur to challenge the Holder somehow? Demon-wisps sounded like the perfect protection against the unknown power of the Holder. I needed to find out.

As I stepped out to call my gang, Saby looked thrilled.

"That will definitely do! I love the bodice…wait, where are you going? Who are you calling?"

"Just a quick phone call, Saby. I'll be right back."

"No, no, no! We still have more shopping to do. Eve. Help me out!"

"Kaylie. You can't leave me alone. Saby will try and turn me into a MILF."

We laughed.

"Okay, okay. I'll stay."

The Demon-wisp questions would have to wait.

CHAPTER THIRTY-ONE

PERDONIC SHOUTED, "Let's go, people. Top rankings won't wait around."

After repairing my gear and restocking flasks and elixirs, I met the others at Driftor's Cauldron. It was a six-master dungeon. I had studied the strategies that Ilusas and Riscanth had posted, but the execution wasn't going to be easy. Dozens of other groups had been working in the lair, studying posts and previous attempts. No one had finished the course to claim the title and the ranking bump-up toward the Stakes.

"Everyone's here," Riscanth said. "Let's move."

The vortex welcomed us, teleporting us in a swirl of light. We stood between the walls of a great hall. The domed ceilings and elegantly carved parapets formed a vault fit for royalty. Groups of enemies, Eldylia sorcerers, barred our path.

"Let's try to skip this. Potions of invisibility, now," Risc ordered.

We drank the liquid. Our bodies grew transparent, and we moved. My Demon-wisp followed me, somehow undetected as well. The potions gave us sixty seconds of invisibility. Silent concentration overtook the raid. The Eldylia were a race of gigantic caterpillars, and they half-snoozed as we sneaked past. One by one, all twenty of us made to the wall. Riscanth pulled a lever, and granite doors in the shape of kingly statues creaked open. A bridge lay before us. The scores of scorpions and winged reptiles on it swarmed the archway.

"Let's get some crowd control," Findail said. "Loxy and Furtim, go."

Furtim laced his dagger with a sleeping potion and dazed several scorpions while I shackled others. Rangers shot down the flying reptiles, and warriors slashed any survivors. Beyond the bridge, we followed the path to a staircase ascending into a large throne room. Beetlegiants moved back and forth, oozing and spraying poison. A stinger stuck me from behind, and a spray of yellow poison brought me to my knees.

"Noooo! Loxy!" A critical healing wave rushed from Brambt and covered my alias. "Phew. That was close. You okay?"

"Yes. Thanks."

"Hey, Loxy. That's *my* personal healer," Risc said.

"It's true." Brambt nodded. "I do have an unresolved attachment to authority. Risc, you've always done it for me."

Our laughter echoed in the throne room. More beetles advanced. Blasts of color flashed on the walls as we called down a wave of damage onto the beetles. We fought until the floor was covered in their yellow poison. And we arrived at the first master—Hyrdo-Blisk, an elemental master who could hurl torrents of water. We avoided the torrents and his ice-breath by dividing into several groups. We defeated him and the second master—the Calisto Twins—by swapping in and out, taunting and provoking the masters to keep them distracted.

"Rowley, are the traps disarmed?" Risc called out.

"We're good to go."

King Porathas came after the Twins, then Tuag the Inscriptionist, who was lethal. He had the ability to inscribe tablets and from them bring to life any species he could describe. We never knew what would come next. He was tricky but not immortal. The easier mobs in between the masters' rooms gave us ample chat and rest time. Syntax's weapon glowed orange and purple as he drove a meandering rat away. Idle chatter filled the channel.

[Flogg]: How'd you do that, Syn?

[Syntax]: You gotta be me!

[Flogg]: Overpowered!

[Windvar]: Hey guys, what should I eat? Cheese sticks or cinna sticks?

[Grimm]: Cheese sticks with mozzarella sauce.

[Thrill]: What? Cheese sticks with cheese sauce?

[Grimm]: Yes.

[Thrill]: You're just asking for constipation.

The laughter buzzed.

When we arrived at the fifth master's room, the chatting ceased. Nalarah, a shapeshifter, had taken deadly form—the Maltese tiger. With a slash that could bring our strongest protectors to their knees and tear the rest of us apart, Nalarah was the biggest challenge of the series. If we could get past her, we'd down the last master easily. She was our checkmate.

Perdonic whispered on a private channel, "Loxy. It'd be nice to have your Demon-wisp on this one. I know it's not a good idea for you to use him until he's been bound to you awhile, but if you feel comfortable, we need this. Nalarah summons an orb around her—a shield—if her life gets too low. If that shield forms, it radiates a blast we won't withstand. It would only take one touch from your Demon-wisp to stop her shield."

"On your mark, Risc," Fin called out.

Risc charged in, throwing an axe and taunting Nalarah to come to him. Nalarah lunged at him: her saber teeth flashed and her blue body, all coiled muscle, rippled. His block missed, and he braced himself as she sliced a hole in his chestplate.

"She hits like a truck!" he groaned.

"Kite her, Risc!" Fin yelled.

Risc started a path around her throne room. Nalarah

turned and lunged toward one of our mages, fighting from behind her. We were making progress: Nalarah got desperate as her health dropped. Tigerlings appeared from corners of the throne room. I knew the time had to be soon. I took a deep breath and called out to Lixur. The great demon-spirit swayed closer to me. He energized, drawing power from somewhere. My alias's life started to drain. He was awakening—but at the expense of my own energy. The aura around my alias flickered; the required amount of time had not passed. It was too soon, and it was killing me. I tried to stop him from channeling, but it was too late. Lixur fed until he was rampant with energy, then tore away from me after Nalarah.

Nalarah was growling and biting at Risc and Fin as the Demon-wisp reached her. I had to keep him from touching her before her shield formed. I called out and beckoned to Lixur. The Demon-wisp looked to me, jeering. But when he turned back to Nalarah, the orbs were just forming a shield around her. Lixur reached out, and his shadowy essence touched her. The cat screamed out in pain. Nalarah's summoning shield evaporated, and the raid took the advantage. As soon as Nalarah dropped to the floor, her throne room moved and shook. Tremors pianoed across the floor. The walls moved to reveal a back door. My alias was weak and staggering as we crossed the hidden threshold. Perdonic motioned me ahead of him and nodded with approval.

The door opened on the lowest level of the cauldron,

where the pathways narrowed. Lava of a putrid green color seeped through cracks in the ground and dripped from the walls.

"Quiet, up ahead. We're here," Fin said.

The molten rock entrance left little room in front of Master Lavarkin—an earth elemental master, waited on a stone stage opposite us. The lava gurgled underneath our feet. We waited as officers discussed the fight in quiet voices. The lava periodically burst, spewing up through the cracks in the floor.

Risc cleared his throat. "Listen up. We know the lava spews in the same pattern. It will ripple across the area, there, in front of the master, and then back again. We have time to follow it as it moves toward each wall. When the lava wave passes the first time, healers, I want you to run to the stage and heal from there." There was a moment of silence before the team started in again.

[Flogg]: They're gonna get owned.

[Findail]: Quiet.

[Riscanth]: I will have a hold of the master by then, Floggnut.

[Perdonic]: Exactly. The rest of you, let's dance with the lava.

[Riscanth]: All right, ready check to pull.

[Aerum]: Get your tap-dancing shoes on!

[Findail]: Go.

The lava spewed as we ran in and took up positions behind the next wave. The master came down from the stage, gliding right through a lava burst. Covered in lava, his tall form was almost bloblike, lit up in hot, green goo.

[Brambt]: His Rock Kick. Watch out, Risc!

Riscanth blocked the blow with his shield, all the while moving backward, taunting the master to follow him and staying away from the lava.

[Findail]: He's going to cleave! Wait, wait. Now! Everyone back! The spews are changing direction.

[Riscanth]: Get away!

[Findail]: Can one of the shamans conjure a protection shield?

We moved in cadence, careful to stay together and to miss the lava rippling back and forth across the floor. Flogg fell behind.

[Findail]: Flogg!

The lava caught up to him. The hot green covered him, and his life dropped to nothing.

[Perdonic]: Lost one! Come on. Keep it together. Focus.

[Riscanth]: Dance, people, dance!

[Findail]: Get behind, get behind him! Do you want to die too, Syntax?

[Lekar]: Lava coming up behind us and fast.

[Rowley]: Guys, it's the same pattern. Move faster.

We moved in a sequenced pattern, swinging or casting our attacks.

[Brambt]: We almost got him.

[Riscanth]: Don't celebrate yet. Concentrate!

The lava was coming faster. We adjusted to miss the bursts. The healers fought to keep everyone alive with umbrellas of protecting and healing light. We continued unraveling the master with a barrage of spells and siphoning blasts.

[Riscanth]: And he's down.

[Flogg]: Nice job.

[Brambt]: Nice for you, lying dead while we do the work.

Brambt knelt by Flogg and applied cantrips to revive his alias.

[Findail]: We deserve some celebration tonight, folks. That was a hell of a raid. Well done. Really well done!

Taby's Tavern was in a roar.

[Perdonic]: What a night!

[Windvar]: I'll drink to that.

[Riscanth]: I got at least fifty slams there at the end.

[Syntax]: When the next expansion comes out, I'm never stepping foot in DC again. That dungeon sucks.

[Windvar]: You mean if it comes out. We didn't get the last expansion for months. It was delayed twice. All because Deluvian Games has a control problem.

[Riscanth]: It's not the company. It's the maniac who runs it.

[Thrill]: Developers are either burned out or dumped. The owner's a freak about corporate security.

[Ilusas]: Sarkmarrs.

The rumbling ceased as Ilusas entered the group chat.

[Ilusas]: How'd the night go?

[Brambt]: Ilusas. Welcome.

[Findail]: Flogg took a nice swim in lava.

[Brambt]: We surely could have used your expertise in there today. We had a few close calls.

[Perdonic]: Risc almost got his face melted by Nalarah.

[Flogg]: I thought I moved in time! That was such bull!

[Lekar]: Flogg, when you gonna stop being the noob?

[Flogg]: I thought I had a chance when Loxy joined, but nooooo, she had to go and get a Demon-wisp and shine shine shine.

A ripple of winces circled the room. Risc sucked his teeth, Brambt put his hands to his mouth, Perdonic shook his head. Everyone stared at Ilusas. The Archnigh officer had gone rigid. His eyes were wild, like a storm's anger. Rowley dropped his head and glued his gaze to the floor.

"Curious. I thought I just heard Flogg say that Loxy got a Demon-wisp. But that couldn't have been right." Ilusas turned to me. I thought his eyes could have ended me right then and there; they glared so dark. Before I could speak, Flogg opened his big mouth again.

"Yeah! She can step outside and summon Lixur right now? Want to see?"

I wanted to shrink from the room. I had done well and should have been proud, but I wasn't. It felt like I'd taken something precious from Ilusas. Without knowing why, I felt guilty for having visited Vile Xors.

Perdonic put his arm on Ilusas's shoulder. "Sarkmarr did a lot in that raid tonight. Let me tell you about it." The two officers walked to the bar.

It was more than uncomfortable now. I waited until there was a chance to slip outside and then made a break for it.

"Hey, Loxy, wait!" I bit my lip and turned. It was Fin. "Perdonic asked me to give you a message. He said, link in tomorrow night. Videoconference with the Holder."

"Do you know what about?"

"I don't. Though it's always important business with the Holder, huh?"

CHAPTER THIRTY-TWO

"GREETINGS GENTLEMEN," the Holder said, "And lady." I couldn't see his face very well. The videoconference was dark; the lamp in the background did not light him well. I could see the outline of his face—a good jaw line, messy hair. "You've achieved this status on your own, and you should be proud of yourselves. Remember that when you clamor to thank me for what I am about to tell you." He paused. "Thousands have wanted to be where you are today. Where they failed, you succeeded. I am very pleased to tell you, the five of you have been deemed the pinnacle of Sarkmarr. And you'll be competing in the Stakes."

My gasp was one of several. Whooping and clapping followed.

"Perdonic and Ilusas will accompany you. They have been through it all before, and they will prepare you. Congratulations. Don't disappoint me."

"Lorgen," Rowley's tone was unfriendly. "You're saying that Perdonic and Ilusas will be there, but will not be competing? Leaving us with who? Loxy? With all due respect, I don't think that's the best idea. We want to win."

"Rowley." The Holder's cold tone sent chills down my spine. The Holder allowed an uncomfortable pause. "Where were you two years ago?" Rowley didn't answer. "Exactly. I won't exercise the same kindness again."

"I'm just saying—"

"You're saying nothing. Loxy reached tier three in half the normal time. She obtained a Demon-wisp. What are you saying to those accomplishments?"

"As far as experience goes—"

"Dwell on the current achievements, Rowley, rather than on who you think is expendable."

Lekar tried to hide his laughter. "Rowley just got owned."

"Where were we, Ilusas?"

Ilusas answered the Holder methodically, "You were just telling us to not disappoint you."

"Yes. The competition is Friday and Saturday, November seventh and eighth. That leaves us more than a month to prepare you as a team. Get your things in order. All of you will be flying out the sixth. That is all."

The video stream switched off, and the view of the Holder went black.

When I signed into the game, a private message from the Holder was waiting for me. It read: "Don't let anyone intimidate you. You worked hard to get here. You surprised even the worst of your critics. Good work."

For hours those words—so meaningful and warm— flashed in my thoughts.

Chapter Thirty-Three

Moltov's was a great place to kick back and relax. Danny and Eve had named it as the welcome-back spot for Gage and Elliott. The green chili and hot wings were to die for. All of us dug in to the platters of spicy appetizers.

"So how did the gigs go?" I asked.

"It was great. They actually asked us to come back for another show this weekend."

"That's great," Danny said.

"But that's in three days. You just got back."

"A gig's a gig, Kay."

"True. Well. Congratulations. Are you going again too, Elliott?"

"We can't go without him anymore. We realized how badly we needed a techie when Elliott straightened out our soundboard," Gage said.

Danny looked at me. "How's the plan going, Kay? We need some updates."

"Yeah, we've been away too long. We're starving for updates here," Gage said.

"Well, there is one thing...." I suddenly felt excited. I wasn't sure how to explain all that had happened.

"Come on, spill it. Nothing too stressful, though, with my lady in her condition." Danny patted Eve's rotund belly. "Don't want to upset her."

Eve slapped Danny's shoulder. "What is it, Kaylie? Go ahead."

"The Holder announced who's going to the Stakes. And I'm one of them."

"Whoa!" Danny said.

"Oh my god, we did it!" Gage started to howl loud enough for a couple of barstools to turn our way. "How did we do it?"

"This is huge! Congratulations!" Danny said.

"Thank you. Congrats to all of us."

"No really, how did we do it?" Gage asked.

"Well. It could have something to do with the Demon-wisp I recently procured."

"WHAT?" Half the restaurant looked our way again. "Are you serious? You just became the third on the entire continent, and sixth in the world, to get a Demon-wisp."

Gage and Danny started sputtering and laughing to each other, but Elliott looked upset.

"What's the matter, Elliott? I thought you'd be excited."

"Why's that? I wasn't excited about the plan from the beginning. I didn't hide my feelings about it then, and I'm not going to now, either."

Gage and Danny stopped talking.

"What could happen, man? Calm down," Gage said.

"The worst could happen. Ever think of that? The Holder offers us all something unique—something we can't get anywhere else. A world of power and perfection and the promise of fulfillment and respect. You're threatening its whole existence. And what about Kaylie? You're acting like there is no risk for her. Are you forgetting about all the people out there backing him? We're getting Kaylie involved with the most calculating aliases in Ylora. Ever think of that?"

"Elliott, no one is risking anything that we didn't all agree to, including Kaylie."

"Danny, Sarkmarr members like things the way they are. We mess with that, they'll come after us."

"I think everything is going to be fine," Gage said.

"You always think everything's going to be fine, Gage. Your answer to everything. Well, I don't agree with it. I think it was a stupid decision." Elliott grabbed his cell phone and keys, shot up from the booth, and left.

The four of us sat still for a moment.

"He'll cool off," Gage said.

"Will he?"

"Don't worry about it, Kay."

"We back you, Kaylie. And Elliott does, too," Danny said. "Good god, seriously though—'grats. The Stakes and a Demon-wisp? Man, I would lose it if I found out I was going back to the Stakes."

"You, honey? Lose it under pressure? Thanks for that lovely image," Eve said, touching her belly.

Danny scrunched his eyebrows.

I thought of Vsin and the e-mail I had composed for the Shade.

"Danny. You said the Shade, Sillek, asked you about the Holder, but did he ever say anything else about what you could do to help find the Holder? I've been doing some research, and it seems like Demon-wisps are good for AVE but were specially made for alias-to-alias matches."

"That's true. You'd be powerful in AVA duels."

"Perhaps Vsin could use me and my Demon-wisp..." As the thoughts came out loud, I hesitated. I realized I was even more unsure about what to do.

"What, Kaylie?"

"Oh, nothing. Just thinking out loud, I guess."

"I wish we could go to the Stakes." Gage shook his head. "I wonder if I'll have a chance to stream it."

"I'm sure you'll hear plenty about it when you're done with the gigs. They sold out all thirty thousand tickets to the Stakes in, what? Less than an hour?"

I looked at Danny. "Thirty thousand?"

"Ignore the number. It's just a number, Kay. Don't psych yourself out."

"You've come so far in six months," Gage shook his head. "It's unreal how fast you've risen the ranks. Everyone wishes they were you right now."

Danny grabbed his glass. "To the Stakes!"

We all clinked glasses.

On the way home, my windshield flung my thoughts back at me in devil's-advocate arguments.

This competition isn't just some pony ride; it's the Kentucky Derby. And, I'm about to be neck-deep in its mud. I'm completely out of my element. How can I possibly do this or be ready for any of it?

CHAPTER THIRTY-FOUR

[Aerum]: I did it guys. I can't believe I just did that.

[Brambt]: What did you just do?

[Aerum]: A morphis mission.

[Furtim]: One we know?

[Aerum]: Ex Marks the Spot.

[Lekar]: Ouch. What did you have to tell her?

[Aerum]: That I was fine with the divorce. I blessed her new marriage. And she was right about the cat.

[Furtim]: Hardcore.

[Aerum]: I've never felt so humiliated in my life. That was awful. Just awful. I gotta head out, though. See you guys later.

Aerum summoned his mount, a huge mammoth, but I stopped him on a side channel.

"Aerum, wait. Can I ask you something?"

"Hey, Loxy. What's going on?"

"Why did you do it, Aerum?"

"What?"

"Why did you do the morphis?"

"It was just part of the job. Of course I was going to do it."

"But that was uncalled for. A marriage is intimate; no one can possibly know what is good or bad for the relationship except the two people involved. How arrogant to assume—to presume—what someone else should do."

"Loxy. Brianna and I had a world of issues we didn't agree on. And she didn't want to try anymore. I admit I didn't try very hard, either. She was going nuts and so was I. It's been awkward silence between us for months now. The Holder, knowingly or not, made me broach that silence. It's kind of a weight lifted. But, hey, no divorces in Edannair! Thank God."

"I still don't think it was right."

"Look, after the divorce, Sarkmarr—well, this whole place—has given me a new perspective. A break like this after a long day's work—it's invaluable. I wouldn't give it up. It's where my home is now. If I have to call my ex and tell her a few lines I don't believe, so be it."

"But it wasn't true. You don't bless the marriage, and you were not fine with the divorce at all."

"Maybe I should have been."

After speaking with Aerum, I wandered the Ruins of Threen—a sister to a Roman coliseum, it had the ruins of gladiator arenas and vine-covered archways.

What will I do if the Holder asks me again—makes me do something that revolts me?

"We meet again, Miz Loxy."

I spun around, startled, at the sound of the authoritative voice.

"Vsin."

"Ah. You remembered."

Adrenaline ripped through me. "Kind of hard to forget the first Shade you meet."

He smirked.

"How's Shade business, anyway?"

"Times have been better. I hear congratulations are in order."

"For who?"

"Are you not officially a competitor at the Stakes?"

"How did you—"

"Ah. We try to remain in the loop. It is, after all, our job to keep you safe."

"Right."

"But there are areas where we lack information."

"What kind of information?"

"Locations. Names. Hangouts. Where a person might spend time."

Vsin was looking in my direction but not directly at me.

"You wouldn't know of anyone that could help us with that do you, Miz Loxy?"

"I don't know. Maybe."

Vsin anxiously looked around and then grabbed hold of my shoulders. His voice changed. "Loxy, if you have any information about the Holder...I'm begging you."

"What's wrong, Vsin?"

"Please. I—I'm not supposed to tell you any more. If you know anything...tell us. Everything depends on it. Look this is my *job*, okay? I work for Deluvian, and if I don't find and stop the Holder, I get fired. I'm running out of time."

"What do you mean?"

"We're the good guys trying to uphold safety in the game. The Holder is jeopardizing all of it. Please, Loxy. Someone like you could be very helpful."

"I might be able to get you what you need."

"You are doing yourself and every alias in Edannair an honor. Take this."

I opened the folded note. *Marked* was written on it.

"Send that word to the number on the other side, and I'll find you within the hour." His arm straightened to the ground, his fist curling. The dirt and pebbles reacted, turning white. He vanished, leaving a bleached imprint where he had stood. The Shade's remaining aura shimmered beside me, and I suddenly had the feeling that someone else was near. Some presence....

I turned around and something caught my eye from behind a crumbling pillar. It looked like....

It looked like Ilusas.

CHAPTER THIRTY-FIVE

THE CLOUDS HAD GATHERED AN IRON SHROUD over the sky. They sailed so low I could nearly touch them. It hadn't rained in months. Maybe it's because I grew up in the rainy Pacific Northwest, but I've always felt reassured by precipitation. It's the only thing that can sort of refresh and restart me. But here in Austin, drought oppressed me.

Halloween at dusk, and I was already exhausted. The reckless truth whispered to me over and over again. I couldn't stop questioning myself. Was I wasting time in a pointless power struggle in a made-up world? No ... I'd come close to feeling renewed. For brief moments in the game, I felt healed; I was surrounded by people who respected what I'd done—how far I'd come. But outside of it, reality still waited. And inside me, reality awaited too: I still was processing my emptiness over and over again, the loneliness and isolation and grief. It never quieted.

Downtown was a zoo, and for Austin's party scene, that's saying a lot. I attempted to convince myself to find something fun to do, to let go of heavier things. Yet the clouds were heavy, too, and rumbled in heavenly conversation. The idea of a storm comforted me.

"Ugh. It better not rain tonight!" Saby moaned.

Our matching stiletto boots clicked the pavement in quick stride. Our pink stockings peeked out above, and I tried to focus on Sabrina, following her down one-ways that had been blocked off for pedestrians. We walked into pubs and then back outside again to rendezvous at another. There were so many people; Sabrina seemed to know all of them. We hugged and cheek-kissed Robin Hoods, princesses, naughty nurses, and nice knights. The streets bled fake terror as grim reapers, vampires, and witches surged through the crowds. It was a shoulder-to-shoulder masquerade. I thought of Arano and his claustrophobia—how terrifying it must be. But the incoming storm's subdued rumblings fed me energy.

Sabrina saw Eve and Danny waiting at the meetup spot by the Old Brewery. As soon as Saby saw what she was wearing, she cried out, distraught, "But we need our third Harlequin Girl."

The clouds grumbled again, and this time burst open, showering us in dense rain. The crowd gasped as one and fled. My friends darted out of view with the rest. Everyone began disappearing indoors like ants burrowing underground, sparing their costumes and makeup from ruin. I didn't join them. I couldn't move. I was a statue standing in the rain. The water poured all around me. I closed my eyes and lost myself in the power of it. The rain found its way through my clothes to my skin. The drops clung, soaking me. It felt good, like I was closer to nature somehow, or closer to my soul and all I'd left behind at home.

CHAPTER THIRTY-SIX

NOVEMBER ARRIVED. For weeks we had trained for uncountable hours, and any hint of failure made me go cold with worry. If I couldn't hold on to this, what would I lose next? With every dungeon, arena, and battleground—it didn't matter which—the sense of camaraderie built in me, bolstering my strength. When I was with Sarkmarrs, that's all that existed. That moment was the only moment. The only thing that existed was the team and winning. Even with all the assignments and surprises the Holder put us through, Sarkmarr brought the feeling of success.

"Form ranks!" Ilusas yelled. "If you don't hold your positions, the Kiigeons will cut you off one by one."

In the middle of training, my cell rang. It was a number I didn't expect to see. My home number. It wasn't Hunter's cell or Mum's, but the home phone. I hadn't changed the caller ID since Dad disappeared, and now his name showed on the display. I pressed the phone against my chest. I wanted so much to hear from him. I couldn't help but listen for his voice.

It was Hunter. He was upset. "You have to come home now. I don't know what to do anymore. I can't handle her anymore!"

I pulled Ilusas aside. I was afraid to ask, but knew I must. "This is the worst possible timing with the Stakes around the corner...."

"In three days, Loxy."

"Yes, I know. But it's my family. It's very important. I wouldn't be asking if it wasn't."

He studied me suspiciously, as if I might be lying. But when he finally agreed, I was on my way, flying home. I wasn't sure what would be waiting for me.

I FOUND MUM like Hunt said she would be. Her fingers were dry and discolored from constant cleaning. She looked empty, like a zombie.

"Mum?" I kneeled beside her. "Mum, look at me."

"Kaylie?" Something changed in her eyes when she saw me. "You're here? Well, let's get some supper started."

"No, Mum, I'm not hungry."

"Tea then," she said, getting up. She tried to hide her weakness behind a blur of activity, but I could tell something wasn't right.

"Can we talk, Mum, please?"

"Nonsense, you and your brother are here together. We need to celebrate with something. Tea will have to do."

For the rest of the evening and into the morning, she

avoided conversations and hovered around as if Hunter and I were toddlers again. When I started repacking my bags, Mum was surprised. "You're leaving?" she asked.

"My flight is today."

"No, it can't be. You just got here. Stay. We'll get you another ticket for later in the week."

"I need to go, Mum."

"Why? What could be more important?"

"Nothing's *more* important. But I have somewhere I have to be."

She inhaled slowly.

"I'm sorry, I have to go home."

Her face lost tension. "This is your home, Kaylie Ames."

"I just meant I need to go back."

"Well, I don't see how you could go now. It's so easy for you to see your brother like this." She motioned at my brother sitting at the kitchen table. He was eating a bowl of cereal.

"Like what? Hunter's fine."

"We need you to stay, Kaylie. I need your help, your brother needs you."

"Hunter is going to have to heal his own way."

"Heal. What do you mean heal?"

"Mum, stop! You are so caught up in your own denial you're poisoning us, too. We can't fix everything. All we can do is try to cope. If Hunter wants to get lost, then maybe we should stop looking."

"You're saying things that don't even sound like you, Kaylie."

"No, I'm not. I sound like Dad. And Dad would be proud of me."

"Is that right? You think because you found your way out of your family and into some online fantasyland that he would be proud of you?"

I looked at her in surprise. And glanced at Hunter. His smart-ass expression told me how she found out. "As a matter of fact, I think Dad would be proud. I qualified for the finals—out of everyone in the world. I'm competing in the largest gaming network of its kind. I was afraid to tell you, tell myself even, because I thought it would remind us all of Dad too much. Well, maybe that's good. Maybe that would help. Maybe it would help all of us."

Long seconds of silence. Always silence. Always ignoring the topic. Throbbing in my temples. Anger took over, and I lost control of my tongue—"Nope, that's right. We don't talk about this do we, Mum? Close up and close off! Don't speak about him, like you never do! It's like you're ashamed you were ever married to him!"

The hard smack against my cheek stung immediately. My eyes were already welling with grief, but her slap made the tears fall. Time stopped, and we stared at one another with shocked eyes; appalled at each other, appalled at ourselves.

Mum's forehead furrowed, and her eyes were cold and intent. She dropped her gaze to the floor and said,

"Your father meant everything to this family. Before you two, we didn't know anything but us existed."

It felt like I was an intruder in my own house. I was surrounded by family, but everything felt distant. All of me was sadness. The thought of Mum and Dad happy together knifed me in a place I'd thought I'd guarded. I suddenly understood the kind of unbridled grief that forced Mum to put on a blank face.

I fumbled for the brochure in my bag and placed it on the table. "The competition is being broadcasted. Here is the information, and here's the city and hotel where I'll be staying."

CHAPTER THIRTY-SEVEN

NOVEMBER SIXTH—TODAY IS THE DAY. My head rested on the airplane window. It felt as though a clone of me was flying to Chicago for the Stakes. The flight attendant offered me a bag of cookies. I passed. I couldn't eat; I could barely breathe in regular intervals. Grabbing the marble from my purse, I turned it over in my hand. As I looked at the small sphere, I realized that I still couldn't grasp that I was going through with this competition. Up to this point, it was all kind of a grand scheme—a way to occupy my mind on nights when everything reminded me of days that would never be again.

The past week I'd been on an airplane like a businessperson, day in and day out, flying from state to state. But I couldn't think about where the last trip had taken me or how it went. I let the details of this trip fill my mind instead. It was all so extravagant, wasn't it? Star treatment—more so than I had imagined. Everything had been arranged beforehand. Sarkmarr's team, Rowley, Lekar, Merksril, Ilusas, Perdonic, Arano, and I, each had flights rendezvousing at O'Hare. And our accommodations were at a five-star hotel.

We were to meet that evening at six in the Great Room off the lobby to set plans for the next morning. After laying out my clothes and toiletries in the hotel room, I pulled a warm sweater around my navy halter top and made my way downstairs.

This is the first time meeting the rest of my team in person, I thought. *Odd—we interact with each other so often, it feels like we've met already.* As I walked through the taupe hallways, with their gold-framed mirrors, it wasn't my curiosity that I noticed as much as it was my nerves. Ilusas hadn't wanted anything to do with me since Vile Xors. Would he be any different in person? Would the Holder be here? What would Rowley be like? I passed the lobby bar and found the Great Room. Double French doors opened into it.

"Hey, Loxy." Perdonic greeted me with a wave from the other end of the room, his curly hair even longer since last I'd seen him. He stood against the wall in the corner. A few coffee-colored seats had been arranged in a semicircle around him. As I dodged through the maze of leather couches, I noticed someone else pacing back and forth. One hand holding a cell phone to his ear and the other holding a few rolled-up maps—it was Ilusas.

Our eyes met, and his jaw tightened. I didn't want to move. I wanted to run from the room. Forcing myself to continue, I tried to act natural. He stopped talking as I passed, and his icy blue eyes narrowed. Ilusas looked taller and thicker than he did on the live feed. And he had cut his hair short in a military style.

Perdonic gestured for me to take a seat. "Sit anywhere you'd like. And welcome."

"Thank you."

"Hey! You must be Loxy!" I looked up, and there was a young man of Chinese descent slouching in his chair and grinning at me. "I'm Lekar."

"Nice to meet you. Anyone sitting next to you?"

"No, take it. You're the first to make your way over."

"Have you met everybody?" I asked as I sat. The chair was pillowy soft.

"Ilusas and Perdonic are here. And Merksril, Rowley, and Arano are still back at the bar."

"I'm a little nervous to meet the others in person," I said. "You're not helping any, Lekar, hiding in your chair like that."

"What?"

"You're hunkering down in your chair like you're hiding or something."

"Well, there are some people coming today worth hiding from."

I leaned in, my mind fluttering to the obvious choice. "The Holder?"

"You'd think so, wouldn't you? But from what I hear, he is not half as scary as you-know-who...." He leaned close and lowered his voice. "This *girl* they said was coming. She's supposed to be sca-he-he-herrry, if you know what I mean."

"Oh really?" I said, smirking.

"Her name is Lox— Hey! Wait a second, that's you!" He palmed his forehead. "Now I've done it. Pssst. Perdonic! Pssst." He pointed his thumb toward me. "It's Loxy. Loxy's here. Just wanted to point that out."

Perdonic shook his head and turned back to Ilusas.

"So, you ready for this?" Lekar asked.

"I think so. You?"

"Heck no. We have to go up against the best teams in Ylora with the Holder's watchful eye on our backs. That's some kind of pressure."

"But, that's why they picked us. They know we're good."

"Oh, is that what they told you? Hmmm. Mmmm." Lekar chuckled and straightened up in his chair. "Ready or not, here they come." He motioned toward the door.

Ilusas nodded to a guy in a gray beanie. "Rowley." My stomach tightened.

Lekar leaned toward me. "Now there's someone worth hiding from."

"Perdonic," Rowley said, shaking his hand. "Good to see you."

They walked into the semicircle together. Rowley had his hands in his jeans pockets and had pushed his shirtsleeves up to his elbows. Along with the beanie he wore sunglasses. Perdonic motioned for him to take a seat. Rowley turned and appraised us before sitting down. Lekar stood up and stepped toward him to shake his hand.

"Rowley. I'm Lekar." They shook hands. "You know Loxy?"

I waved and stepped forward. "Hi."

"What's up," Rowley said, shaking Lekar's hand and then mine. It was the quickest and limpest of handshakes. He sat back down, got out his phone, and started punching buttons. Lekar looked at me and shrugged. Merksril walked in with Ilusas and Arano, and the seven of us filled the crescent of chairs, save one that was left empty.

Merksril was a robust man—both tall and wide, and somewhere in his early thirties, I'd guess. He looked like he had just walked out of a monthlong wilderness excursion. He had a thick, long beard that hadn't been tamed for weeks and a full head of messy brown hair. Arano and I exchanged comradely glances. His gaunt frame looked like a mouse's next to Merk. Their real-life sizes were exactly opposite those of their aliases in Edannair.

"All right. Let the Stakes begin." Merk's booming voice matched his girth.

"Everyone's here." Ilusas spoke in his normal, firm monotone. "We made it. Hoorah. However, we're not on vacation. This is not some reunion where we're all going to drink and party together."

"Bummer. I think I got on the wrong plane." Lekar looked around, but no one laughed.

Rowley shook his head, eyes still hidden by sunglasses.

Ilusas continued, "We're here for one purpose: to win the Stakes. Not only do we walk away with the quarter of a million dollars, but we win the title, sponsors, and a ten-page spread in *Deluvian Games Magazine*."

"I'm looking forward to that," Merksril said, patting his potbelly.

"A win gives us the first-place ranking throughout the world. We will be featured and recognized in every relevant website, review, and forum. You get the picture. As always, be prepared and be discreet when you are approached with questions about Sarkmarr and the Holder. The publicity's important. It will continue to keep Sarkmarr as the number-one sought-after group throughout Ylora's millions of subscribers. If you're shy, now's the time to get over it. Just watch what you say.

"To the newbies here, this all may sound overwhelming. And for good reason. It is. If you're not nervous, get nervous. You may think you're the best, but that is only because we've been training you for weeks. We've put every possible scenario before you to hone your skills and reaction times. Tonight we'll go over blueprints and plans, and we'll review once more last year's Stakes and what might be expected this year."

Perdonic helped Ilusas unroll the paperwork onto the coffee table.

"Last year's Stakes Raid." He pointed. We all leaned in. "The entrance at this corner had a thousand-foot drop right off the bat. If Rowley hadn't been paying attention, even for a second, the entire raid would have fallen right then and there. We would have been finished. Everyone dead. When you wipe, you're out. Disqualified."

"Remember, these raids are nothing like the dungeons we're used to in Ruinnlark," Perdonic added. "There are no betas where we can learn and practice our strategies before the content goes live. There are no websites or live feeds where we can compare other strategies. There's nothing. We go in completely blind. It is working together as a team, using each other's strengths, that will get you through. So no one better die. If someone does die, Merk, res 'em fast."

"You got it."

"Do not resurrect by life guardian—that takes too much time. We need every second to stay ahead to win. Each of you has a refined strength that enhances the group composition."

"Each of us?" Rowley muttered.

"Rowley, for example, has the detail. He can sense things coming before they appear. He can spot a trap before another rogue even senses one exists in the room. Rely on his instincts. With his skill and perception, you'll be off to a good start. Lekar does great damage but is also our best hybrid. His ability to switch from dealing damage to healing will be essential if Merk gets trapped or mind-controlled. Merksril's heals are strong; he can get you through anything. We have Arano, now. Although fairly new to Sarkmarr, he is not new to what he does best. As the protector, he put his old group on the map. He's better used with us, of course, and his burst damage and critical strikes are beyond any capabilities we've seen in protectors thus far. He's a secret weapon. Eludan, Bararm, or any one else won't see that coming."

"Perdonic's right," Ilusas said. "Protectors can't push that kind of damage while taunting the masters, but somehow Arano can. His additional damage will shave off extra seconds and get you that much farther through the lair, that much quicker, than our competitors."

"And last but not least, we have Loxy," Perdonic said. "Even though she's new to Edannair, she has shown her skill. She's extraordinarily resilient and can control enemies both defensively and offensively. With her Demon-wisp, she can disarm enemy targets quickly, discover their weakness, and control them longer than normal." Ilusas's eyes met mine. He looked like he wanted to strangle me. I wasn't sure if I should look away. "Together, obviously, you make a very strong team. All nine AVE groups will begin when the bell sounds. Each team has six hours to progress through the maze. In those six hours, you have to defeat all masters. And you have to do it quickly, without missing any of the time limits."

While Perdonic continued, Lekar leaned over to me and whispered, "Too bad the Holder won't just use his Pixie Dust in the Stakes, huh?"

"He could do that?" I whispered.

Rowley's voice rang out in a sarcastic cackle. "Ilusas."

"What is it?"

"I think Loxy-girl has a question."

I closed my eyes for a moment. *Damn it, Rowley.*

Ilusas looked at me. "Loxy, you have something to add?"

"No. No, I don't. I was just asking Lekar a question."

"What was the question?"

"Oh it was nothing. I'm sorry to interrupt."

"Are you saying you don't understand something and you are not clearing it up?"

"It was nothing."

"Nothing would have been you listening silently. Lekar? What was the question?"

"She just asked about the Holder. Well, it was more a continuation of my comment when she asked her question."

"Lekar. Any day now."

"We were just wondering whether or not the Holder could use his Pixie Dust in the Stakes the same way he can in Edannair."

"You mean cheat?" A voice rang out from nowhere. We all turned to see where it had come from.

CHAPTER THIRTY-EIGHT

BEHIND US STOOD A FIGURE—a dignified minaret of a man. I recognized the shape of his face. It was the Holder. He looked ungodly confident. His towering form stood perfectly still, his hands resting on the back of Arano and Merk's chairs. No one had sensed his arrival, but he had been there. He spoke right into the conversation.

"I don't use my knowledge to manipulate the outcome in the Stakes, Lekar." He spoke with a polished, almost royal voice. "I handpicked each of you because I know your abilities and composed a team that can win this year's challenge on Sarkmarr's talent alone. And to each of you there is no equal. You are the absolute best in your category, and together there will be nothing Deluvian can present that you will not annihilate."

The more he spoke, the more I noticed his delicate but tenacious tone. His body looked strong—not body-builder strong, but toned. His skin was flawless porcelain, smooth, but sun-kissed. His sharp jaw defined a strong face with a well-shaped mouth. His tousled hair was a sandy blond with strands that brushed his eyelids. His eyes were still and dark. I couldn't help but stare at him. He was beautiful.

He looked at me as if he knew I was inspecting him. His expression was neutral—or more accurately, balanced equally between cold and warm. He looked untouchable, unchallengeable, but in tune with the moment. I looked away before he did and found a refuge in the blueprints on the table.

"You will be unbeatable. You will be the gods of the Stakes and take everything. But behind all great things is preparation and work. Self-discipline before victory. Please, Ilusas, enough from me. Continue."

Ilusas nodded to the Holder. "Thank you, Lorgen. Now, we know Deluvian likes to use a few of the same enemies mixed in with the new. This year should be no different, so use the same tactics with the ones we know. Draegons. They cleave, they tail swipe—both avoidable. The key is to keep them on the ground. If they threaten to fly, Loxy comes in. You must keep them on the ground."

I nodded.

"Braden warriors. We've seen them each year, and for good reason. They're a bitch to handle. Iron Breach will knock anyone to the ground. Their Sickle Darts are enough to kill anyone in a few seconds. Merk will have to heal you immediately, or it will be fatal. Rowley's interrupts are the best bet on those. We did get wind of one new master they may be using this year."

Each of us perked up in our chairs.

"A multiheaded thing—Enigmas they've been nick-named. All speculation and rumors of course, but it doesn't hurt to be prepared. Supposedly they are half-insect, half-man. They sit on a scorpion tail with four cloaked heads. The rumor is each head can target individual group members. With a normal master, it's easy to see who's going to get attacked because it will lean or turn. With Enigmas—nothing. There won't be any advance notice. They can target anyone randomly and independently, and each head is equipped with different abilities and immunities. Arano, do what you do and more. Anything to keep all eyes on you.

"As far as anything else, you're on your own. Drodges, Imoogis, and Limeracks, all common, but probably won't be seen in there. Use what you know, and when that doesn't work, think methodically and do not panic. Get some rest. Tomorrow we'll meet bright and early. Perdonic. Does Deluvian need anything else from us?"

While I listened to Ilusas and Perdonic iron out the final details, my eyes wandered back over to the Holder again. I couldn't help but study him. He wore a black blazer over a thin Bondi blue shirt, and dark denim designer jeans hugged his profile perfectly. But more than his tailored appearance, it was his proximity that lured me. His focus was on Ilusas—his dark eyes unmoving—but his lips held the smallest curve of a sagacious smile. He seemed beyond present in the conversation.

"Lorgen. Anything to add?" Ilusas asked.

"We've rolled you through dungeon after dungeon, examining how fast you react to and kill masters." The Holder paused. "Know and use your entire range of skill. Trust nothing, and assume everything."

Perdonic clapped his hands together. "That's the game, kids. You've done it over and over. Now do it again."

"Hmmp," Merksril muttered. "Except this time in a raid no one's ever seen before, fighting new masters with nasty abilities, live, in front of thousands of people, against nine other gifted teams. Yep, sure sounds the same."

Rowley leaned forward. "And it's timed."

Arano took a deep breath.

"We got this, little brother." Merksril patted Arano's shoulder.

"Let's get it done, boys," Rowley said.

"And girls, don't forget," Lekar added, smiling at me triumphantly.

Rowley shrugged. "Whatever."

CHAPTER THIRTY-NINE

WIDE AWAKE IN THE HOURS BEFORE DAWN, I stared into the darkness of the hotel room. I divided my time between eyeing the clock and painting pictures in my mind against the dark canvas of the blackout curtains. I imagined gold and white universes and faraway stars. I touched my cheek, remembering the hard sting of Mum's hand. She was so angry; I'd never seen her lose control. I shouldn't have spoken about Dad that way, but I wanted to speak freely for once.

What is it that you have to say? I heard my father's words clearly in the stark quiet of the hotel room, as if he were sitting on the foot of the bed. *Take your time, Kaylie. Whatever is bothering you, we can figure it out together.* His support seemed tangible. I tried to let the memory of his voice comfort me and block out the memory of Mum's outburst, but knowing I had failed her and Hunter made my solitude worse. Feeling empty and alone, I turned over. Trying to sleep was torture, and I raged at myself for wasting time in bed. I got up and threw a sweater on over my pajamas.

A hotel employee nodded to me as I passed the ice and vending machines. I took the elevator to the ballroom and event center floor. It was nice up here, and for a moment I imagined hosting a fancy party in a place like this. How fun it would be to dance and sing the night away, surrounded by family and friends—everyone lost in the enchantment of the evening. I looked up as a ballroom door ahead of me opened. I recognized the man who passed through it. He held an open book in one hand and shut the door with the other. It was Ilusas. I turned on my heel and walked—almost jogged—back to the elevator.

"Hold it right there."

I turned back around to face him. The book slapped closed, and he stopped just short of knocking into me. His hand wrapped around my wrist, and with a hard twist he forced me backward against the wall next to the elevator.

"Ouch, let go of me. What are you—?"

"You." His voice was harsh. "You are not welcome here. Do not assume for one second I have forgotten about your visit with that Shade."

The confirmation of what I had seen that night shot through me like a thousand needles. *What would I say? What could I say?*

"What did you tell him? Answer me!"

The elevator stopped at our floor and dinged. Ilusas released my wrist but kept his intense gaze on me. A couple exited the elevator. I had to get away, now! "Hold the lift, please!" I moved from the wall—it felt as though I was ripping away from nails holding me there—and slipped inside the open elevator car. I hit the button. And hit it again, and again. Ilusas looked at the strangers and back to me. I didn't look away from him until the doors closed.

My room was now a haven. My heart pounded and my mind raced. What was I going to do? Ilusas knew. Panic flew through me; everything was compromised. He *knew*! If sleep came at all now, it would be of little use. I watched the clock tick and asked questions I couldn't answer.

THE PHONE SHRILLED IN THE DARK. Its ringer was louder than I had expected. Sitting up made me dizzy, and I suddenly felt how tired I was. But thoughts of the competition jolted me into action. As I dressed, I told myself to focus on the positive. But I couldn't help thinking: *This is it. Everything rides on this weekend. Better not mess up.*

How was I going to do this? I was about to compete in the Worldwide Deluvian Tournament with competitors from all over the world, live before thousands of people—with the Holder watching. I thought over my role. *Keep the masters on the ground. Anticipate. React. Can I use my Demon-wisp? Have I been bound to him long enough? How long should I channel his attacks?* I buried my face in my palms. What had I gotten myself into?

I heard two raps on the door. I zipped my jeans, shoved my marble in my pocket, and cracked the door open. The bright hallway lights were less than welcoming.

"Good morning. I have your breakfast. Where would you like it?"

"Oh. There must be some mistake. I didn't order any food this morning."

"The note says for room 1206."

"That's me but—"

"There is a card here."

I reached for the note and opened it.

Breakfast is on the house. There will be no excuses for error, so eat up. We'll see you outside the hotel at 6:30 a.m. The car will take you to Deluvian Games Conference Center.

The Holder

I looked from the card to the room service attendee. He waited politely.

"Um, of course. Come in."

Facing a trolley full of fruit, meats, eggs, toast, and waffles, I picked at each item, tasting as much of each as the butterflies in my stomach could stand. Then I took the elevator down and walked outside into a breezy, brisk morning. I gave everyone a nod but bit back my friendliness when I saw Ilusas arrive in a limousine. He gestured for us to climb in. I tried to act normal. We rode in our white stretch limo for a good thirty minutes. It was my first time in a limo. It was huge, but somehow I still felt cramped. My teetering confidence raked my mind, and the air felt too concentrated. Rowley's attitude made it worse.

"Get your coffee, Loxy? Today wouldn't be the day to fall asleep."

"I'm fine, thanks."

"You look nervous."

I wasn't sure how to respond, so I didn't.

"I would be too, if I were you. Going on what? A few months in Sarkmarr—must feel pretty awkward."

I clenched my teeth.

"She's been here longer than that." Lekar glanced from Rowley to me. "You look fine, Loxy. Besides, today is just the dry run."

I forced a smile and looked back to the window. I let the buildings blur past me and kept my focus inward. We pulled into the parking lot of a huge silver-and-white convention center. The driver took his time letting us out. The tension hemmed me in.

We followed Perdonic and Ilusas around the building's oval shape until we reached a side door marked "Competitors' Entrance." I felt my stomach drop. I was here. I was really at the Stakes. Who would have thought the gang and I could have made this happen? Not to mention that this was the first time Sarkmarr had a female competitor. I choked the urge to say out loud, *This is cool.* Rowley would eat me alive.

Two men guarded the entrance. One, in his early forties, wearing motorcycle pants and a leather jacket, sat with a magazine at his waist. He had a lantern badge with the name *Rick* printed across the bottom. I couldn't see the other one's name, but he seemed fresh out of high school, wearing baggy jeans, a Deluvian Games baseball cap, and a shirt to match.

"What team?" Rick asked without looking up.

"Sarkmarr," said Ilusas.

Rick's magazine dropped to his thighs, and he looked up with expectant eyes. The younger one looked up at the same time, but with a flashy hypertensive smile and an eager wave. Rick's face changed when he saw Lekar and me. "Hmm. Not the same team this year, huh?" He handed some papers to Ilusas.

Ilusas ignored Rick.

"They're a great team," Perdonic said. "Don't worry about that."

Ilusas looked at me, then questioningly at Perdonic.

"I'd hope so," Rick said. "Deluvian held nothing back when making this year's maze."

"Is that what you heard?" Ilusas said drowsily as he signed page after page.

"Said it's the hardest set of masters yet."

"Even trumps the Rancids," the younger one blurted.

"Shut up, Kevin." Rick rolled his eyes.

Ilusas handed back the pen and papers. "Don't they say that every year?"

Rick took the paperwork. "You're good to go in—" Rick gestured at the door— "and your setup is to the right of Eludan, past the statue display."

It was almost seven o'clock, and only a few guests dotted the place. The convention center looked oversized. The vaulted ceilings and skylights soared at least thirty feet above me, making me feel like a shrunken version of myself. Potted trees and plants decorated the place like a garden display. The carpet was woven with the Deluvian Games insignia and "The Stakes." Concession stands had been fitted into cubbyholes along the walls, and their managers were setting out menus and stuffing napkin holders. I almost didn't notice my team walking away from me. Hurrying to catch up with them, I passed magazine and comic-book stands coloring the walls. Past those, video game companies and their studios had set up tables of flyers and flat-screen TVs. The Sarkmarr crew walked past everything without slowing, and I kept falling behind like a tourist.

Thinking I saw my alias's name on a table, I stopped for a moment. It was a long, fold-out table with a Deluvian Games tablecloth and clusters of action figures. There, in large calligraphed letters, was *Loxy*. I looked around, but no one was stationed at the table. Above me hung a banner: *Alias Collectibles Here!* Lekar, Arano, Merksril, and Rowley's names were next to mine, and behind the nameplates were exact replicas of our aliases.

"Hey, guys! Check this out! It's us!"

Arano and Merksril looked to each other, smirking. Rowley rolled his eyes and kept walking. Lekar was the only one who stopped.

"Awww yeah. Pretty cool, huh? Anyone who competes gets one of these. Did you ever think you'd see yourself as an action figure? A couple years ago I was buying these up, all of my favorites." Lekar smiled. "I can't believe I'm here now, competing with my idols at the Stakes."

"It's pretty incredible. This whole place is incredible."

"Yeah, it is. Come on. We're almost to the competitors' side. See that roped-off area up ahead? That's ours."

Halfway around the building, Perdonic and Ilusas were speaking with a security guard. A ring of dividers surrounded the competitors' areas, and steep-walled paths led between the bleachers to the center gaming area. I caught only glimpses of the game stage, which was partially blocked by all the seating, but it looked like a megaplex of computers, with rows and rows of towers.

Beyond Perdonic and Ilusas were colorful medieval tents for the competitors, fit for kings. Banners hung above each, a claim for every group: Bararm, Nerodic, Eludan, Sarkmarr....

Deluvian Games staff were everywhere. As we approached, one of them waved us by. The tent hosted tables, chairs, a computer, a couch, and beverage and snack platters. My team settled in as though they had been here a hundred times. Perdonic laid out paperwork on one of the tables, Rowley got comfortable, Ilusas was already on his cell phone and pacing, and Arano and Merksril pulled out two chairs and started shuffling cards. Lekar joined them. I stood for a couple of seconds, looking from the corners of the tent to back outside of it. Suddenly, the nine o'clock start time felt like a painful countdown. Sitting on the couch only worked for a little while, as I grew tired of my own nervous hands. I got up and walked to the entrance, but Ilusas stopped me.

"Where you off to?"

"I was just going to have a look around."

"Don't talk to anyone," Ilusas growled.

"And don't be gone long," Rowley said.

Even though I was at the Stakes, it didn't feel like I belonged. I walked out, glancing left and right. We were pretty much smack-dab in the middle of the other teams' sections. Ahead of me there was a pathway, a sort of tunnel through the bleachers. There was no rope keeping gawkers away, so straight was my direction.

It reminded me of the canyon that NBA players run through to reach the court. *These bleachers will very soon be filled with fans*, I thought. When I reached the center, an armada of computers unfolded before me. A decadent slice of technology. Hundreds of computers covered rows and rows of tables, with the bleachers forming an intimate enclosure around them. *I truly am an outsider here*, I thought. I was never a fan, never even played computer games. I came to Edannair by a completely different route. I let my finger trace along the row as I walked past. Five computers had been set up on each table. The smell and look of new hardware filled the stage. Everything was brand new, from the mouse pads, mice, and monitors to the gaming machines themselves.

Ticket holders were entering the convention center in groups now. I could hear their voices merging into the room's soundtrack. The convention center still didn't seem any more personal, and the fans' eager voices ricocheted in the giant room. Some of them ooh'ed and pointed around the place, their reactions similar to mine.

The hairs on the back of my neck rose. It wasn't just me in the inner ring anymore. Three boys were chuckling to each other, glancing in my direction. Their T-shirts matched. *Must be competitors*, I thought. They kept pointing at me. As I was about to go over to them, someone else addressed me.

"Guests are not allowed in here yet, ma'am."

I whirled around. "Oh. You scared me. I didn't see you."

"Sorry about that ma'am. But you can't—"

"Oh. I'm not a guest; I just left my team to get some air. I'm with—"

"Come on now, ma'am. Return to the other side, back by concessions. Seating opens in half an hour."

"No, I'm competing."

"Whose team?"

"Sarkmarr's."

The security guard laughed hard. I looked around to see if he'd drawn attention. The boys were watching us.

"That's a good one. Where's your badge then?"

I reached in my pants pocket, forcing my hand to the bottom—skinny jeans being relentless. Nothing but my marble. "I must have left it—if you give me a second I can grab it." I moved toward the competitors' stalls.

"No, no, no you don't." The guard said, grabbing my elbow. He started ushering me the other direction.

"I'm telling you"—I pulled away—"I'm part of Sarkmarr's team."

"Are you saying that *you're* the girl Sarkmarr included this year? Loxy?"

"Yes. That's what she's telling you."

That voice. I turned around, almost closing my eyes in the hopes that it wasn't him. But it was. The Holder. He had squared off with the security guard, unmoving as a statue. The guard fumbled with what to say. He stared at the Holder a few seconds and finally let me go.

"First time Sarkmarr's had a female competin' here. Just threw me for a loop, I guess. Sorry about that, ma'am."

"First time for everything." The Holder's words fell off his tongue in silken tones.

"Well. I'll be gettin' back to my rounds then. Good luck to you both."

The Holder walked with me. I couldn't say anything. I couldn't even look at him. Instead I looked everywhere else. Up and around, just not at him. Why was I so nervous? Why did he have to be the one coming to my aid, anyway? And the way that guard acquiesced to him— without one single question. He had power over everyone.

"You draw a lot of attention, little Zana." His voice sounded like music.

I shrugged. "This place is a pretty big deal."

"It's become the rave of if its time, I guess you could say."

I nodded, and we walked onward, both letting the silence linger.

"It's yours, isn't it?" I asked.

He looked at me—unmusically.

"The Stakes, I mean. They told me the idea was yours? And Deluvian capitalized on it?"

"Where did you hear that?"

"Around."

"Interesting."

"What is?"

"Months of complexity drizzled down into a summation like that."

"So it's true?"

"There are some questions not worth your time, Loxy."

"Some people say you're a menace to Edannair."

He stepped in front of me, his eyes direct. "Some people say you shouldn't be at the Stakes."

My mind went blank, and I stood gape-mouthed. He smiled and continued walking. We entered the tent, and as each of my team members looked up, they jumped to their feet. Lekar stood up so fast he hit his knee on the table. He almost screamed out in pain, but held it in, staring at the Holder.

"Lorgen! What are you doing here?" Concern riddled Ilusas's voice.

"It's fine. I was escorting Loxy back after she had explored the premises."

"Someone could have seen. You know Shades are crawling around these events after you."

"Ilusas. It's fine."

Rowley sighed. "This is why we don't go running around 'exploring' like a little girl. A little girl who can't even keep a hold on her own badge." Rowley lifted his hand. My badge dangled from his fingertips. Everyone stared. Embarrassment flushed my cheeks. Rowley threw it at me. I caught it and clipped it firmly to my shirt. "Way to start off the day, noob."

"Rowley." The Holder spoke with an edge. "Enough." Rowley looked from me to Lorgen and took a seat. The Holder did not look away from Rowley until he had been sitting quite a few moments. "I'll leave you to your review." The Holder turned to me, but I didn't look up at him. He stepped toward the exit.

Lekar suddenly lurched toward him. "Lorgen!" The Holder narrowed his eyes, and Lekar stammered. "Holder. Sir. Pardon me, I was just wondering, are you, um, going to watch?"

"Of course."

"But, f-from where?"

The Holder smiled at Lekar and looked at Ilusas. Ilusas mirrored his smile—faintly sad, but mostly resigned.

The Holder took a deep breath. "From the shadows, of course."

There was nostalgia in his last phrase.

CHAPTER FORTY

THE AVA TEAMS had been the first to compete. Duos, trios, and teams of thirty against thirty had battled for the title of AVA champions. We watched as the fights brought the computer armada alive. With two hundred aliases dueling for the best of three rounds in every category, WAMs had been the very spectacle of chaos. Somewhere out there, Sorkah was probably thrilled about the Holder's decision to pull our AVA team. Her passion for Eludan was the same as Danny's. And at the end of the day it had been Eludan's AVA team that swept the thirty-on-thirty. Volatile had won the three-on-three, and Hethos had won the one-on-one.

After a night of poor sleep, I dragged myself out for the second Stakes day. Raid day. There was a different energy to the crowd. The raid would feature unleaked content, places and enemies that no one but the developers had seen before. The boisterous thunder of thousands of fans circulated through the convention center and threatened to drown out the announcer's voice.

"Let's hear it for your AVE teams!" The crowd roared.

"Put your hands together for Nerodic!" Lined up outside our tent, we watched as each raid team entered the inner ring. "The runner up at last year's Stakes, put your hands together for Eeeeeludan!" The crowd screamed as Eludan's players entered. I pictured Danny at this very place years ago. The announcer continued, "Now let's hear some noise for the amazing reigning champions—" My stomach twisted in knots and I could barely breathe— "the winners and carriers of the Stakes title, Sarkmarrrrr!" The crowd erupted in rolling roars.

Arano jogged ahead, I followed close to him. He waved, so I waved. I could hear Merksril behind me yelling to the fans. "Yeaaah! That's right! We're back and showing no slack!" The screams hit new volumes. We paused at our stations, taking it in, waving to thousands of screaming fans of every age and from every part of the world. Merk kept waving while the rest of us took our seats.

When he finally turned around, he said, "I guess I'm the only ham on the team. All this publicity ... you can bet your ass I'm going to soak it up." He blew a kiss to the crowd.

The last few teams entered, and the announcer asked for all aliases to load.

"When you're ready, push this green button. That locks you as ready," Arano said, pointing at a flashing button next to my station. "Check to make sure you have everything: potions, flasks, food, water, wand, and weapons."

I ran through a final check, ending with my Demon-wisp, and then took one more deep breath and locked in. I looked up at the projector screens. There were four hanging above each section of the room. Nine team names flashed green under the main screen, showing they were ready. The lights dimmed. The crowd hushed. Adrenaline poured through my veins, threatening to turn me inside out. I double-checked that the marble was still in my pocket. It was there.

The announcer continued. "All teams have indicated that they are locked in and ready. Who will win the AVE championship this year? Deluvian Games founder and president, Mr. Charles Luvi, will do the honors of kicking off the start of this amazing race, so we can find out!"

A powerful, confident-looking man walked in between the players to the middle of the stage. He had a few grays, enough to show maturity. He waited for a few seconds before beginning.

Lekar pointed at Mr. Luvi. "There's the man obsessed with two things: keeping his online empire alive and neutralizing the Holder. Little does he know, he can't have one without the other. Word is, he's a real tyrant at Deluvian. Fires anyone—developers, janitors, whoever—for anything. Bet he'd fire players if he could."

"Welcome back, everyone, to the second day, raid day! We come together once a year to witness the most talented gaming legends in the world. We enjoyed some really great battlegrounds yesterday with the AVA tournament. But today—today, even our developers will be on the edge of their seats as our AVE players go up against the most unforgiving content ever created!" The crowd cheered. "Some teams are new this year, some are our beloved veterans, but they are all here with the same mission: to prove their worth, their abilities, and their right to the place at the top. Who will claim the Stakes and set their position as the number-one world AVE team? We are about to find out. Teams: now is the time to prove how exceptional you really are. The Stakes Raid, begin!"

IT WAS HARD TO SEE in the near-blackness of the dense forest. I stood frozen, afraid to move—to even breathe. Slowly, ahead of me, the ground began to glow ever so slightly, and I could see the outline of where we stood. Weeds and mossy vines hung like fishermen's nets from low-hanging branches. Growing along the vines were tiny flowers whose petals glowed in a holy white aura, creating points of light in every direction.

I inched forward. I almost forgot that Lixur was following me. The Demon-wisp's powerful darkness swayed silently in my wake. Before I took another step, I saw a small shadow flicker ahead of me. It looked like the outline of a dwarf—Merksril.

"Merk—"

Before I could finish the word, a hand grabbed my face and covered my mouth, muting my alias. The Demon-wisp reacted. His dark aura expanded and seethed and twisted around my captor. Rowley dropped his hand

and staggered backward. "Get off me!" The Demon–wisp released him, and Rowley raised his fist at me. "Keep that thing in line why don't you?" His voice was forced, cold, and crisp, but I sensed fear. "Follow me."

Why did Lixur attack? I hadn't channeled or linked to him. For a second, the spirit had acted as though our bond was sealed, reacting intuitively on my behalf.

The grove loomed. Our only light came from the glowing petals at our feet, and those lit only a yard or two ahead of us at a time. Rowley took the lead, creeping ahead as darkness covered him. He paused, hunkering low to the ground, and whispered, "We'll move in formation." His voice was so low it was barely audible. "Merksril, watch our backs. And each of you watch our sides."

"Rowley, want Ilumny?"

"No, Merk. Keep your staff dark. Light could wake something. It's this dark for a reason. We'll follow this path. Move as a unit, facing every direction. Weapons ready."

It was natural for us to listen to Rowley. He had the most experience, and Ilusas and Perdonic often praised his ability and instincts.

It was unnaturally quiet for Edannair. The only sounds were whispering grass under our feet and the occasional insect's song. We crept deeper, our eyes watchful and hands gripping weapons. A rustling in the trees startled us. A cracking, followed by the crash of a tree nearby. It sounded like a logging crew from my native Pacific Northwest.

Rowley stopped.

There was a darting movement around my feet. I glanced around but saw nothing. I searched what little foliage I could see—the vines and luminous petals. The outlines of our aliases were barely visible, but I saw Rowley sidestepping and hunching as he moved. I looked down again, thinking that I saw the ground flinch a second time. Looking and looking, I couldn't find anything. Arano walked beside me, his large Quarlin body moving carefully.

"Did you see something, Arano?"

"Hmmm?"

"Just now. On the ground. I thought I saw something."

He shook his head.

Suspicious, I started tiptoeing over the ground. I tried raising my head while keeping my eyes on everything in my periphery. It moved again. It whipped almost as soon as I lifted my head. A vine! Moving toward Arano's ankle.

"Merk. Halo!"

"What?"

"Do it now!" I ordered in a hoarse whisper.

Merksril threw his staff in the air, and a golden beam grew and circled his hand, and then flew out above us. The light from the spell lit the forest, singing out like a firecracker. The ground came alive with whipping and curling vines. More woke, slithering and snatching their tentacles toward us. The light of the spell seemed to awaken and anger them. They attacked without inhibition now.

A cold, damp tendril wrapped around my ankle and slid up my calf; I could feel the vine coiling as it reached around my leg, pulling me downward. I screeched. Rowley leaped to me, slicing at the vines with his dagger, and they loosened and slipped away in lifeless sections.

"Merksril, I'd say we're ready for Ilumny now." Rowley looked at me. "And you. Try not to panic, and cast something useful. Your Demon-wisp asleep all the sudden?"

"I can't channel him—"

Rowley motioned me away, yanking at another vine.

Merksril uttered a chant and whipped his staff forward. The head of his staff glimmered, and the brightness grew into a full bulb of light. He moved to Rowley, who was hacking away at two more vines that were threateningly close to him. Lekar and Arano were sawing at the vines with their weapons as well, but the vines were entrenching us.

"I can't draw these vines to me!" Arano said, smacking his shield against the green fingers that slithered everywhere.

Lekar conjured an earth shock and began hurling torrents of soil to stun the vines. The more that dirt covered the tightly netted green floor, the slower the vines attacked.

"Loxy, any day now," Rowley growled.

Vines can burn. I took a deep breath, focusing. Fire-Bray's red-orange heat manifested in my hands. It grew larger and larger, blustering, until it formed a fountain of fire. Thrusting my hands together, I shaped the fire into a funnel that flew forth and burst. An umbrella of fire-rain crackled through the forest. Sizzling vines shrunk back.

"Nice job," Lekar said.

"Nice job? The time it took her to stop panicking will get us killed next time. Get it together. Be quicker."

"Take it easy, Rowley."

Rowley looked at Merksril, aghast—then back to me with a glare.

"I'm sorry," I whispered.

Suddenly we heard a cracking and breaking of branches. The distant rustling was growing louder, and fast.

"What have we woken now?" Rowley froze. We stood listening as it closed in. "A master."

Lekar gulped. "How do you know, Rowley?"

"Because I know."

A giant mass of vines came into view. Its massive plant body moved toward us, consuming the undergrowth with its long tentacles. The forest seemed to awaken, quivering in the master's presence.

"Merksril. Get Patchy?"

"I've got my hands kind of full here, Lekar. Plus, I don't see any water. The vines are the only things green. It looks like they sucked this place dry."

The vines below us started rippling. "These vines are not separate mobs. Look."

"They're coming from…" We looked to where Merksril pointed his light.

The living roots and vines were snapping and breaking away from the floor. Our eyes followed the vines to the base of the giant master. Its roots had grown along the ground and tangled together to form an unusually long reach for the master. The jungle beast pulled itself toward us with its vines. Branches and twigs snapped under its weight. I heard a spitting and gnashing amongst the brush and the sounds of dead leaves crunching at our feet.

"Shit," Lekar said, looking up at the master.

As the master stretched its green mass above us, white flashes of grinding and gnashing teeth threw vine-spit on our coats and armor. Eyeless, but with a head split by a gaping, oversized mouth, the monster was an oval glob of weaving and towering foliage.

"Arano…"

"Got it." Arano moved to the front. He closed his eyes for a second and whispered an enchantment. An inch of white light rimmed the edges of his shield and axe. He clanked them together, and a spray of white sparks flew at the vine-master.

The master waddled toward Arano. It whipped at him with short thorny vines. The Quarlin didn't flinch as he parried blows with his shield and slashed back with his axe. Rowley leaped behind the master with Lekar at his heels, and they both attacked the master with blades and mace. Merksril kept everyone alive while I hurled Fire-Brays.

"Lekar! Loxy!" We looked to Rowley. "On my signal.

Lightning Arrows and Black Fire to the back of its throat. Together, start your casts!"

Lekar took up a position in front of the master, and the lightning arrows sparked in his hands. I grew the black flames. Heat and ash spewed before me.

"Grow it. Keep it forming," Rowley yelled. "Wait for my signal. Wait." He pulled another dagger from its sheath—it dripped with black, pungent ooze. He thrust it into the vined master, which threw its head back, revealing hundreds of teeth. The tentacles went stiff. The dagger's stun potion had worked.

"Now!" Rowley yelled.

I shot my hands toward the master's mouth. Lekar did the same. His blue lightning streaks crackled through the air, and the black and orange of my flames roared, meeting at the back of the master's throat and bursting together. Pieces of vine, thorns, mucus, and teeth flew everywhere. The green master sunk like a heap of wet grass onto the veined floor. The darkness lifted as soon as the master fell. We could see the mouth of the forest ahead of us.

"That's our cue. We're on to the next."

Lekar and I, immobilized by awe, stood for a second before we followed Rowley.

PAST THE FOREST WAS A BASILICA of caves…an enormous labyrinth of tunnels and domed ceilings.

"Bats above!" Arano called out.

Purple-bodied bats with long, triangle-tipped tails swooped from the high reaches of the cave. They darted up and down, grazing our heads.

"They're just a distraction." Rowley glanced left and right. "Ahead. There. You see it. The mouth of the cave opens. That's our exit."

We poured out into a starkly different landscape. Our feet sank into masses of loose sand. Lekar dropped to his knees and ran the sand through his fingers. "A vast sand desert. Grrreat. How are we going to know which way to go?"

"Be quiet," Rowley said.

The open canvas of sand and sun blared on forever. I couldn't see anything but desert in every direction.

"Glad our aliases protect against sunburn," Merksril yawned. "Up for a trek across this?"

I hung back as we broke our line through the sand. My Demon-wisp hovered behind, sometimes so close to my side that I felt antsy, like he wanted something from me. Rowley pushed us through shifting trenches and over sand dunes. When he hooked a sharp turn, the earth started to move unnaturally. It rumbled quietly at first, then louder. The sand slid away as the ground around us reared up and dropped away—a hill was forming.

"What in the world?" Arano squatted and searched the ground.

"I don't know, little brother, but be mindful where you step," Merksril said.

The ground continued to fall away; first in ripples of sand, then in chunks, larger and larger. Faster and faster the ground fell until we felt ourselves being lifted into the air. Something was moving underneath us, something strong and wide enough to lift the five of us easily. Sand slid away to reveal granite and stone. Carvings and archways started to appear. A monument was rising, as sand poured from its edges.

As we rose into the sky, Egyptian columns sprung up around us. We were standing in the middle of a vast new city.

Arano and Merksril looked at each other. "Anubis soldiers," they said together.

Rowley nodded.

"This will be fun," Merksril snorted.

The sand twisted and fell, turned and formed the shrine, until the last wall, far out in the sand-sea, unfolded. I glanced around in the blinding sunlight. Sandstone towers lined the rims and corners of this monument. Rowley pointed to some stairs opposite where we stood. At the top of the flight, between four columns, a giant golden key glittered from halfway out of an urn.

"That's our key to continue. Right there. Are you seeing the pattern? Always a puzzle, and always some way to trigger an exit. The vine master barred the way out. When we killed him, voila, we got here. Now. That key will be our way down from this sand hump."

"Sand hump? We're like thirty stories high, Rowley!"

"Sand dune?" Merksril suggested.

"Sand buggy?" Arano asked, twisting his smile.

"These are freaking sand towers! And I'm afraid of heights!" Lekar screamed.

"Close your eyes, Lekar, and get your shamanism ready. We're not alone," Merksril said, tilting his staff.

Triangular doors spilled sand as they opened, revealing Anubis soldiers that started emerging in formation. Dozens of them filed out, cold-faced like zombies.

Rowley darted into one of their lines and slashed one, then the next, with his dagger.

"He wastes no time," Merksril said, backing up to the stairs and conjuring a healing barrier around Rowley. Lekar and I cast spells to smite the Anubii one after another. More emerged. Their numbers seemed inexhaustible.

"Rowley, I can't keep you healed. Too much damage! Pull back!"

"Not now, Merksril."

"Arano," Merksril pleaded. "A little help!"

Arano crossed his hands, whispering. With axe and shield, he struck the ground. A ring of violet spread around him. The darkened circle grew and distracted the Anubii as it swept through the sand under their feet. Lekar conjured a poison potion and laced it over the purple of Arano's circle. The Anubii weakened as soon as they crossed the threshold of poison.

"I'm coming to help, Rowley!" Lekar sprang to the side of the overwhelmed rogue.

Beyond the battle, a large stone door slid open and sand began to pour from it. The walls of the edifice shook and cracked. The Anubis soldiers paused and trembled for a moment.

"I think we've got a master," Arano called out.

"Now?" Rowley yelled.

A pharaoh emerged from the doorway. He wore a nemes headdress and carried a golden rod. The pharaoh master was a giant compared to his soldiers, and they cowered at the sight of him.

Arano's voice cracked. "I'll get him."

He jumped over the Anubii and taunted the master. The pharaoh raised his rod, and the sand around his feet began to twist and whirl, moving faster and growing higher until a funnel of sand obscured him. Lekar, Rowley, and I continued striking down more formations of soldiers.

"Start on the master, Loxy!" Rowley called out.

I looked at my Demon-wisp. He swayed eagerly, locking a deadly gaze on the Anubii. *I can't. He's too powerful.* Images from my spell book flipped through my mind. *The master is earth-based. He lives in sand, in desert. He will be immune to earth spells. What can we use that's water-based? Think! Think!*

"Merksril!"

"A little busy healing here, Loxy!"

"We need Patchy."

"What?"

"Can you summon your Seeing Eye?"

Merksril glanced behind him. "Yes. There's a fountain back here."

"Do it!"

Merk closed his eyes and mumbled something in whispers. A bubble the size of a fist appeared. It bounced and whistled as it found the water; the overgrown eye splashed and dived until it had grown from the size of a fist to a beach ball. Patchy blinked open his eyelid and shook like a wet dog, sending water droplets everywhere. Then the muttering, sputtering Seeing Eye streaked back to dance in the air next to Merksril.

"Merk, send it to the middle."

"But I can see the middle."

"Send it!"

"We're getting overrun here!" Lekar yelled out, smacking at the Anubis soldiers swinging weapons wildly around him.

"Fine." Merksril touched his forehead and commanded the Seeing Eye forward. It zigzagged its way, taking the longest path possible. "Patchy. Don't procrastinate!"

The eye turned up his lid and wiggled its way along, finally reaching the middle of the fray. Patchy turned to face Merksril, sputtering, "Ta-da!" just as the Anubis soldiers broke past Lekar and Rowley. They encircled us, closing in for a quick suffocation. Arano was taking massive blows from the wind-tunneled pharaoh, and the sand whirlwind deflected every spell I threw. The ground at our feet started rippling, in the opposite direction now. The sand that lifted the monument from the earth was reversing its course. We began sinking. Sand from the urn rose around the key, slowly obscuring it.

Rowley yelled out, "Time's up. We gotta move!"

"Merksril, now!"

"What?"

"Dismiss Patchy!" I yelled back. I fought to keep my ground against the funnel's powerful outbursts of wind and sand. The eye shook ferociously.

"I just got him out!"

"Just do it!"

"This is gonna hurt." Merksril closed his eyes and dismissed the Seeing Eye. Patchy let out a high, deafening howl and began spinning. He reached an uncontrollable, blurred whirl and then exploded, and water blasted in every direction. Anubis soldiers cried out and fell to the ground. Merksril moaned and grabbed his head with both hands. The force of Patchy's explosion hit the pharaoh hard, collapsing his whirlwind. *Now*, I thought. *The master's vulnerable.* The glow of emerald magic grew in my hands. As I threw the seeded spell at the master, I heard Rowley too late.

"Wait. Loxy, don't!"

The green light hurtled through the air and hit the pharaoh, then fluxed and disappeared inside him. A moment later a green aura burst through the master. The pharaoh lost balance for a moment and fell to one knee.

But the master steadied himself, turned, and aimed his rod at me. A barrage of small, thin bullets exploded from the rod. Like darts thrown at a target board, the needles flew through the air and buried themselves in my chest.

"Merk! Heals on Loxy!" Rowley yelled.

Merk's rain of light splashed over my dead body with no effect. The screen had changed. My spirit levitated over my alias, and I saw my teammates through a colorless lens. Arano jumped toward the master, but struggled against the rising tides of sand. Rowley and Lekar joined him, shoving their way through.

"Res her now, Merk!"

"There's way too much damage! If I stop healing Arano for one second, he's gone. And then you'll be gone, too!"

"God damn it."

Rowley and Lekar slashed and cast against the master, then turned to attack the remaining Anubii. The sand rose until it was impossible for my team to navigate. The sand changed viscosity and moved like liquid, and my team looked like apparitions within it. Rowley and Lekar called out coordinating attacks while dodging blows. *I'll find a res. There must be a life guardian around here somewhere.* I steered my spirit through one of the triangular doorways used by the Anubis soldiers. I checked for any sign of a resurrection place.

Outside, Arano yelled to Rowley and Lekar. "On my mark! I'll weaken him. Then attack!"

I looked frantically around. *Where's a life guardian? I need one now!*

I scrambled down tunnel after tunnel inside the sand tower but found nothing. Arano called, "Now, now, now!" My teammates' attacks rang out in a cacophony of sounds, and I heard the pharaoh smash into the ground with a shuddering roar.

"Phew. Let's not do that again," Lekar said. "Where's Loxy?"

"We have to go now!" Rowley said. "The key is disappearing! Loxy?"

"I'm looking for a life guardian."

"What?" Rowley hissed. "Merk, don't tell me her spirit's—"

"Out of range, yes. I just tried rezzing her. I can't. Where are you, Loxy?"

"I'm below you guys. Inside the sand tower."

"Oh no." Merk said. "Rowley look."

"Shit. We're almost out of time! Loxy. Get your ass up here now!"

I turned around and started back up the tunnel. Lekar called out, "Buy some time with me. Dig the sand out from around the key!"

Twisting and turning, I followed the tunnels back up through the triangular doorway. My spirit flew threw the doorway and hovered over my alias. Merk kneeled beside me and started to meditate. In seconds, he revived me, and the moment my view returned to normal, we lunged toward the key through sand that flooded around our legs. Rowley was the first to reach it. His alias evaporated the moment he touched it; sand and air whiplashed around where he had stood. I stared at the now-empty space.

"Go Loxy," Merksril said and motioned toward the key.

The moment I touched the key, there was an intense sucking noise, and everything disappeared.

CHAPTER FORTY-ONE

"A THIRD TEAM JUST FINISHED within the sand time limit. Let me get confirmation here ... yes, it is confirmed. Sark-marr has passed the sand key with only moments to spare!" The announcer's voice sounded muffled and far away. "So, ladies and gentlemen, getting into our second hour, the competition is getting more and more intense. It's a close, close race, and there is no way to tell who will continue to make the time limits and who will start falling behind. We have Bararm in first place now, with Eludan in second, and Sarkmarr in third. And Nerodic and Sentimental right on their heels."

The audience was already yelling. "Come on!" "Sark-marr's losing?" "Go Bararm!" "Hurry Eludan!"

"Nice, Loxy," Rowley was livid. "Hear the crowd? That's all because of you. What were you thinking casting that spell? With Arano's hands full with the pharaoh, it didn't occur to you to watch what spells you cast? No one could have kept that pharaoh off you, not even him. And then trying to find a life guardian? Did you not hear a word Perdonic said before the Stakes?"

"I'm sorry. I panicked. I thought I was helping—"

"You thought wrong."

"Rowley, let's move on," Arano said.

"We made it to the key in time at least, right?" I said.

"In time? Are you making a joke? That's exactly what you cost us. Time. Time we can never get back. How do you think these things are won? By seconds, *Loxy*. We've lost the lead, and it's your fault. Enjoy that thought."

The crowds were relentless, and their shouts only banged the reality of Rowley's words into my head. Between the gasping, the sudden boos and cheers, and the ardent clapping, it felt like we were at a boxing match. A match I'd botched. People kept shouting, moving in and out of their seats, popping in and out of my periphery. I could see the projection screens and flashing cameras, heard the tangle of high and low voices. The fans were cumbersome, and I strained to focus. I clutched the marble in my pocket, but nothing could keep the tears from welling up in my eyes. *I'm costing us everything. I can't do this.*

Lekar must have noticed me. He took off his headset and leaned over. In a low voice, he whispered. "Loxy. Don't sweat it. Otherwise, you'll really get overwhelmed. What matters right now is the next part of the Stakes." He pointed to our monitors. An icy mountainland lay before us.

"Look. What are those?" I pointed above us. Four shapeless ghosts—white-cloaked—were circling. Stormy black

340

clouds wreathed the sky, and the phantoms stood out starkly against it. They even seemed to glow. One stopped in its pattern to stare.

"Banshees, maybe. It's the Stakes, who the hell knows?" Merk snorted.

We climbed toward ice- and snow-covered peaks. The wind stung my ears. The cloud cover thickened and darkened, cracking thunder and throwing bolts of cobalt lightning. The sky looked alive and agitated, and it was amassing ever-stronger power. The white banshees streaked above us. Even though their faces were covered, their essence emanated heaviness and despair.

"That wind has a sting," Lekar said, registering some damage to his ear.

"I don't think it's the wind," I said. "It's them." They were wailing—a soft, high-pitched song, solemn and hollow.

A woman's voice with a foreign, authoritative accent sounded behind us. "Do you know where you are?"

Chills spilled up and down my spine. The five of us looked at each other before turning. When I saw her, my eyes widened. She stood at the door of a castle made of glass—a castle that hadn't been there a moment ago. Her body was white like the snow, and black markings striped her feline head. Her eyes were like a cheetah's, but solid black, with the same dark markings drawn from her eyes down her face. Her neck was feathered, and her back supported wings. She had the body of a horse, but the feet of a lion.

"I am Master Nimphana. And I ask you again, do you know where you are?"

She spoke from the other end of a platform, at the base of glass towers that reached seven or eight stories high, nestled into the cliffside.

"We're either in the Misty Mountains or their twin," Lekar answered nervously.

Master Nimphana turned her head curiously. "Not quite." She extended her wings, her neck feathers rising. The white drifts of snow danced in a cloud underneath her. "Do you see the Narrovix?" she asked. We looked around the platform—it now extended out from the amethyst mountains like palms of a hand in offering. Barely visible beneath the snow were traces of ancient symbols.

"Them?" Rowley said, pointing to the banshees above us.

"Tsst, tsst. No, fools! The Narrovix! They wait here at the spirit's gateway, their harbor of rest in the afterlife." We looked but saw nothing but the floor between Nimphana and us. "Soften your eyes. Look again."

When we looked again, something was appearing. Rows of translucent jewels hung in the air, and tied to them were dozens of ghosts like the ones above, but leashed. Their jingling jewels looked like artwork—a deathly artwork fit for a cemetery, with the ghosts as their own tombstones.

"Ah, you see it now." Her voice was melancholy. "You

are standing on a burial ground. A sacred place. You've come uninvited and with weapons—both insults to our spirits."

Rowley reached for his daggers. Before he touched them, they cracked and shattered. Our weapons followed, turning to ash as they fell at our feet. "Neither your magic nor your weapons have power here, swine."

"What are we here to do?" Rowley said.

Nimphana howled a witch's laugh. "Here to die." She spread her wings and flew into the air. "There is one way to survive," she said, hovering above us. "But I'm not so sure I want to tell you. You don't deserve it, coming here as you did."

"Master Nimphana," I said, stepping forward. She looked appraisingly from her large, slitted eyes. "We're deeply sorry for coming unannounced as we did, and with our weapons." My voice quivered even in its softest register. "We did not mean to disrespect the spirits. Please tell us how to pass through."

"Tsst. Tsst." She landed at my feet. I looked up at her as she stared at me. She was taller than a draft horse, and her wings stretched high above her back. She lingered, looking me over, then examining the Demon-wisp that levitated at my side. "You may have saved or damned yourself, swine. Get through the Narrovix without breaking a pendant, and I will let you pass alive."

"Thank you. Thank you, Master Nimphana."

She pointed to the banshees above. "But they will

343

not be so understanding," she snapped. "You're walking through Syucooma—their heaven. They will want their revenge. If they do not take you first, I will spare your lives, but you do not touch them." A cloud of diaphanous snow whirled as she lifted into the air again. She flew high and quick and disappeared behind a glass steeple.

I glanced from the banshees to the crystal chateau. One at a time, the ghosts paused in their circling flight pattern to gaze at us. "Don't touch, don't cough, don't breathe—just move carefully," I whispered.

I took a step toward the Narrovix, and my Demon-wisp followed at a distance. A banshee screamed, and the sound was deafening. We doubled over, grabbing our ears. With another step, and another, we inched our way into the burial ground. Another shriek—paralyzing.

We kept moving. The Narrovix gazed at us from colorless faces. They were naked, translucent, and only faintly humanoid.

The banshees changed their pattern to an erratic dance. The wind whipped harder and tunneled past us. We strained for balance; it was impossible to walk in a straight line. The banshees arced through the air and began dive-bombing the ground. Swooshing by our ears, like birds protecting a nest, they charged but did not make contact. Between the wind and the wailing, we were reduced to hand signals as we warned and directed each other. A Narrovix watched me with sunken, sad eyes. It reached for me, but the pendant locked the spirit in place.

As a gust of wind whipped through the Narrovix, Lekar, ahead of me, sidestepped to catch himself.

"Lekar! Be careful!"

It was too late. He stumbled right into a Narrovix. The spirit screamed. The pendant broke; the spirit flew up, swirling and shrieking. All of the entombed Narrovix looked up as the ground began to shake. At once they pulled their pendants taut, reaching—scraping to be freed as well. The banshees above us huddled into a formation and streaked down in attack.

"Run!" Merksril said.

We ran in single file, zigzagging and dodging the grasping Narrovix.

"The banshees are going to kill us!" Lekar was looking up, afraid, and stumbling.

"Shut up! Run!" Rowley yelled.

We reached the stairs of the glass castle from which Master Nimphana had first addressed us.

"Now what do we do?" Lekar said.

"In. In! We can't stay here!" Rowley said.

We pushed on the glass doors, enormous in height and incredibly narrow. Their hinges moved with a sound like grinding glass. Ducking inside, we shoved the high doors closed and panted for breath. For a moment, we didn't notice the strange hallway before us. Everything was glass—prism glass—but something enchanted this place. The prisms morphed from a rainbow of refracted colors to mirrors, and then to reflections of animals—

the eyes and faces of eagles and doves, lions and foxes, appeared and disappeared around us.

At the end of the hall we came to a fork. We followed Rowley. Faintly, and then louder, a husky, labored gurgling sound overtook us.

"What the...?" Arano said.

"That wasn't you, was it, little brother?" Merk smirked. "I'd wager we took a wrong turn. Let's go back the other way."

We looked to Rowley automatically. He nodded. We turned around but were shocked with what we saw. The prism hallway formed a new wall that blocked our retreat. The same growl rumbled through the walls again. I glanced around, trying to glimpse anything.

"Quit standing around," Rowley hissed. "You bunch of little girls. We'll keep moving this way, then."

"Who you calling a girl?" Merksril rolled his shoulders.

Rowley ignored him, continuing in the only open direction.

"Lost?" A whisper hissed from the walls. The accent was familiar—Nimphana. We followed the hallways left, then right, then left again, hearing the whispers over and over. "Very lost it seems. Very lost."

"She's toying with us," Arano said.

"This is taking too long. We're not getting anywhere. Come on." Rowley moved to the wall. He pulled two new daggers from his boots and struck the prism reflection. Glass shattered across the floor. Reds, pinks, and blues flitted from the blades as he drew them back. Rowley peered into the shattered opening and then stepped through the cracked hole.

The walls suddenly transformed from reflective prisms to an inky liquid. A black, gluey substance spread over the wall, trapping Rowley's leg and rippling as it moved up and around his body.

"What's happening, Row?"

"The glass is like glue all of a sudden. I can't—I can't get through." Rowley shrugged and wrestled, struggling to free himself. The mirrors now reflected the faces of hideous, mutated creatures, all of them glowering at us.

"Rowley. Get out of there!" Merk yelled.

"I'm trying, you idiot. I can't."

We saw movement in the walls, distant but edging closer. The world beyond the mirrors was a space of its own now, one with great depth—and something was drawing near. The formations were physical beings, something...

My stomach dropped.

Skeletons. Armies of skeletons marched toward us from beyond the walls. The army's first ranks breached the surface and struck at us with their spears. Two of them immediately engaged Rowley.

"Ghouls," Lekar said. "And probably resilient against magic, too."

"They're coming through from everywhere!" I called out.

"Get behind me," said Arano. "I've got this." He lifted

his shield. The ghouls stalked to him with hunched back-bones, their arms dangling lifeless at their sides. Arano struck at the one nearest him, but the ghoul blocked the blow with its spear. Dozens more trailed through the walls and encircled us. They pushed us back, cramping our position against the wall. We had backed up to within an inch of the sticky wall when we heard her voice again, cackling.

"You did not pass through the Narrovix without disturbing them, swine. You did not think I would forget, did you?" She whispered a command in a tongue we couldn't understand. The skeletons charged, ravenous—coming through the inky walls in larger packs now.

We met them head on. Every spell bounced off of them as if they were surrounded by a force field, and we were forced to rely on physical weapons only.

"Rowley, there's so many. I can't take this many!" Arano hoisted his shield to block another spear blow.

"I know! I'm thinking!" Rowley growled as he struck at the skeletons. But his dagger strikes were like mere pinches to the undead. They felt nothing. And we had no way out. Meshed together, the ghouls had us trapped.

Without warning, my Demon-wisp drifted between the skeletons and us. His sinuous spirit expanded to form a barrier. A ghoul brushed against it and collapsed.

"Did you tell him to do that?" Lekar asked.

I shook my head.

The ghouls backed away, scared and calling out in a strange tongue. Nimphana rasped a command back to the ghouls, and they reluctantly moved forward again. One stepped toward Lixur and plunged its spear into the shadow. The spear went straight through, but the Demon-wisp did not flinch. Instead Lixur made a sound—that cursed whisper, a sound that could only come from an underworld creature. Lixur reached his spirit arm toward the ghoul. At his touch, the ghoul crumbled to a pile of bones. The Demon-wisp touched another and another, stretching its essence and tangling its energy around more ghouls. The skeletons collapsed in waves.

A movement—something caught my eye on the ground beside me. A lap of water—no, it was sliver liquid slipping in around my feet underneath the wall.

"Rowley."

"Not now, Loxy."

Hundreds of skeletons rushed the Demon-wisp, swinging their spears. He expanded farther, and wisps of essence flanked to wrap in and out around ghouls.

"Rowley. Look!"

"Not now—"

"But the wall, there! It's different. Do you see underneath that part there?"

His eyes darted to the section I'd indicated. When he saw the silvery water, his expression changed. "Yes. Go, there!" Rowley shouted. "Through that part of the wall only!"

Lekar and Arano, then Merksril, jumped through. As soon as they touched the black wall, instead of clinging to them, the wall sucked them through to the other side.

"Loxy, hurry."

I looked from Rowley back to Lixur. "You go, Rowley. I'll follow."

Rowley nodded and slipped through the enveloping space. I beckoned to Lixur. The Demon-wisp's glowing eyes glanced at me before it pulverized another ghoul. I asked again. And again. *Come on! I have to step through now!* The Demon-wisp flew to me, and the ghouls came crashing after him. I closed my eyes as we dove together through the wall just as the sliver of water disappeared.

WE WERE UNDERWATER, but protected, encased somehow in the middle of an ocean. Ribbons of water flowed over the invisible barrier. We moved slowly, baby-stepping our way along the ocean floor. It was clear that we had arrived in an ocean-cluster. I had heard rumors of new zones like this—vast orbs, entire marine ecosystems under the sea, somewhere near the southern islands.

We traveled a pastel world of water orchids and coral labyrinths. Some kind of water-bird swam past us; it looked like a raven, but with a fish's mouth instead of a beak. A forest of water flora grew in tall clumps amidst the coral. Sea creatures hummed—we could hear them clearly from all directions. Strange manatees that walked upright came out from behind shells and water-trees, and a few stopped at the barrier to watch our passage. More emerged from behind kelp beds and coral reefs and stood like a crowd watching a parade.

A series of gurgling vibrations pounded through the water. We looked at each other. Some evil was coming. I searched the water. The strange manatees called out to each other as if in a warning. They turned and swam quickly for refuge.

"Uh-oh," Lekar said, pointing out into the water. "What are those? And another, there!"

As tall and wide as a four-story house, with orca markings and wings for fins, some kind of enormous whale-dragon hybrid was swimming straight for us. A second and a third appeared. The last one was different from the others. It was bigger, and something else—it had two whale heads.

"Careful! I doubt they are friendly."

The first pair paused at the barrier and waited. The two-headed one plowed into the water-wall. The barrier broke and water poured forth, careening and smashing around us.

"You have to take a water-breathing potion!" Rowley yelled.

We each quaffed a vial of liquid, and immediately an air bubble grew around our noses and mouths. Within seconds, the water had closed over our heads in an avalanche of power.

THE WHALE-DRAGONS WERE RUTHLESS. Running out of strength and ideas, we fought to stay alive. Arano dodged their forceful swipes while Lekar and I attempted spell-casts. The water was unforgiving to all of us but Row-ley, for it eradicated almost all of magic's normal potency. One of the whales snapped at Arano's ankle and snagged his boot. The sea monster began dragging him away into kelp and coral.

"No!" Rowley called out. It was the first time I had heard his voice that frail. "We can't lose Arano!"

Wrestling through the kelp, I swam after the whale, panicked. *Ground them*, I suddenly remembered. *I must ground them!* Concentrating on the whale, I muttered cantrips, and a leaden weight hammered down on the whale. It fell, pinned to the ocean floor, and released Arano. Lekar and Rowley were trying to hold off the others, and the weight of the spell would soon expire. We were falling behind.

CHAPTER FORTY-TWO

IT WASN'T UNTIL LEKAR'S LIGHTNING TOTEM gained enough power to electrify the water that the whale-dragons finally retreated. We fought several more aquatic masters in the ocean-cluster, the last of which reminded me of the Loch Ness Monster. Flying creatures that looked like lotus flowers pulled us from the depths and dropped us before gates at the base of a mountainside. The inscription on the gates read *Mors Gate*. When we stepped inside, Braden warriors nearly sacked us, but we made it through and entered into lower levels of the mountain.

My hands and head ached. We must have been on our fourth or fifth hour. All around us, statues were carved in the mountain's granite stomach—animals and Buddha heads. It was like a sanctuary and sacrificial altar at once. Ahead of us, where the paths ended, sank a crater. A stream of some dark liquid trickled along the walls around it.

At the bottom of the crevice it stood. It had to be the Enigma master.

It almost looked asleep; it seemed so calm and tranquil with its hooded heads bowed. Half-insect and half-man, the creature had a scorpion tail and long limbs ending in pincers. The four cloaked human heads on its shoulders were eerily still.

"How do you wanna do this one?" Merk asked. There was exhaustion in his voice as he stared at the Enigma.

"Let me go in first," Arano said. "I'll take it where it stands."

"Wait," said Rowley.

"We don't have time to wait. Eludan could be fighting this thing already."

"Wait. Something's not right."

"You're thinking it's a trap," I said, studying Rowley carefully.

He nodded.

"How do we reveal it?"

"I don't know. I'm thinking."

We waited silently. The crater was too quiet. The only sound was the faint trickling of water. It felt as though the mere sound of our thoughts could wake something in here.

"We could try Patchy again?" Lekar suggested.

Rowley shrugged. "I don't see any harm in that."

Merksril summoned the Seeing Eye. Patchy bobbed up and down along the walls drinking the water and finally coalesced, sputtering and blinking defiantly. Merk put his hand to his forehead and sent Patchy toward the Enigma. The Seeing Eye lollygagged down the steep face of the crater. Merk spouted curses, but Patchy continued to bob down the incline at his own pace.

A slight hissing came from one of the dark faces, and its hood tilted upward. Patchy wavered and dropped to the ground. The Seeing Eye shook and seized before exploding at the feet of the master.

"Patchy! That thing just killed Patchy! Are you happy, Lekar? There goes my Seeing Eye. You know how long it took me to raise him?"

"Quiet!" Rowley said.

"I have an idea." My team looked at me. "Lekar, give me your hat."

"But I never take off my hat."

"Lekar, please. I have an idea." He handed over the pointy wizard hat. "Arano, hand me your hammers, and Rowley, your extra knives. Give me anything with weight. Give it to me." Lekar's hat had ample room for the items. I tied a strap around it, securing all the items inside. Then I tossed the hat into the crater.

"What are you do..."

The hat hit the ground and rolled, thumping along the ground in its awkward shape. Spikes shot up from the ground, caging the hat in front of the Enigma. The walls started to shake and crack, and animal-head statues moved from their embedded places in the walls. Cackling echoed all around us, and small cherubs appeared, scurrying out from holes in the ceiling and flying around the room. They were not the chubby, healthy-looking winged children. They were ugly, wicked, red-faced things with bat wings.

"Without that hat experiment, we would have lost

Arano. Good work." Rowley nodded to me.

"Duck!" Merk yelled and sidestepped an attack from the devil-cherubs. There were armies of them now, flooding around us.

"Open fire," called Rowley.

"Don't spread too far out. Healing Canopy, incoming!" Merksril's entire body began to glow. He threw his hands in the air, and beams of yellow light shot toward the cave's ceiling. The rays knit together in a brilliant gold umbrella of healing light. Our strength and agility levels were restored, and every cherub turned its eyes from the light. But when the healing light dimmed, they sneered at Merk and charged him.

Arano tried to draw them off by bashing the ground with his shield, but nothing could lure their focus from Merk. "Drop the healing shield! I can't get them off you," Arano said.

"I've got to keep us alive!"

"So do I!"

The devil-cherubs swarmed Merk, knocking him back. The umbrella of light disappeared as he hit the ground. With Merk down, we quickly began losing our strength. Frantically, I scanned the room, looking for a ledge, a second floor, anything to get us leverage. Nothing but statues filled the room. *Wait—the statues.* There was no other feature in the room but the statues—they had to be important.

"Cover me, Rowley," I said.

"Why? For what?"

"I need to check something."

"Now?"

"Now."

I ducked to miss an attack and shot a ball of fire toward a cherub as it veered toward me—the barreling blast knocked it dead. Lekar summoned currents of a violet essence and whirled them toward the master. The Enigma hissed and moaned, an unnatural guttural sound.

I struggled to scale the curves and ledges of the animal statues. When I reached the mouth of a serpent, I looked for anything different, out of the ordinary. *There has to be something. Ah, there!* The tongue of the serpent was some kind of lever. *It must be rigged for something.* Grabbing the lever, I heaved and pulled. It gave way with a heavy click and locked into place at the front of the serpent's mouth.

In a domino effect, each statue moved further out from the walls. Rock and dirt cracked and fell in large chunks as the statues awakened. The cherubs panicked. Spitting and growling at each other, they flew and scurried, and finally disappeared back into the holes in the ceiling.

As the statues inched closer to the middle of the room, the Enigma channeled a powerful aura around itself. I scaled back down and ran to meet my team. The master hummed, and its hooded heads turned and stretched as if locating where each of us stood. Its scorpion tail started to twitch like a cat's. A dark lulling sound came from inside the hoods. "Death. Your time to die." It sounded alien. The Enigma raised one of its scorpion claws—and Arano flew back fifty feet from us.

"Did you see that! He wasn't even close to him!" Lekar screamed.

The other claw lifted. We all were knocked backward as if a rug had been pulled from our feet. Each time we stood, the limbs knocked us back. A cyclone of amber-colored energy blasted from one of the hooded faces. Arano lifted his shield and blocked at the last second; the energy surrounded his shield and ate at the metal like acid. Another hood moved, and two wisps of white and black air, crisscrossed like lace, spewed out from the dark face. The laced essence moved and slithered like it was alive. It wrapped around Lekar's body and lifted him off the ground. Rowley struck at the air, but his daggers went straight through the essence—completely useless.

"It's immune! It's taking Lekar!"

Arano and I blasted fire and ice toward it. It deflected everything.

"Try focusing on the hood, Loxy!" Rowley yelled.

I aimed my fists at one of the heads: my hands turned over and under, and coiling auburns and fuchsias shot through the air and blasted the hood. The Enigma reeled and jerked, releasing Lekar.

Lekar hit the ground hard and started crawling across the floor. The master sent more lacing energy to grasp him again, but Lekar recited a silencing enchantment, and for a few moments the Enigma went still.

"Gather behind me!" Arano yelled.

We ran to Arano just as the master began to move again. Torrents of electricity sliced the air from one of the dark hoods. We blasted spells from behind Arano as one of the pincer claws touched the ground. The floor grew ice. Merksril levitated us before we were frozen in place. I threw my mace to the ground, and from it flowed a circle of heat. It melted little more than a small circle, but it was enough for us to stand in, shoulder-to-shoulder.

Suddenly, all of the dark hoods bowed at once. Electric white currents blasted out from them. Arano struck the ground with his axe, and a white barrier formed in front of us, cutting off the blasts an instant before they hit. Smoke started seething out from under the hoods; gray wisps rose like warm breath in a cold winter morning. The vapor slipped past Arano's barrier. Like shrouds, the gray smoke wound its way around each of us. Our aliases weakened to near-paralysis.

"This reminds me of Crux poison," Rowley said. "Summon, now!"

We moved our hands in the memorized pattern. And from very far away came a whinny—Nillekmas were coming.

The toxin was taking our energy fast. We didn't have but moments left. We were going to die, and the Stakes would be over for us.

"Hold on. Hold on," Rowley whispered.

"Come on, Nillekmas. *Hurry*," Lekar pleaded.

Five bronze-furred steeds plowed through the tunnels. They ran to the Enigma in a stampede of galloping hooves and reared and pawed the ground in the crater. Rowley whistled, and his Nillekma immediately answered to him. We did the same, and our Nillekmas flew to our sides, holding their horns low to the earth. As soon as their horns pierced the cloud of toxin, the cocoons around us evaporated. Our energy meters sprang back as clean air surrounded us again.

The Nillekmas charged the Enigma, which snapped its claws and hissed. The equines reared and pawed, utterly brave, and charged the Enigma, piercing it with their horns. The toxins absorbed by their horns ate at the Enigma's impenetrable skin, which cracked open to reveal a squishy layer of tissue.

"Lekar, Wind Burst, now!" Rowley yelled.

Lekar twisted his wrists, and a sheet of wind gusted toward the Enigma. Rowley jumped into it. His body lanced through the air like an arrow, his daggers in hands stretched over his head. His body whirled between two Nillekmas, and in a blast of wind and blades, Rowley slammed into the master. His knives lanced between the cloaked hoods, and horrid screams rose from the dark faces. Rowley buried his daggers in the exposed flesh and let the weight of his body drag them downward, ripping the Enigma's insides to shreds.

For a moment, Rowley lay limp against the fallen scorpion master. As we helped him to his feet, our monitors dissolved into black and a different noise erupted.

CHAPTER FORTY-THREE

IT WASN'T FOR A FEW MOMENTS that the sound registered.
It was the fans. They were roaring. The entire convention
center shook with clapping and cheering. The audience
poured forth around the gaming stations like a rush on a
football field. We stood slowly. My legs were numb from
disuse. Fans shoved pens, papers, and cameras in our faces.
We moved in a daze through the crowd, accepting congratulations and praise. It was finished. We had won.

We were ushered to the announcer's table. It was hard
to hear anything over the crowds. The bigwigs of Deluvian Games presented the $250,000 check and trophy.
I stood transfixed as Rowley and Merk held the giant
check and Arano kissed the trophy. My father and brother
flashed in my mind. The way Hunter had stood just this
same way at the skateboarding tournament. That incredible smile on Hunter's face. And Dad, beaming with pride.
They had always been the competitors of the family. They
were the ones who could always handle the pressure. My
gaze found the ceiling.

Here I am, Dad, I whispered. *I made it. I competed and won, just like you always said I could.*

"Hey. Loxy."

The furious tone of Rowley's voice made me wince. I turned, fighting back the sting pricking my eyes. "Yes?"

"Get over here." His tone suddenly warmed, and he flashed a wide grin. "You were great. In the end."

I smiled and threw my arms around his neck.

"Whoa, whoa, I didn't say anything about hugs," Rowley said, laughing. "Seriously, though. We coulda bogged down bad with those ghouls. You saw that opening, and your wisp kept 'em back. So, good work."

"Back up! Back up!" A man with a microphone called out as he pushed his way through the shoulder-to-shoulder fans. "We're live in ten seconds!" The crowd shifted barely an inch or two at his command. The cameraman counted down on his fingers: three, two, one....."We're live at the Stakes competition sponsored by Deluvian Games, and as you can see, the crowds are going crazy for today's winners, Sarkmarr!" The audience cheered and their volumes reached another octave. "Tell us Sarkmarr team, what does this win mean to you?"

A DOZEN MORE INTERVIEWS and photo shoots later, we were still moving from person to person, answering questions and getting congratulated. One interviewer was asking too many questions about the Holder, at which point

Ilusas, with his customary forceful demeanor, pulled us away and excused us from the winners' ring.

We escaped in another limousine aimed back to our hotel. Ilusas and Perdonic laughed during the ride back, enjoying Rowley and Lekar's argument about how difficult it was—or was not—to reach the Holder's Stakes Party. I gathered that anyone attending the party had to endure a labyrinthine screening process. Every guest had to arrive at a certain address to be inspected and questioned. Then they got the number of a decoy hotel room where a password was required to obtain the actual hotel suite.

WHEN WE ENTERED THE EXECUTIVE SUITE, I realized it was larger than my entire flat. It smelled like strawberries and champagne. My phone started beeping text message alerts. One, from Gage said, "Now's your time to make it happen." And another, from Elliott said, "You did it. That's enough. Just enjoy your evening and forget the plan." Any response I could imagine texting back made me nervous. So I put the phone in my pocket and sat quietly, smothered between Lekar and Rowley on a small couch. Perdonic had already downed a few drinks and was chatting incessantly, regaling his listeners with past Sarkmarr adventures. Arano and Lekar urged him to continue every time he said, "But I'll stop now with my stories."

"Tell the one about when we got incarcerated by twelve Shades," Lekar said.

Perdonic doubled over with braying laughter. "I've never had more pity on those bastards."

"What was it, five hours?"

"Like they would have believed Lorgen hid away on Shade Island under their very own dimwitted noses!"

Rowley choked on his beverage and glared at Perdonic. "Why don't you shut up with the stories now?"

My eyes widened. *That's it. That's where the Holder resides. That's what Vsin needs.* Trying to act nonchalant, I excused myself and headed for the door. I could step out and message Vsin. Two minutes. No one would notice. As I moved through the sea of guests, shreds of doubt gutted me. *Am I sure about this?* Now that the moment was upon me, I wasn't sure that humiliating the Holder or aiding Vsin were the right things to do. *Without the Holder—the Enigma master of Sarkmarr—what else would we lose? Look what he's made possible. No. It is better this way. It's deserved.*

Just as I touched the handle, I heard his voice.

"Running off already?"

I turned around. The Holder stood there, his gaze searing mine, his face said that he knew what I was planning to do.

Chapter Forty-Four

"WHAT IS IT?" I asked. The Holder had appeared so quickly that I was unsure of where he'd come from.

"I think you know." His words were silky—soft.

"No, I don't."

"Is there something you're on your way to do?"

I tried not to let the surprise in my mind show on my face. "I—I got all these texts from my friends. I want to reply before they think all *this* is going to my head." He smiled like he was seeing straight through me. I was nervous and angry at once. "You know, I notice that you never really say anything. You just imply and let people fill in the blanks for you."

"You're speaking as if you've decided something about me."

"I have. And way to prove my point, by the way."

"A few weeks ago, this malice was not in your voice." He didn't take his eyes from me. All I wanted to do was hide. My heartbeat felt a thousand times too fast. "Let's move somewhere more private," he said.

I hesitated, fighting between wanting to flee or obey

him. How dangerous was he? At the sight of his retreating back, I maneuvered through the crowd after him. His finesse was sickening—the sea of guests parted for him. We went through a corner door into another room. It had more windows than walls and lavish couches piled with maroon pillows.

"So, tell me. What are your exact conclusions about me?" He moved to another connecting door and closed it.

"I might damage your pride."

Our eyes met. He grinned.

"Please try."

"All right. In that case, you're bored. And lonely," I said. The words weren't what he expected, and he furrowed his brow. "You're a miserable ten-year-old bully in a twenty-something-year-old body who somehow finds satisfaction in bossing people around, especially those with low self-esteem. You think of us as puppets. You feed on the misery of others because it makes you feel powerful. But there's something you don't know, believe it or not."

"What's that?"

"It's not worth it. The people closest to you won't stay around. They don't love you—they're afraid of you. You'll lose everyone if you give them half a chance to leave. All that will be left is a circle of misery. You may have your power, your manipulation, whatever this circus is that you're running, but it's not right and it won't last. You cannot manipulate people forever. Your so-called power is nothing but an overgrown teenage bully's ego, and you ought to just get over yourself and grow up. Until then, you are powerless."

"Really?"

I turned to the window. I didn't want to look at him. As sure as the thought entered my mind, he voiced it.

"Look at me, would you?" I sat still until the urge to obey won, and I turned to him. "You called it ego. I call it talent and passion. I got rid of my ego a long time ago— all I have now is conviction."

"Well your conviction is to hold power. What does that tell us about you?"

"No. Very few people can define their lives as precisely as that, and neither do I. All I know is that people want to be inspired to seek that definition, that purpose."

"Your promises don't do that. You manipulate people—my friends!—for the pleasure of watching them humiliate themselves. Look at Brambt. Syntax. Rynq." My voice was starting to shake. "And Arano and Asillus. I can't stand watching them suffer. You know what they've been through, and you make them retrace their fears, that agony…Arano went through therapy, for god's sake."

"You were assigned to escort Arano? Isn't that right?"

"I was seconds from calling the ambulance for Arano."

"And what was the result?" The Holder's eyes hadn't left mine. That look in them—superior and expectant. His tone went sharp. "And Syntax. He couldn't eat for two days, so what? He's three hundred pounds. And Rynq? He's afraid to fail, always has been. So I make him fail more."

"That's why it's wrong."

The Holder moved to me. He pressed his hand into the skin of my shoulder. "And you. You are so afraid of the past, of being hurt again, that I asked you to face your fear. And you did it for nothing—a simple tier two."

"It's still wrong."

"Yes. And what's the harm in that? Sarkmarrs climb the tiers and get what they want. And I get what I want. It's a fair and mutual exchange."

"It's a façade," I said, moving away from him.

"How? My members become famous and respected. My manipulation, as you've candidly labeled it, is just an invitation to do what your subconscious wants you to do anyway. Don't you see? I help you get your egos out of the way so you can channel your talent and passion. If it weren't for me, every Sarkmarr member would be just another gamer. Out of tens of millions of players, whose names are recognized? In Sarkmarr, you are transformed."

"And how convenient. You're absolved of responsibility."

"On the contrary. Why do you think I keep such a watchful eye on everything? Why do I require Sarkmarr's age limit to be eighteen? Why do I know my members just like parents know their children? Like parents *should* know their children…" The Holder's face changed, as if all arrogance drained away. For a moment, his gaze drifted away to the wall behind me. "I take responsibility. That's the point. That's the whole point. My presence in the game both threatens Deluvian and enhances it. I draw in more players and give them thrills. I deal them out like a deck of cards, for a purpose."

"Your own purpose."

"Yes. Of course. And how is that different from what any other leader does? Citizens follow their president, students their teachers. Leaders seize power because followers offer it freely. Leaders become the people they have always dreamed of being not by compromising, but by stealing. Case in point: Deluvian Games. The stories are true—an owner gone mad with a dream so embedded in his consciousness that he'd demolish anyone, friend, family, employee, anyone who might threaten it. And behold. Out of his insanity, an empire is born. Reared like a beloved child, Edannair lives in the wake of destroyed lives. For now."

I looked at him confused. "For now?"

"Your mistake, Loxy, is to think my actions—the morphises—were ever intended for the players at all."

"If not for the players, then … so you're … all this is because you're after Deluvian Games?"

"The moment you stop providing your followers with the basic necessities for growth or personal satisfaction, you lose all credentials to lead. The moment you expect your followers to provide for you, getting nothing in return … Let's just say, it takes a while for rot in the heartwood to show in the leaves of a mighty tree, Loxy. Something very real is eating at the heart of Edannair, and the casualties aren't pixels—they're the artists and designers and coders and strategists who create it. The talents of

369

Deluvian's finest employees are being sacrificed to Luvi's obsession with Edannair. It doesn't matter that he's built an empire. He's forgotten those of us who laid its foundation. Amends must be made. And they will. One way or another."

The Holder locked eyes with me. He swallowed hard and adjusted his coat, looking as though he was fighting not to lose his guarded demeanor. I stared at him. The curve of his mouth, his sandy hair framing his dark eyes... something was shifting in my heart.

"My will alone does not give me power here," he said. "I ask for obedience in exchange for thrills to achieve a higher purpose. What *you* say that means is irrelevant. What matters is the effect it has. How do you think you were perceived when you came here? Your concern, passion, motivations... they had me intrigued. I took an interest in you and started your assignments early. You did well in them—you're good at this game—but you and I both know you shouldn't have passed your first morphis that day."

"Why did I pass?"

"Something you said. It was about your father." He stared at me differently now. Unsure, without defiance. "Your fate changed, and now look where it led you."

The blood seemed to drain from my head as I tried to digest what he was saying.

"Don't overthink this, Loxy. Grasp the opportunities I can offer you. You wanted to get to me this whole time, and your initiative and the speed at which you've adapted to this game to do so are impressive. Your empathy is a strength. People are not a mystery to me. But there is something in you I have not seen before. Think of it as potential. Can I count on that? Can I count on you?"

"I don't know."

"Shift your focus. What I do has nothing to do with the reason you are here. You are here to become more than you currently are. To face what you fear most. You found a home in Sarkmarr, and its members found a home in you."

My head was swimming. He sounded so convincing, but I wasn't sure what I was being convinced of.

"Tell me. Since you have been here, have you been sleeping better, or worse?" My gaze flew to his. I couldn't fathom how he knew anything about that. He seemed amused. "Trust me when I say it: I know you. And I know that in here," —he put his hand to his chest— "you would ally with Sarkmarr."

"What do you mean?"

"Don't act ignorant, Loxy! War is coming to Edannair. The morphises are only the beginning. I've seen you. The interest you have in the officers, in their discussions and duties. Always asking questions, always wanting to know more."

"I—"

"Your observations are sharp. Why not help me mold and shape Edannair? I think you know that part of our purpose is to carve the world around us. And with me you can do that. Here you can take a stand against unethical practices, against wrongful terminations. You will help restore credit and honor back to those of us who've built Edannair. People like Vsin won't have to lose their jobs."

He looked at me as if he was handing me the world. Like my parents had looked that day on the ski slopes.

"As long as the Holder remains ubiquitous, Edannair has a chance. You can build a legacy in Sarkmarr, apart from anything and anyone. Think about it. Here you become the competitor and the leader you were always meant to be. Edannair will live, so that people find themselves in it—like you did.

"Look at me, Loxy. Join my revolution."

A polite knock sounded on the door. Brambt peered in, "Excuse me, sir—the victory speech, it's time."

My skin went cold. Thoughts raged like wildfire. The victory speech! Danny. Gage and Elliott. What about Vsin?

With a wave, the Holder dismissed Brambt and then extended his hand toward me. "There is nothing wrong with becoming the person you were meant to be. Shall we?"

CHAPTER FORTY-FIVE

WHEN I WALKED OUT OF THE HOLDER'S SUITE, Perdonic was waving my cell phone toward me. "Hey, Loxy, your phone. It's been ringing on the table for the last several minutes."

I grabbed the phone, excused myself from the party, and into the hallway to scan my missed calls. Nine calls from the home phone. I stared at my dad's name on the caller ID. Even after this much time, seeing it created a cruel hope.

And yet...why that many calls? Had Hunter gone missing? Was Mum still furious at me? I couldn't handle any of that right now, but I had to call back. Dad's name popped up again on the screen as I rang them.

I pressed the phone tightly to my ear. "Hello?"

"Kay, hey! We saw you on TV!" It was Hunter. "You're on speakerphone: here's Mum."

"Hello. What a surprise to see you, Kaylie," Mum said.

"Hi." Their happy voices caught me off-guard.

"We watched the whole thing," Hunter said. "You were brilliant, sis. Who knew you could be such a competitor!"

"Thank you, Hunter."

"Kaylie?" Mum asked.

"Mum, listen. At home, I shouldn't have said what I did. I wasn't planning—"

"Kaylie. It's fine. You were right." It was as if the whole room froze. I braced for a million things I wanted to hear but was afraid to hope for. "I know I haven't done the best at coping—might as well say I've been the worst of us, closing up that part of our lives like I did." Her voice started to tremble. I wanted to comfort her. I wanted to reach through the phone and hold her hand. "The moment I slapped you, the moment I broke your trust, that was the moment my eyes opened. The sting on my hand stayed for what felt like days. I can't apologize enough. When your father never came home, I did the things I did because I felt we had to. It was for the good of the family—the family we had to become. Once I started to move forward, I couldn't stop." Her voice sounded fragile, and for the first time in a long time she began to cry.

"The truth is, I miss him, too. I think about him all the time. I keep imagining the door opening and your father walking in." She cleared her throat. "It's so difficult without him. He was our light, wasn't he? We knew this world was only better because we were together. We knew we could make it through anything because of that. And when I say your brother needs you, I suppose I'm saying I need you too. With you at the university, and then Hunter disappearing, it's this feeling that there's no return."

"I'm sorry, Mum. But we're still together. No matter if I'm at school or Hunter's acting out. You're not alone. I love you."

"I love you, too." In that moment I heard the mother I hadn't heard in months. That was the voice I grew up with. That was the voice I loved.

"Kaylie!" Hunter said. "Guess what? Mum and I were talking, and seeing that I'll be looking to start college next year, we thought we'd start by looking at schools in Austin. Mum even made a comment about looking at houses maybe."

Wiping the tears from my eyes, I cleared my throat. "Really?"

"Maybe Austin Community College. I know it doesn't sound like much, but I think it'd be all right."

"That sounds incredible. I don't know what to say."

"Well, we can talk about the details later, Kaylie," Mum said. "But your father … he would have wanted us to give life another chance. He lived his life the way I want us to always live our lives: with vigor, surrounded by family. Now, go enjoy your night. We want you to celebrate your victory."

The world was moving again—in fact, the whole room felt alive. I exhaled. Relief fell in a sort of healing aura all around me.

"And Kaylie?"

"Yes?"

"Your father would be very proud of you."

She hung up, and I stood there staring at my phone. I felt like I had just finished running five miles—euphoric. It was time. Mum was right. I knew Dad was proud of me, and inside he was telling me it was time. I located the home-phone entry in my contacts list. I pressed edit and began deleting his name. *I will always miss you, Dad, but I know you are here…in my heart.* I replaced his name with one word: *Home.*

I pressed the phone into my chest. The ceiling had somehow become the sky. I felt larger than life somehow. I was still standing there, trying to absorb what my mother had just said, when I heard the question.

"Have you made your decision?" the Holder asked. I didn't know how long he had been standing beside me or how much he had heard.

"Partly." It all seemed different, like I was looking through a new viewfinder. Edannair could use my help, and I could use its help too.

"What part?"

"My father used to tell me to treat life like a tornado and to choose my tornado's path carefully. If you think I can be of some use to the community in Edannair, I do want to help. But I won't agree to anything until you agree to change the morphises."

He mused. Finally, he answered. "I see. I believe an arrangement could be made. I'd ask that we push that discussion to another time. Right now, your first task awaits you. If you're ready for it."

"Okay. What is it?"

"Collect the paperwork on the desk in the suite. It compiles my extensive research on players and strategies for duels, threes, and thirties. Let's see what you can do for our AVA team. Get to know those pages as well as I do. Know them like you know your own eye color. And let's see if I was right. How much can you inspire in our teams?"

I FOUND THE PAPERWORK where he said it would be. There were papers rolled and tied like ancient scrolls, as well as manila folders, envelopes, and books. I felt unexpectedly excited to be working on Sarkmarr's AVA team.

And that night, out in the lobby, I said good-bye to my raid team. Even though we were going back to our own lives, hundreds or thousands of miles apart, we had a bond with each other. The Stakes had made us a family.

GAGE, Elliott, Danny, and Eve waved as I walked into Luii's. I felt strange. My gang seemed to be on an opposing team suddenly. I felt a loyalty to Sarkmarr.

"How did it go?" Gage asked.

I tried to explain the best I could what happened. But none of them looked satisfied.

"How did this happen?" Gage asked. "You were right there in the same room with him. You could have had the Holder by the balls. Instead you sided with him?"

"Well, I—"

"We're still just pawns in the Holder's game, and now she works *for* him!" Gage screeched at Danny.

Danny looked deep in thought.

"What does he want you to do?" Elliott asked softly.

"My first assignment is to help with the AVA team."

"Well." Eve slapped her palms on the table. "The Stakes plus the Holder breathing down her neck? That's a lot of pressure. I remember Danny saying his nerves could have killed him."

Danny returned from his thoughts and looked at Eve. "That's true. And now we have someone even closer to the Holder and more of a chance to find out what he's plotting."

"So what," Gage said. "That was our last chance to tell the Holder off. We'll never have that kind of opportunity again. You blew it, Kaylie." Gage stood up, shook his head at me, and walked out.

Elliott got up to go after Gage. He looked at us. "I better go. It will be okay, Kaylie."

"Don't worry," Danny said. "There's more to this than we thought. You were right to throw out the plan."

AT HOME, as I unpacked my suitcase, I reached for the paperwork I had gathered from the Holder and flipped the pages between my fingers. I was learning more about myself through him than through any college class. It was his group and his trials that had taught me I could believe in myself—that I still had some fire left in me. The way the Holder referred to me as inspiring…he had to be speaking about my family and me. He made me feel that I now had even more to offer. His passion for Edannair and its makers….

For the first time in a long time, I felt needed, part of a great movement. Edannair offered ingenuity and a place to bond when I needed it most. When college life seemed too limited and shallow, Edannair brought the vibrance of a worldwide community. When I thought I had lost the ability to feel, it gave me something new to care about. I talked, laughed, cheered, and sometimes cried in this game. And that's the point. It wasn't me watching others live life while I seemed to be swallowed up. Through Edannair, I was actually learning about myself—how to forgive and how to grieve. It wasn't just investigating the Holder and helping Elliott. It was a real-life res for me.

And now, with all that I've learned, and with my family behind me and my father watching over me, I was ready to start anew. Just like Mum and Hunter. To start a brave new future, unafraid and not alone.

EPILOGUE

Okay, let's see. Folder one. Here we go. My fingers followed the paragraphs as I looked through the papers in the first envelope. The handwritten notes and lists at the top looked to be several years old. *Xuvy, Kronx, Martigan, Micayah, Logos, matched up against Silucus, Rawstone, Leushin, Vinns, and Atorion.* Some of the names had been circled, and some were crossed out. Words jotted above and around the names formed some sort of tracking system for progress or potential.

I stopped reading. Something unusual stuck out from between two other manila folders. I grabbed it. It was a leather-bound book. I opened it and flipped past the first few blank pages. The first marked page read, with underlining, "The Math Book." I turned another page, and there was a drawing—a sketch, rather—done in pencil. The shading was incredible. The details around the faces...a boy, seven or eight years old, holding a fishing pole in a pond, looked over his shoulder at a man I assumed to be his father. But the father wasn't looking at his son. Instead the man stared at an object in his hand, maybe a jewel. The lines in the father's face created a disturbing, almost unnatural expression. Behind the eerie shading lay familiarity…where had I seen this person? The Stakes stage flashed in my mind. *Charles Luvi…and the boy?*

I turned another page, and then another, as if they could pacify my rampaging thoughts. There were several more sketches. A portrait of a woman with ringlet chestnut hair and an exquisite face. She was so beautiful, but her eyes…her eyes held pain, as if she was screaming silently.

I turned another page and then another, faster, until the pages were flipping through my hands. The drawings changed to chapters of notes and mathematical equations. Lines of code and programming edits filled the pages before something else caught my eye. I stopped and turned back, one page at a time, until I found the page again. "Demon-wisp: code cracked and inhabitable. Testing underway for observation and info gathering." The handwriting…*It's the same as the Holder's AVA team notes. This was his—*

The book dropped from my hands to the floor. My head swarmed, my fingers went numb, and suddenly, instead of my chest, my stomach seemed to hold my heartbeat.

What exactly had I picked up from the suite that night?